The Eternity
Train

First published in Great Britain in 2023 by M. Ahsan Al-Haadee

Copyright © M. Ahsan Al-Haadee 2023
Cover illustrations by Katarina Naskovski

Paperback ISBN 978-1-916848-02-3
eBook ISBN 978-1-916848-03-0

Typeset and interior formatting by Abdul Rehman

Acknowledgements

God-willing, this book has finally come to a reality. I'd like to extend a special thanks to my two brilliant editors, Eduardo Hormazabal and Jasmine Wolffrath for their impeccable attention to detail and wonderful suggestions.

Most of all, I'd like to thank all my beta-readers and students. This book wouldn't be here without them; Adil for his kindly ear, Shamus for his multifaceted views (often nonsensical but somehow always helpful), Uthman for being Uthman, and the inspiration for The Librarian no less.

Thank you to Allison Muniz and Fiona G. Otsu who helped develop the story onwards and upwards.

A huge thank you to Rebecca for always believing in the story and the writing, and equally to my students who tirelessly read and made suggestions even when they had their 11+ exams ahead! Huzaifa, Joshua, Lucy, Qiaoya helped tremendously, as well as Diya with her eye to detail!

Last but not least is the guiding light for this book, my wife—so an eternal thank you to you, Dina.

To all of my students—past, present, and future

Table of Contents

PART III

PART I

Chapter 1

Riyul

Riyul jerked awake.

Wooden boards creaked and groaned under his shifting weight as he remembered where he was. He righted himself, and threw his legs over the edge of the moving carriage.

Riyul blinked hard. A blur of dark trees and countryside streaked before his tired, narrowing eyes whilst he tried to get his bearings.

The unmistakable clangs of metal on metal could be heard from all around.

How long was I asleep?

He rubbed his heavy eyelids with calloused and cut hands. His eyes narrowed, taking in the smears of earthy brown, woodland green and dark purple sky as the countryside whizzed by, the crescent moon shining down upon the rushing vista.

The perpetual cacophony of clangs and groans and heaves—these sounds were something Riyul once despised, but as time had gone by, they had become something more akin to a moderately irritating lullaby: a metallic pounding that seemed to simultaneously come from underneath him, above him, and around him; whistles and sirens (barely audible over the ceaseless clangs) blared from some distant part of the train—a part of the train that unfortunately did not concern him, for Riyul was alone.

Complete solitude. Bliss, some might consider it, in this compartment, secluded from all else. Riyul didn't find it to be bliss. For Riyul, he was in prison.

It was difficult to be certain how long he had spent on this train. Had it been a month? Two? The passing of days, much like the passing of the world outside, seemed to become one endless blur.

It still looked around midnight outside.

The wooden boards he was sitting on groaned in protest as he heaved himself up, abruptly lolling his legs over the edge of the carriage and back into the compartment, and stood up to full stature. All around him were the telltale signs of a man who had quickly made home out of near-nothingness. It was dark. Wooden crates were scattered around the box-shaped carriage; clothes were strewn around the compartment, covering the wooden boxes as though creating children's play tables. A makeshift bed carefully constructed out of miscellaneous clothes and hay took up a third of the living space; on a rusted nail hung a solitary lantern, bathing the compartment with a sickly yellow light—jerking and twisting with the slightest turn and sway of the train.

As he glanced at his bed, contemplating whether he should give up on the watch and lie down, Riyul heard the scurry of tiny feet. He edged forward carefully, and out of his pillow (once a pair of his finest trousers) poked a miniscule nose, followed by snow-white whiskers and fur.

'Eli!' cried Riyul, rushing over to the mouse before he could escape. 'I was wondering where you were!' Eli twitched his nose affectionately as Riyul reached down and picked up the rodent, who began nibbling the inside of his palm.

'I haven't got any food for you, I'm afraid, Eli,' Riyul said, walking over to the other side of the carriage.

Gazing down at the innocent creature in his hand rekindled a gnawing feeling inside of him—a feeling he did not want to resurface. He watched the playful animal scurrying around, and a powerful ache began to well up from the pit of his stomach and flood his body. Eli was the only other living being Riyul had in the world now. The sensation of helplessness stuffed his lungs and throat, and suddenly swallowing seemed difficult.

He had remembered again. Eli was now his sole companion; and as for his real friends and family—he did not know where they were. Were his sons okay? The ache reached inside his chest and twisted, making Riyul falter and his vision blur for the millionth time.

So he pushed their memories away.

The wooden wall panels adjacent to his makeshift bed were littered with carvings, endless deep scratches indicating what Riyul hoped were days passed. The only thing was, every time Riyul woke up, it was night. The lines he carved every so often were his best guess at what may have been twenty-four hours. But were there hours in the train? He had been riding the train night after night, week after week, without a single ray of sunshine peeking over the moving forest outline. And yet he felt sure that there were days—days that were just waiting around the corner. He just seemed to never catch them. Riyul always fell asleep, no matter how hard he tried, before daybreak. And he always reawoke in the depth of night.

If daylight could finally make an appearance, he might be able to understand another piece of the puzzle…

It felt as though it was just yesterday that he was running to Moor Street Station, praying that he was not too late for departure. It felt like just yesterday he had taken his ticket, unceremoniously waved it in front of the ticket inspector and proceeded to sprint helter-skelter to Platform 2. It felt like just yesterday he was in the world he knew and understood, outside of this nightmarish, disconcerting misery—and yet his world of just yesterday felt like a lifetime ago.

Riyul was deep in thought when he realised something was wrong. The playful nature of Eli came to a halt: whereas he was but a minute ago scampering around Riyul's splayed hand, mischievously hiding behind box and blanket, he had now stopped moving. Instead, Eli appeared to be staring at something far off in the distance. Riyul turned around to look at the opening of the carriage, near where he had been earlier.

His eyes grew wide.

There, standing in front of the rushing trees and night sky, on the very spot Riyul had been sitting half-asleep just minutes ago, stood a shadowed figure.

'Who are you?'

Chapter 2

Adam

Daffodil stumbled through the woods.

She looked around as the towering forest trees swayed around her in the night breeze. She had arrived at a circle of clear unbroken woodland. A strange white glow radiated out from the centre of this patch of clearness—an eerie luminescence where no wood dared to grow.

A light flickered from the centre of the circle. Or … a pair of lights?

An owl hooting somewhere above, as if in warning.

Daffodil squinted, trying to find what was in the centre of the glowing circular patch. The light was intense. She blinked to keep her vision from wavering—through the pain, she looked to where the luminosity was strongest and most intense, to the epicentre.

And that's when the screams began.

***

Daffodil thrashed about. She was screaming. She looked around her, eyes wide.

Walls. Her bedroom walls.

Where was the glow, the woods, the sounds? Sweat covered every inch of her body. She raised her hands, looking at them, splaying them, turning them, touching her bed, duvet and arms.

She was in bed.

A sigh of relief. She was at home. As she let herself slump back into her bed, she thought back to the nightmare. It was already fading, but she managed to grasp on to a few blurry images: a figure in the woods, a strong light, and her brother. But before she knew it, the dream slipped away.

'All in your head, Daffodil,' she whispered to herself.

These dreams were becoming far too frequent. Night after night, strange visions of endless woods and that figure which seemed to be her, looking for something. Then, the dream would suddenly end, and she'd find herself in her bed again… screaming, sweating, shaking. Yet she didn't ever remember exactly what happened, nor why she was screaming. Her parents never heard a sound either.

Daffodil sighed. No, she was not doing this, not tonight. She rubbed her temples and decided to get some water downstairs to get her mind off things.

She reached the landing and realised something was wrong.

The kitchen.

There was a stream of light from the top of the kitchen door. As she listened—yes, she was sure of it. She could hear clinking sounds from within.

Who on earth would be in the kitchen at this hour, at the dead of night? She checked the clock.

3.14AM. Surely it wasn't a burglar robbing her parents' things and stalking through her home?

Deciding to not waste any time in case the burglar escaped, Daffodil grabbed the closest object she could find on the landing—her mother's blue and white china plate—then, armed with nothing but this piece of porcelain in her shaking hand, she proceeded to the kitchen door and slammed it open.

'Aaaah!' shrieked a voice from within the room.

'Aaaah!' Daffodil screamed in response, raising her plate in both hands, ready to smash it over the head of the screaming burglar.

'Daffodil! What are you doing?! It's me!' the voice shouted, higher-pitched than she had expected from a thief.

An ambush, surely! Wait—how did the shrieking thief know her name? But as she quickly realised, it was not in fact a burglar; this wasn't a thief or intruder of any kind—shrieking or otherwise. It was a young boy in a baby-blue sleeping top, with a jigsaw piece still in hand, eyes wide, frozen in shock, presumably at the thought of being hit over the head with mum's favourite china plate.

'Oh, it's just you, Adam,' said Daffodil, a wave of relief washing over her.

Her little brother remained frozen, smiling nervously—as though in shock.

'Can you not smile like that please? It's unnerving,' said Daffodil.

'But you still look like you're going to hit me with that plate,' breathed Adam, motioning at her circular instrument of death quivering mid-air.

'Oh, right.'

Daffodil gently placed the plate on the small table near her, from where it clattered to the floor (whilst somehow not breaking). She tried to look composed—though she wasn't too sure how to look composed after nearly bashing her brother with a plate. Consequently, she proceeded to smooth down her pyjamas.

'Why are you smoothing down your pyjamas?' Adam asked, motionless. 'Are you trying to act nonchalant? Also, they're really sweaty.'

'It's my new style. I like the sweatiness. And I'm trying to make them less crumpled; I want to remain elegant and graceful when fending off intruders like you,' said Daffodil, believing this was a great comeback. She smiled to herself. That was a good retort. Her brother had always been the clever and funny one, but she had a quip or two of her own. Her chest puffed out. What she had just done was quite brave, actually—not only brave, but her quick thinking was also elegant and graceful. She nodded to herself and grinned again.

'Why are you grinning like that? It's terrifying,' said her brother.

She stepped forward, not caring about his teases, smiling wider, happy with how this had gone, and broke the plate.

'I think you broke the plate.'

'Yes, thanks Adam.'

'So,' Adam said, pulling out a second chair at the table, 'are you going to tell me why you're up at 3 AM?' He was now concentrating on his puzzle whilst Daffodil poured herself some water.

'Weird dreams, Adam. Weird dreams,' she replied, pulling out a seat.

'Do you want to talk about it?' asked Adam, raising an eyebrow, still focusing on his puzzle. It was mostly complete. Perhaps a hundred pieces left. The entire puzzle looked around five thousand. Goliath for most. Nothing for her baby brother.

'Not really. What are you doing anyway, at this time of night?'

'Is it not obvious? I'm scheming to take over the world.' Adam squinted at his puzzle. 'Aha!' He placed a piece in the middle and picked up another.

'Huh. But you're nine.'

'Hey! That's ageist,' he exclaimed in feigned shock. 'I'm a perfectly suitable candidate to take over the world, Pinky.'

Daffodil smirked.

'Anyhow,' he continued, 'I'm not really planning world domination. Not yet anyway. I'm just trying to figure out how to put this ridiculous train together.'

Daffodil watched him work on the puzzle for a few minutes, tongue ever so slightly poking out, contemplating how to connect the two-dimensional bits of track and wheel. Oh, her brother was amazing. That much she was sure of. Despite his years, the kid was an absolute genius. But perhaps more important, at least to Daffodil, was that along with his intelligence, he was a good kid. In fact, he was and had always been her friend, even when perhaps Mum and Dad hadn't. Now he sat there, in his blue nightwear, forehead creased, his brown hair poking in a thousand different directions: the very picture of childhood innocence—and the apple of her eye.

His cuteness was misleading though, Daffodil had always thought. The cute appearance did not tell of the vast intelligence lurking beneath. She thought back to the day when her dog, Fluffy, died five years ago, and Adam had promptly decided to console her by developing a robotic replacement. She remembered when letters had streamed in offering him a chance to study at universities such as at Bath and Cambridge, despite his age. Most of all, she remembered how he had always been there whenever she needed someone to talk to. There was a lot to love about her baby brother.

'I think you need to just—' Daffodil stood up, picked the piece out of his hand, 'put that piece … there.'

She added the piece to the right place, but in the process knocked over the china plate with crumbs from the counter. It smashed into a million pieces on the tiled kitchen floor.

'Ah, yes, I guess that works. You know what's just happened, don't you?'

'I showed kid-genius how to solve a simple puzzle?' she said, laughing.

'Well no. I was going to place that there anyway. Also, you did just break yet another plate in a three-minute period. No, I mean tomorrow.'

Daffodil's laughs dried up.

'There's a reason you're up at 3AM. There's a reason you've been having nightmares the last few days. And there's a reason that you're down here, doing puzzles with me and not in bed—I mean, you don't even like puzzles.'

'What? That's not true—I don't dislike puzzles.'

He stared at her.

'You literally told me yesterday that puzzles are the most boring thing in the world.'

'Yes. Boring. Boring! Not that I dislike them. I mean, sometimes I like being bored!'

'What does that even mean?' he said, shaking his head. 'Anyway, there's a reason you cannot sleep. You don't want to go to school tomorrow.'

'School? That's ridiculous.'

'Oh, come on, Daffodil. We're not stupid. I mean, I get it. Nobody likes starting something new. Who would? It's literally a new school! It's big and unfamiliar and absolutely terrifying.'

He gently placed a hand on her arm, though continuing his puzzle with the other. 'It's okay. I get it.'

This boy, Daffodil thought, shaking her head in incredulity. *It's like he's my older brother.*

'No, Adam,' she whispered hoarsely, 'You don't understand. I mean, yes, you're right in some ways: I'm worried about being different and making friends and fitting in. But it's not that. It's just … I feel like Mum and Dad need me here. I don't want to be away at this time, not with what's happened.'

'Ah, I see,' Adam said kindly. 'You're worried about being homesick. It's a little early for that, isn't it? Considering you're currently still at home?' He grinned that goofy grin of his. 'Look, I may not be fourteen like you yet, but I can appreciate that boarding school is a very different proposition to just switching schools. It's far. You have every right to feel homesick at first. But remember why you are doing it.' He took a deep breath and put down his puzzle piece. 'Who is the one that absolutely smashed the entry exam?'

Silence.

'Me,' Daffodil mouthed.

'And who's the one that beat all odds, even after we moved across England, and got into one of the top schools in the country?'

'Me,' she smirked.

'And who is the one,' he stood up, and Daffodil grinned, 'that is going to go on the train tomorrow to Rarley School—' Daffodil was beaming now, involuntarily nodding along to the impromptu speech, '—and finally—once and for all—is going to stop breaking all the blooming china plates?'

She scowled. Though the twinge of a smile threatened to break out of the corner of her mouth. Not letting it out, she turned and slowly paced back to the door.

'Thanks for the chat, Adam, but I think it's time for me to get some rest,' Daffodil said, sighing.

'Yeah.' Adam nodded in his ridiculously adult way. 'Big day tomorrow.'

She turned to him as she made her way out.

'Big day indeed.' She smiled sadly. She blew her baby brother a kiss from the doorway, and left.

Chapter 3

Puzzle

Daffodil slammed the door and ran. She was running and running and running and running.

It was all a blur. The street. The houses. The people.

She ran, tears blurring her vision. Down her road. Towards the bus stop which would take her to the train station. Past the streaming pedestrians.

Time itself cascaded around her.

She had to run. She had to get out of that house and move. When you move, you leave all of it behind, she thought through an onslaught of tears.

Daffodil was sprinting now, red jacket flapping in the cold morning air, suitcase clanging along the pavement after her, barely keeping up. Pedestrians were staring as she bolted past, but she didn't care. Just get as far as you can from the house, thought Daffodil. Get on a train and get out. Go anywhere. Just move.

She had argued with her parents again. She knew that much. But that's all she knew; she was too distraught to focus on the details—she only wanted to get on a train and out of Birmingham.

She'd not go in to school today. She'd bunk off. Go somewhere. Stratford, New York. Didn't matter. Anywhere at this point.

Still running, she swiped at her eyes, her vision continually blurring, hoping to come up with some kind of plan. Her train to Rarley town-centre would depart in fifteen minutes. Yet that was the last thing on her mind after what her parents had done. But did it really matter which train she caught? Once she went through the turnstiles, she could board any train to any of the nearby destinations, and, so long as she could dodge the ticket inspectors (who never appeared this early in the morning anyway), she'd be fine. Even if she couldn't, she didn't care. She could hop on one of the trains and spend the day at Stratford-upon-Avon or London or anywhere—she just needed to move and get out and clear her head.

What her parents had said was terrible. But no, she wasn't going to think about that again. Come to think of it... what had they... Ugh, it was blurring again, like her vision. Her fists tightened around the handle of her luggage as she turned the corner towards the bus station. She stopped. Deep breaths. She squeezed her eyelids shut, trying to calm herself down.

Darkness. Her synaesthesia was kicking in. Sounds of ... screeching rubber?

She heard it before she saw it. The bus pulled into the stop and opened its doors with a light hiss, letting out a deluge of passengers. An old lady in pink, a man in a tweed suit, a lanky teenager listening to music. Normal people going about their normal Mondays. Not a crying schoolgirl who didn't know what to do or where to go. Daffodil looked around. Nobody left but her to go on. She blinked away the last of her tears. She decided then and there she might not take the train to Rarley this morning, but a train somewhere would be best to get her mind off of things.

So she boarded the bus into the town centre, and began the journey towards Moor Street Station.

***

The door, and by extension, the whole house, shook with such force after Daffodil left that it seemed as though the entire front of the house had been rumbled by an earthquake. Seconds passed, yet the window panes, walls and doors continued to tremble.

'Well, perhaps we should have seen that coming,' said Zakariyya, leaning against the kitchen table, watching the front of the house shake.

'This wouldn't have happened if you didn't bring it up,' said Clarice, tears in her eyes, arms akimbo. Her soft, round face was glaring, though more out of worry for her daughter than anger at the situation. She knew they had to say what they said.

He tapped his foot lightly against the ceramic tiling of the kitchen floor as he wondered about the decisions they'd made that morning. Frowning, forehead creased, he looked perpetually in thought. Clarice walked over.

'You're right,' she said softly. 'We had to bring it up. I just guess I didn't expect her to react quite like that.'

'Ah, you remember what it was like being fourteen,' Zakariyya said, holding his wife's hands. 'You feel like the world is against you, particularly your parents. Add to that what we actually said, and I don't blame her for reacting how she did. She's been through a lot.'

His gaze fell on a puzzle piece on the kitchen counter.

As gently as possible, he picked it up, recognising the piece, and delicately twirled it between his fingers. He smiled. She loved this puzzle set.

Clarice sighed.

'Yeah, I just hope she'll get to school okay.'

'She'll be okay,' said Zakariyya, gently tapping the jigsaw piece against the counter top. 'We have to have some faith in her—she's caught buses and trains before. We know she can do it.' He placed the piece down and looked up at Clarice. 'We just have to trust she'll find her way.'

He gave her a thin smile, squeezing her hand one more time, and walked to the front door, placing the puzzle piece back in its original box with Daffodil's things.

Chapter 4

Courage

Daffodil's head was buried in a book, though for once it was just a façade. She wasn't even reading. Her head was spinning with what had happened at home, when her parents had said…

No.

She shook her head. She was not going to think about it.

She just needed some space.

The bus began to slow down, judder and squeal. Raising her head a little, she peered over at the throngs of bus-goers standing up and making their way towards the exit—some slowly, some in sudden bursts of roused awakeness, all realising their stop had come. It wasn't her stop. Yet, involuntarily, her mind whizzed back to her argument with Mum and Dad, how they'd said those horrible words which made her heart hurt. How she was riled to run and move and get away, as though the truth had come out in one giant flood of tears and heartache. No, she didn't want to sit on the bus; she could walk the rest of the way.

***

The reassuring, satisfying sound of her shoes clacking against the pavement confirmed Daffodil was back in the outside world. She began walking through Birmingham's town centre, Digbeth, winding her way around the complex thoroughfares towards Moor Street Station, when she spotted the homeless man.

At first, she couldn't fathom why someone had just discarded a pile of clothes on the side of the road—with a red patchwork quilt on top, no less. But then the bundle of clothes moved, and she realised it was a homeless person—a homeless person who caused a bit of a scene.

The movement of some clothes appeared to have terrified one of the passers-by, a busy-looking man in a posh suit. The businessman had consequently screamed and nearly spilt his coffee over his expensive suit.

Daffodil giggled at the sight. The man didn't giggle, though. In fact, once he had composed himself and seen the cause of his fright, he began turning a bright shade of plum, and now looked like he was going to explode. He had doubled back, after shrieking, and now stood, fuming, with one hand to his ear, ending a call, and the other to his heart. His fallen coffee cup was forgotten and began a slow roll across the pavement. The man took a deep breath.

'What on EARTH are you doing, you disgusting tramp?' he shouted.

The homeless man scrambled back towards the wall. 'Sorry, sir, I was just getting up, after—after a hard night on the road,' he said feebly.

'Well, go somewhere else!' barked the man. 'This city has enough of an infestation without you adding to it.'

How dare he speak like that? Daffodil thought, stunned. *More importantly, why is nobody saying anything?*

She looked around; people simply glanced and walked around as though it had nothing to do with them, watching the commotion with awkward sidelong glances.

All these adults are just … ignoring it.

Daffodil bit her lip. She had to do something, particularly considering nobody else was. But she was only a little girl; what about these adults? She waited a moment and hoped somebody would step in. Yet they continued to walk on. The people weren't doing anything. They just kept going along with their lives, pretending it wasn't happening.

Well, one thing was for sure: she couldn't stand here and do nothing.

'Hey! Mr!' Daffodil said loudly, feigning confidence. A few people began slowing down, hesitating in their brisk morning strides, watching the new change in dynamic. 'You sure are a lot more noisy after seeing all that frightened you was a person moving. Why were you not so loud before you saw it was a homeless man? Why only raise your voice when it's someone you think you can bully?' Daffodil gestured at the man on the ground, half-propped up on his elbow, mouth open in a mixture of shock and happiness.

Daffodil smiled as kindly as she could as he looked at her incredulously. She glared at the man in the suit, who seemed equally flabbergasted at what was happening. 'I mean,' Daffodil continued, 'All I'm saying is that you weren't like this when you shrieked a minute ago.'

People had begun gathering around now. It must have been a sight, Daffodil thought—this scene between a young girl, this suited and irascible man, and the poor homeless man on the ground. Before the man in the suit could respond (a pink tinge had appeared on his cheeks), others from the crowd began to call out in support.

'The girl's right! Leave him alone!'

'Yeah! I saw what happened. You have no right to speak to anyone that way.'

'Yeah. Move on, Suits! Let the homeless fellow be.'

Everybody seemed to get involved after Daffodil made the first step.

Suits opened his mouth to say something, but no words came; just expressions of disbelief. He shot a glaring look at Daffodil— though he did not look at the homeless man again—and stalked off, shaking his head and starting another phone call.

As the small crowd began to disperse, the other man got up. Turning to him in worry, Daffodil realised his clothes were in tatters, and his frizzy, auburn curls were wild and all over the place. She thought he might be angry at what had happened, but suddenly he broke out into the biggest smile she'd ever seen.

'Thank you so much,' he said, beaming at her.

'That's okay. What's your name, Mr?' Daffodil asked.

'James. I get that a lot, being who I am…' James pointed his thumb to the general direction in which the man in the suit had walked off toward. 'Not many people have stood up for me before, let alone such a young and brave girl like you!'

'It was nothing,' Daffodil said, feeling her cheeks flush a fiery red. 'Well, that's tragic you have to go through such abuse. So … you're very welcome,' she said kindly as he coughed. It certainly was cold this winter. 'I for one just couldn't watch you being treated in that way,' Daffodil said, looking at the taxis and people passing. 'If there's one thing I've learnt from my mum, it's to never let somebody get treated in the way you don't want to be treated. So, if we can do something, we should, right?'

'Indeed.' James nodded, grey eyes twinkling. 'Your mum is a smart woman.'

'Yes—you're right.' Daffodil said softly, thinking back to how she had left her mum in the kitchen earlier. 'She is.'

Chapter 5

The Eternity
Train

Daffodil's mum absolutely loved a good book. Day off from work, mind off of her patients, feet up near the fireplace with a classic in hand. That was the perfect morning.

She had proudly been the primary reason why Daffodil herself had become a voracious reader. They had spent many a night reading together quietly in front of the fireplace whilst Daffodil was growing up—when Adam was just a baby.

Clarice smiled sadly at the thought.

She was in her favourite spot in the very same place in her favourite armchair, on the forty-second page of Crime and Punishment, her mind wandering back to Daffodil, and further to Adam.

Dead silence. The mid-morning sun shining in through the blinds. She had just reread the same paragraph four times, but her mind kept going to Daffodil's exit earlier. Her reading-glasses had just begun to slide—ever so slowly—down the bridge of her nose.

And she had just barely raised her hand to push them back into place when—

Ring-ring-ring.

'Aaah!' she squealed, jumping out of the armchair. Her book and glasses flew away in unison, like birds finally free, landing on opposite ends of the living room: her book on the rug, glasses on the edge of the fireplace, near where Daffodil liked to hang her signature red coat. The coat was not there currently; Daffodil must have taken it with her.

Clarice quickly scanned for her phone, hurried over and picked it up from the mantelpiece, almost stepping on her glasses in the process.

'Hello? Is this Mrs Everwater?'

'Yes, it is,' Clarice said, gathering herself. Where had her book gone? She looked around and saw it was somehow on the other end of the room. She had to find the page again now. 'Who's calling, sorry?'

'I'm Anna, the receptionist at Rarley. I'm just checking you are the mother of Daffodil Winters,' she asked gently, but with something else interwoven in her words—a briskness, closing in on urgency.

Clarice's heartbeat instantly picked up.

'Yes? Is something wrong?' she said quickly.

'We are not entirely sure, Mrs Everwater... It's about your daughter.'

***

The daughter of Mrs Everwater traipsed through the concourse of Moor Street Station.

It was quite something, Daffodil mused. Even in the modern day and age, the stunning red walls and exposed bricks (which must have been modernised from when they were first laid) looked as apt for the twenty-first century as they must have in the previous, or whenever they had first been placed.

There sure was a lot going on. People milled around at the stalls and florists and coffee shops. 'Centenary Lounge', one sign read, an old white-on-black signboard. The walls glistened a burnished ruby as though she had been transported back to the twentieth century. Buzzes from a thousand voices thrummed around; the horns and honks of the cars from the main road just behind the corner.

Where was the platform sign?

The station itself was largely airy and spacious, with streams of light shining through from the mostly perspex slats of the roof above.

She heard the unmistakable swishes of the barriers and people with luggage swiftly making their way to their destinations. Which got her thinking.

Where am I even going?

I definitely do not want to go to school, she thought, standing in the middle of the concourse. But she had to go… She hadn't missed a day before in her life, barring when she was (rarely) sick. She could take the hourly train to London Marylebone if she really wanted to, she supposed.

Daffodil was in this state of deliberation when it dawned on her that the turnstiles were simply open. So, after chewing her lip for a whole three seconds more, she decided to simply walk through and see where the trains were going.

Strange about the turnstiles, she thought, but she presumed there'd be some form of ticket checking later on.

This'll be easier than I thought.

She rounded a few corners and found herself in an empty platform bay.

Trains whooshed past, catching Daffodil's attention, turning her head involuntarily. Here's one. Here's another. Train after train after train after train after train—all going places she'd never really been to. She tried to make sense of the destinations, but she was only familiar with one or two of the stations on the screens.

Coventry or London? Rarley or Reading? Daffodil stood still for a moment, taking it all in. Perhaps it didn't matter too much, as long as she could clear her head, and thus, she decided to jump onto the next train that appeared and go exploring wherever she got off. She'd easily make her way back home after a few hours, when ready.

The rush of speeding trains around her sent her flaxen-coloured hair flying in different directions, and she envisaged, in her often day-dreaming way, what she must look like to the outside world right now: a girl standing still on a platform, the world moving around her, waiting patiently to step into the belly of the very machine that goes on, ceaselessly to towns and cities of all kinds—the humble locomotive that had connected people and generations for as long as it had been around.

She was staring out, eyes blank but mind racing, in deep contemplative resonance, when the smooth body of the silver tube of a train slid right up to her feet.

Without a moment's hesitation, Daffodil climbed in.

As she sat down on the cloth seat, she let out a contented sigh.

It was good to move. It was good to not be still and just go somewhere when upsetting things happen. For this reason, she didn't notice as the lights began to flicker. She didn't notice when the door slid shut behind her, nor the doors at the ends of her compartment.

She did notice that she was strangely, completely alone in her carriage; Daffodil supposed that could happen sometimes, though perhaps not too frequently in the late morning of a working day. She also noticed the shudders that emanated from her seat as the train began—or tried to begin—moving off.

The shudders didn't stop, though.

Odd.

They only got more powerful.

Daffodil lurched forward.

The modest shakes and rumbles of a usual train seemed amplified and jolting and now painful.

The juddering, spine-shaking vibrations seemed to rack the entire train.

The lights started flickering. She looked around frantically. The morning light outside her window seemed to be dimming down, like someone was turning down the lights. She gripped her armrests tightly, her knuckles white when—

BANG.

Blackness.

Chapter 6

Haradan

Chukka-chukka-chukka-chukka-chukka.

The sound was the first thing she noticed. It was present even before her vision, for she was still bathed in the darkness. Granted, she hadn't opened her eyes yet, her head hurt, and the rhythmic pulse of the moving train felt strangely ... soothing. She didn't even want to open her eyes just yet.

What had happened? Did I sleep on the journey?

Perhaps she could remain a minute or two in this black void. With eyes closed, Daffodil didn't have to face her sadnesses.

In the darkness, reality was a world away.

Chukka-chukka-chukka-chukka-chukka. The sound again. That sound was calling her to open her eyes: why was it so loud? Or ... was it loud? Perhaps her hearing was simply heightened whilst her eyes remained closed. Wait... The train. The flickering lights. The shuddering. The blackout. Daffodil opened her eyes.

She was lying on her side, facing the wall of the carriage. Though for some reason, the wall seemed different.

How had she gotten onto the floor? Where was her table?

'You seem to be quite uncomfortable there,' called a voice from the other end of her carriage—a deep, resonating sound that boomed across the space: the voice of a man who hadn't been there before. She winced, trying to look around. Whoever the voice belonged to made her realise that she was actually uncomfortable, and in pain: the left half of her face felt swollen and bruised and puffed up. She didn't even want to deal with this extra stress of blacking out on a train; she had already had enough of an adrenaline rush for one day with the man in the suit and James. She wasn't in the mood for any more drama.

'Uncomfortable? That's probably because I am on the floor of a moving train,' replied Daffodil to the mystery voice, trying to slowly get up.

The voice chuckled, then called out, perhaps a little quieter than before, 'Indeed. Well, I must tell you to brace yourself, my dear, once you're up. Whilst it's lovely to have you, it is often difficult when someone new joins us.'

Joins us? What on earth was that supposed to mean?

Daffodil got up and looked around the carriage she'd got on. She gasped quietly. This wasn't the carriage she remembered.

'Yes, perhaps a little different to whatever you had last seen,' came the voice—but Daffodil wasn't listening. 'Very different indeed.'

'No ... way,' she whispered.

Her eyes scanned the walls of the carriage, which were not the usual grey hard plastic; gone were the modern tube-like structures she had initially entered. They were now made of an impeccable burnished wood, as though she had stepped back into the trains of years gone by. Daffodil spun around. The previously modern train seats with their fabric and royal blue colour had disappeared, seemingly vanished, replaced now with wooden bench-style seats.

'It's possible indeed.'

She turned to the voice.

In the corner of the compartment sat a man with a black cane and a long flowing trenchcoat. His medium-length hair was speckled with strands of grey, and as he examined her from across the carriage, he broke into a kindly smile. He looked old, though Daffodil could not place his age. His face had creases and wrinkles, but his posture indicated youth, as though he were ageless.

Daffodil did not know what to say. Her eyes simply grew wider in disbelief as she swept around her and gasped the more she discovered. Wooden floorboards. Previously, they had been some kind of grey linoleum, she was sure. Lanterns hanging on the wall as if she were on the Orient Express. Scenery rushing past through... Wait... Those weren't windows.

She turned to the man.

'How? What? Where am I? How did I get here?' Daffodil demanded.

'You've... You've come somewhere different,' the man said slowly, brushing his shoulder-length storm-grey hair behind his ears. His grey eyes looked concerned. 'Aethril.'

Daffodil took a step back, almost falling into one of the wooden seats. 'What do you mean somewhere different?' she asked, looking around frantically. Everything was different. Changed. 'I was catching a train from Moor Street. Where's the train I was on?' Her words spilled out of her.

'You are in a different land to your world.' He gestured around. 'This is a place unlike your land. As for the where, well, that will be made clear very soon, but please, as difficult as this sounds to do, and as easy as it is for me to say—please do not worry. Let me just say that there are others. You and I are not the only ones here. We believe you've travelled to another place. Another… plane, if you will.'

Daffodil's heart pounded a million miles an hour. Her whole body felt like one thrumming heartbeat; she wanted to be sick.

'I don't understand what kind of twisted joke this is,' Daffodil said, turning, looking for the exit.

The olden style interior. Benches of a bygone age. Darkness outside. And above—now, that was impossible. Something glimmered above, and she craned her neck up at what should have been the roof of the train.

But there was no roof.

Above her—and her eyes felt as if they could not bulge any more or grow any wider lest they pop - she found the sky. Where the ceiling should be was nothing but the immensity of space—an endless canopy of stars. The walls of the train simply cut off where the roof would be. And in its place were a billion twinkles, sprinkled across a deep purple inken sky.

Daffodil gaped. Then she caught herself and looked back at the man. He was exactly where he'd been before. The drum that was her heart pounded harder and harder in her chest.

'You've kidnapped me! You! You did this!' She was shouting, getting away from him as far as possible. When she realised he was not making any attempt to come at her, she slowed her breathing. Still as far from him as possible.

She walked up to the edge of the carriage and gazed outward. They were moving, alright. Bushes, trees, shrubbery. All zipping swiftly by in the beautiful purple darkness of night.

Wait.

Daffodil spun back around.

'How is it so dark?' she challenged. 'I boarded my train in the morning.'

How long had gone by since she entered?

It felt like minutes ago.

'Who are you? How did I get here? How do I get back?' The questions flooded out as she looked around frantically for some clue or sign or escape or something to get back to her train.

He was saying something in response, but it was as though Daffodil could not hear. She felt a warm rush of panic rising as her mind whirled. Realisation began to dawn that she may not be on the train she had boarded. She might be somewhere else—lost.

What train was this? It wasn't hers.

And that sky.

It was impossible. Magic did not exist, yet everything around her seemed impossibly magical. This only happened in books and movies.

Yet as she looked at her surroundings, there was no doubt about it—this train was different to the one she had boarded, and entirely different to anything she had ever seen before.

The man got up with a sigh and walked towards her.

'Look, my name is Haradan,' he said, raising his hands with palms facing forward, signalling peace. 'I'm really sorry you have to go through this, or be here right now. In all honesty, even after all these years I have been here, I can't tell you how you arrived exactly. And I understand you have a lot of questions; you have every right to; but I think it may be easier if I show you a few things.'

'What do you mean?'

Haradan stretched. As he did so, his full height became apparent. He was handsome, although clearly not a young man: grey stubble covered his face, complementing his sparkling grey eyes, and his shoulder-length grey locks matched his well-built frame. He withdrew a small pouch from his trenchcoat and took out small rock-like objects that glittered a beautiful gold.

'These are pure gold nuggets,' he explained, holding out his palm. 'Now, what is it that people in your world, since time immemorial, have wanted to do to everyday objects? Perhaps even to turn everyday things into these things?'

'What on EARTH DOES THAT HAVE TO DO WITH THIS PLACE?!'

'Please,' Haradan replied, his smile gentle and calm. 'Humour me.'

She was breathing heavily. The question was nonsense.

'Please,' said Haradan, tilting his head.

'I don't know. Alchemy? You mean alchemy?'

He nodded. 'What do you know of alchemy?'

Daffodil tried to compose herself and think. 'People have attempted to turn lead and copper into gold.'

'Yes, my dear. All things, to be fair. We've tried to turn all things into gold.'

Daffodil frowned. *What did he mean by* we…?

'We tried to turn many things into many, many other things. But do not let your history books fool you. We found a way.'

He placed two golden nuggets on the ground and extracted a small vial of what appeared to be clear liquid from his jacket, fastened by even smaller cork. The nuggets ever so slightly shuddered with the moving of the train. Haradan removed a cork stopper and poured a singular drop of white liquid onto the closest golden nugget.

The drop fell in slow motion. Or at least seemed to.

And as soon as it touched the nugget, instant change. One moment it was a golden piece of metal. The next, it wasn't. No dramatic sounds or effects. Without so much as a wisp of smoke, as soon as the liquid made contact, it covered the entire golden nugget in a thin white film.

The thin white film then split off and grew into a second identical white nugget, attached by the same thin white line.

Haradan poured a drop of another brown liquid on his experiment, and this turned both nuggets back into the original golden colour, all whiteness disappearing, leaving a second pure golden nugget.

Daffodil stared at the two golden pieces. Then at Haradan, who grinned.

'Duplication balm. The best alchemists have fine-tuned this to work in an instant. The vehicle you have now found yourself on will undoubtedly be different to whatever you had experienced before, in your world. This is a world where things can be made, shaped, reshaped and transformed.'

'No way,' Daffodil said, shaking her head.

She turned and walked past the old benches and impossibly older-still looking walls. 'This is not real. A roof that shimmers? Alchemy? Duplication? This is some kind of joke,' she said, feigning a laugh.

But where was the joke?

Daffodil scanned the surroundings for some kids waiting to jump out and surprise her. She looked around and waited and turned, searching, and waited some more.

But nobody jumped out.

Nobody to explain the prank.

Nobody at all.

It was just her and Haradan.

She turned back around.

This is insane. I need to calm down.

She shut her eyes and embraced the darkness of nothing.

Yet there was not nothing. There was an unexpected brightness there. A brightness that grew every moment.

'Haradan, right?' Daffodil said, opening her eyes.

He nodded.

'I don't know what is going on, but this ... I ... Magic does not exist. This cannot be possible.'

'Ah.' He smiled poignantly. A sad smile—his eyes did not move. 'We do not believe it is magic at all. What it is, however, is perhaps far more complex. Magic would have been a nice and simple explanation to this all.'

He picked up his things, putting them back into his jacket methodically, and stood, facing her. His hands rested on his polished black cane, topped by a ball of glistening silver. He unscrewed it slowly and pulled out a small red sphere, like a marble, but with multiple shades of red gas swirling within. He then withdrew a blue marble and held them both between his finger and thumb. 'You are in a different place. A different plane perhaps, but ultimately it is not impossible, nor is it magical. Watch this,' he said with a wink.

He threw the small red marble against the wall, and the section of wall erupted in flames. No sooner had he done this, however, he threw the blue marble, which formed a rapidly-expanding sheet of ice, dousing the flames and encrusting the wall with a glistening hoar frost.

The more she witnessed, the more truthful this place appeared to be. But was it all just smoke and mirrors? Tricks? Daffodil considered this, walking over to the wall that had just been both on fire and frozen in ice.

'Tell me, what is your name?' Haradan queried.

Her hands traced over the now damp wall; the ice was melting, beads of water trickling down. Cold to the touch.

Can I trust him? There was a lot of power in a name. Her parents had always told her to be careful when talking to strangers. Though she was unsure if the circumstances still applied, considering she was on an unimaginable moving train that defied the laws of nature with a man who had just seemed to have done alchemy.

She ran her fingers against the partly wet wall and looked at her fingers. There was a sheen. It was real. She looked outside the train, where the wind rushed by at inhuman speed. Holding her finger up to get a feel for the wind, she sensed they were moving very, very fast, and she could feel the cold air around them as they rushed through at who-knows-what miles per hour.

To give her name would be to accept all of this. But how could she believe this man, with his seemingly impossible powers in this seemingly impossible place?

'Let me ask you a question,' Daffodil said, voice shaking as she lowered her finger. 'Is there a way off this train?'

He paused before answering. 'Yes—I believe so,' he replied. 'Though it is tricky. But yes, it is doable. I want to help you.'

'And why should I trust you? Why should I trust anything you have said? How did I get here?'

He paused, then smiled that sad, empty smile of his again—as though there were a million memories shifting behind his grey eyes.

'I do not believe you should trust anyone blindly. Indeed, no matter what good you hear of them here in Aethril. All I can tell you is that if you give me a chance to show you your answers, I will try my very best. I am here to help, and that is why I have been looking for you.'

She stared at him, mouth set in a firm line. Once more, she paced across the room, then stopped and looked out at the blur of trees and foliage streaking past beyond the train.

She stood there, steady and unblinking; when she finally spoke, her tone was crisp and unwavering.

'Haradan?'

'Hmm?'

'How long have you been here?' she said, turning to him.

'Me?' he asked, surprised.

Haradan paused again, and looked up at the impossible sky. 'I've been here since I was born.'

Chapter 7

The Endless Carriage

A seagull cried in the distance. And another. And yet another. Positioning himself beside Daffodil, Adam sat beside her on the sand and gazed out towards the endless blue expanse in front of them. The cries of gulls filled the air; a spectacular pink sunset was unfolding across the horizon in mirage-like waves, almost blending into the inky turquoise ocean, as though a great hand had spilt watercolour across a vast canvas. Warm, golden grains sifted beneath their weight as they crossed their legs and played their fingers through the sand. Both stared out in silence at the boats and the docks and the sea.

There was a sharp intake of breath. 'Do you think Mum and Dad are happy, Adam?' Daffodil asked, not taking her eyes off the lapping waves.

Mum and Dad were around a hundred yards down the beach, buying ice-cream for the family. The holiday was all it was meant to be: seaside resorts, great beaches, even a failed attempt at surfing. Daffodil could just make out Dad in his bright red shorts handing money over to the man in the stall, who swiftly disappeared inside to whip up some great ice-cream cones, and Mum standing beside him with her arms folded.

Adam thought about her question before answering. He always did that. Contemplated. He never was the impetuous type.

'I think they carry on. Continue on—for us. They care about us. I don't know if they're happy, but I think in their quiet, shut-up-inside-themselves kind of way, they want to see us happy. And that, by extension, is their happiness. Their kids.'

She looked at him, her baby brother, with his tousled brown hair and ridiculous suntan. He sat there, a walking contradiction to be so profoundly insightful in a body so young. Another bird squawked and took flight. Daffodil squinted due to the remnants of sunlight piercing through the clouds.

'They argue all the time, Adam,' she said. 'Just because we don't see it, doesn't mean it doesn't happen. When we're asleep, or they think we can't hear or we aren't looking, they'll talk. And it's never nice talking. They'll get cross at each other and shout, and sometimes Mum will cry. That's not happiness, surely.'

Laughter from the other children floated over from further down the beach. Daffodil tilted her head, contemplative like her brother.

She lowered her voice. 'I hear them speak about me.'

'Speak about you?' he repeated.

'Yes,' she said matter-of-factly.

She closed her eyes. 'I hear them say my name. When they speak, during their arguments… Or at the start of them anyway. In their hushed voices when they think I can't hear—when they think I'm asleep. That's when the whispers come about. They talk about me.'

The glow of sunset continued to dim, and Adam continued looking on ahead, his face an impassable stone wall.

'Dad talks to me everyday, but I feel like we haven't spoken in years,' Daffodil said, watching him—trying to read him for some kind of response, but Adam's expression was devoid of any noticeable emotion. She knew he was just thinking of the right answer, the right words, but he had such control of himself. She sighed. She wished she could do that. Just switch off. Control her feelings. Her ideas. Her thoughts. Just have some control. How freeing it must be.

'I don't want to do this anymore,' she said, looking away again. 'I don't want to be the reason for their sadness.'

Adam opened his mouth to speak, and then closed it again. Daffodil pretended not to notice, and continued looking on ahead. It seemed that—for once—even her brother didn't have the answers.

By looking ahead, she hoped that nobody would notice the solitary tear she felt roll down her cheek and fall to the warmth of the golden sand.

The sun had now set. And the gulls continued to cry.

***

As Haradan and Daffodil walked past the rows of seats that lined the carriage walls, she reflected on the sky beyond.

So many questions, she didn't know where to start. She guessed she may as well start with whatever came to her first.

'Haradan. Why aren't there any birds outside?'

'Birds? Hmm, well, that is a good question. I suppose it will have to do with the constant night we have on this part of the train.'

So many questions.

'This *part* of the train?' she queried.

'Indeed, my dear. What you need to understand, Daffodil, is that this train is not like anything you've encountered before,' Haradan explained as they walked through their carriage. The sounds of the train were growing exponentially louder as they progressed through the empty aisle.

'It's a bit of a maze. Each compartment can lead to another place, and another place to elsewhere. And you want to remember your route!' he pointed out quickly. 'And the signs of what leads to where! For example,' he said, stopping near a seat, 'there are some places noticeably different from others. Sounds. Imprints. Signs. We need to always be cognizant of our surroundings.'

None of this made any sense to Daffodil, and though she tried to process the information, she was only understanding scraps.

He peered over the back of a seat, running his hands along the wall beside it. The large open panes of what would have been glass appeared to simply be open-air, and the cool breeze whipped at Daffodil's long brown strands.

'Aha!' he exclaimed—though to Daffodil, his perusing hands had found nothing in particular—just more wall. Nonetheless, he pushed against the wood and depressed a part of the wall which was in fact not solid, and somehow, the shape of a door slowly appeared where the wall and open-air pane met. The door itself appeared to simply be a continuation of the wall and the open-air window, but as Daffodil stepped closer and ran her hand over it, there was something distinctly metallic about it. It was cold to the touch.

'What on earth?' Daffodil whispered, bewildered. 'How did you know there was a door hidden here?'

'There are doors all around us,' Haradan said, smiling. 'You just need to know how to find them.'

'Bit cryptic,' Daffodil muttered.

41

Haradan laughed, now fumbling with a silver doorknob, which Daffodil had not noticed previously. 'I've been here a long time. I forget sometimes how difficult it must be to process this all, to conceptualise everything. Even to get around! Though, for me at least the way around this place is not too tricky by this point. Sounds, shimmers, vibrations—all of these are clues, if we remain aware of them.'

His hands were feeling around the edge of the doorframe (though Daffodil was unsure if it could even be called a door). The door itself looked like a hologram almost, an identical replica of the very space it occupied: it not only looked like the wall and open-air window, but Daffodil suspected it very much was part of these, or they were part of it. She wasn't all too sure—but she wanted to work it out; wherever this place was, she needed to understand its inner workings to get back home.

'My life on the train and the lands connected have meant I've been meeting those who end up here for as long as I can remember,' he said, working away at the silvery doorknob once again. 'In fact, I've received word that there is another newcomer, so we have a few jobs to do. Or I guess you could say, we have a few places to go.'

'Where?' asked Daffodil, looking around the empty compartment. As she said this, Haradan pushed down softly on the doorknob, then upward; the door made the slightest of movements, and there was a loud click.

He opened the door.

Daffodil's eyes widened and her mouth dropped. She didn't know what she had expected, but she hadn't expected this, that was for sure.

In front of the door stretched an incomprehensibly long carriage—as far as her eyes could see—with what must have been a hundred thousand seats lining each of the walls with hundreds, maybe thousands of doors dotted at regular intervals on either side.

'We're going to two places,' Haradan said, stepping into the endless carriage. His tone of voice had changed subtly, as though readying for a great expedition. 'Firstly, we need to find the other newcomer, wherever they are. Might even find some birds on the way. But ultimately? We're going to find a man named Gerrihend, and help you to escape.'

Chapter 8

Hoffman

Clarice and Zakariyya squeezed past the stream of people leaving through the doors of the police station. They registered with the clerk at the sign-in desk, sat momentarily, and were then called to enter Detective Hoffman's office.

As they entered, a serious but kindly figure looked up from behind his desk. He wore the look of a man weathered by the responsibility of a hundred duties, and as such, his eyebrows seemed perpetually furrowed.

He wore a simple, yet well-made suit, and wore his chestnut-brown hair in a practical short style, combed neatly to his left side. Upon seeing the pair of them, he immediately stood up, and his weathered blue eyes softened a little.

'Mr Winters; Mrs Everwater, please have a seat.' He smiled and gestured at the two empty chairs in front of his desk. 'I am really sorry to have to meet under the circumstances.'

They thanked him and took the two seats. It was a grand desk, littered with papers. Behind him stood an antique clock with a pendulum that slowly but surely ticked along; on his desk perched a reading lamp that gave off a soft yellow light even in the brightness of the afternoon sun.

For the brief moment before he began, all that could be heard was the ticking of the clock.

'Thank you so much for speaking on the phone with me and coming in. It seems like you are going through what no parent ever wants to hear of, let alone experience. However, I'm glad you flagged this up quickly.' Detective Hoffman spoke swiftly but clearly, as though he had a lot to say but perhaps very little time to say it.

'Most people believe that you need to wait a certain amount of time before reporting a missing person, such as a day or two. Clearly, as you are both probably aware, there is no minimum, and it is important, particularly with children this young, fourteen, to actually begin looking as soon as possible.'

He began to flick through papers in a manilla folder.

Tick-tock. Tick-tock. Tick-tock.

'You mentioned she's not been responding to calls?'

'No, Detective,' Clarice said, her eyes glazed over with a light sheen of tears. She kept her gaze firmly fixed on the pendulum. 'We cannot get through to her at all.'

Hoffman nodded somberly. 'We'll have someone check to see the last time any of her devices were on, and if any CCTV footage was captured of her in public places. Obviously, the main thing that matters is that we understand where she may have been going.'

The pair of them nodded also, paralleling Detective Hoffman's professionalism, but also because they did not know how else to respond. Over the last few hours, they found that their words had dried up.

'So, just to recap, she was due in at school in the morning. She does not arrive at the expected time, the school calls you and you've obviously tried to reach her, but no luck. Is that all right?'

'Yes,' they both agreed.

'Could it be then that she has simply gone somewhere else?'

'Possibly,' Zakariyya said thoughtfully. 'We did argue. Since the incident, she has been harder to predict, perhaps even a little volatile.'

'Ah yes,' Hoffman said, thumbing a distinctly yellow sheet of paper from his folder. 'It mentions it here.' He paused. 'I truly am sorry. But know if she has gone for an excursion elsewhere and is bunking the day off school, we'll find her.'

Both parents smiled kindly and nodded in appreciation. A few moments went by silently.

'CCTV is an interesting phenomenon,' Hoffman explained. 'We'll check footage from the train lines and the stations she was due to travel from to school. Technically, on the trains themselves, all cameras are operating all the time, even when the unit is shut down. Footage is recorded on a hard drive, one per coach, and if there is anything important for us to see, we can see it ten minutes after a train calls in.'

'That's if she was spotted near the train line?' asked Zakariyya.

'Yes. Normally we use the footage ourselves to investigate incidents such as SPAD's—' He stopped himself before continuing. 'Sorry, that's signals passed at danger,' he said, noticing the confusion on their faces. 'Sorry.' He smiled. 'Police jargon. Anyway, we have also used footage to investigate near misses and fatalities. We will also supply footage to the BTP, the British Transport Police, via a designated person who has received the appropriate disclosure training. Again, this is all if she did take the train or a train as presumed.'

'Thank you so much, Detective. We know you will do all in your power to help,' said Clarice, with hope in her voice.

'And is there anything else about her that I should know?'

'Nothing that's not in the file,' explained Zakariyya. 'You know about her synaesthesia, don't you?'

'Ah, yes. That was interesting. Synaesthesia. I had to look it up to be fair. So she can … hear sounds that aren't always there? And see things also?'

'She has the ability to combine two senses. It can be amazing sometimes; I've seen her memorise entire musical pieces by visualising the notes in her mind and work out incredible sums by apparently touching everyday objects around her. Her mind is something very special.'

'She's got a gift,' Clarice agreed. 'We hope we find her soon.'

'That's why I'm here,' replied Hoffman, nodding. He pulled out a stack of legal forms for them to fill in. 'There's obviously some paperwork we'll have to go through too, but rest assured, both of you, we will do everything in our power to help.'

'The main thing to do now,' he continued, his blue eyes twinkling in the light of his desk lamp, 'is to look.'

Chapter 9

Compartments

'Haradan, why is it always night time when we look outside?'

'Ah.' He clicked his tongue. 'Now, that's a question.'

They walked from door to door, as they had been for a while now. Exactly how long, Daffodil wasn't sure. Whether time was even an ongoing process here on the train, Daffodil doubly wasn't sure. Haradan looked out at the night sky, but without perhaps completely looking at it—his eyes were glazed a little, as though he were searching for something far beyond, or considering something.

'It connects to what may be considered to be the beginnings of this train. They say that in the beginning, there was a conductor. This is of course unproven. An urban legend, if you will. Anyway, as the story goes, the conductor is said to have created the train and the larger world, as you will see it, from the walls to the areas within; all that which you see inside, everything you've seen and everything you will see. He did it all through his knowledge of alchemy and transmutation. He took from the real world outside—your world— and tried to replicate or transmute things over into this world. And, as the story goes, he did, overall, very well. At least when it comes to objects. But the thing with transmutation is that objects are easy. They're just a series of particles, which can flow and change.'

They passed by more doors, and the gentle rhythm of the train whirred on. Haradan walked with large strides—the walk of a person who knows where they are going. Daffodil was struggling to keep up with him, both physically and in conversation.

'Sorry, Haradan, are you saying someone created all of this? Including the sky?'

'Yes, Daffodil. At least I believe so. We cannot guarantee who this person was, or if they ever existed, but I believe it. But the thing is, as the legend goes, though he managed to transmute all the solid objects pretty well, when it came to the abstract things, like, say, time, he couldn't get it quite right.'

He must have realised the speed of his gait was too much for Daffodil. He slowed down and looked at her intensely.

'Again, these are all myths,' he said emphatically. 'We've never managed to prove the existence of a conductor or how the train even came to be per se. However, one can hope.'

Somberly, he looked out again at the night sky.

'It seems like you really want him to exist,' Daffodil said quietly.

'Why, yes.' Haradan smiled. 'Oh, I know he exists... somewhere on the train. Somewhere in Aethril. I just hope I can get through to him one day.'

He looked out again for a few moments before marching on once more.

'What do you know about him?' Daffodil asked.

'Know about him?' Haradan replied, laughing. 'It's said he was a loving man. He had children. He built The City for all people to be able to live and prosper. But something happened one day which affected his mind. And his memories themselves began to hurt him.

They say he's hidden away now, never knowing. Never coming back to his full self lest the memories break him. Yet the train, the route to Aethril, lives on.'

He turned to her and smiled.

'Like I said, that's just what they say. As for the sky outside, it's all because of time. How? You see, time is a really difficult concept to… conceptualise,' he said slowly, questioning his word choice. 'It's perhaps the most abstract thing in existence.'

They spoke of all this as they walked, for their carriage appeared to stretch on indefinitely. She wanted to ask more questions, but decided to hold her tongue and observe her surroundings a little.

Haradan continued briefly checking the odd door here and there that he felt may have had some potential to lead them to their next destination. To Daffodil, it seemed arbitrary, but to Haradan, there was a pattern to the doors he was checking. Every time he came close to opening one and checking what was inside, he tutted and decided against it, then continued along their march. Each doorway appeared almost identical, with the faintest of white glows emanating from the outline.

'Time is so abstract,' he continued. 'And yet—' His chin rose and his voice dropped ever so slightly, as though he was about to explain something sinister. 'Everyone seems to agree that it exists. Right? In your world, that is?'

'Time?' Daffodil asked, perplexed at the question. 'Yes, of course. Time exists.'

'Ah. It seems indeed it does… But does it?'

Daffodil frowned, unsure how to respond—or even think.

'There is a man in your plane, in your world,' he continued, looking up. 'Or there was a man, it's hard to say, as you'll soon realise. His name was Heidegger. Heidegger supported some horrible things. I'm not an advocate for his moral positions, but he held some fascinating views. He believed that human beings really were quite tied up in the phenomenon of time. You couldn't live without passing through it, and ageing through it. So, he surmised, human beings in many ways—were time. Human beings, right? What does it mean to be? Lived experiences that do not last forever, Heidegger argues. In his eyes, humans were a number of alive days, and thus their very existence was wound up with the concept of time.'

Daffodil tried to wrap her head around this and find the connection to the night sky outside the windows. Haradan, noticing the look on her face, explained.

'So what if then,' he continued, 'we took time out of the equation? Where would we be? People would no longer grow old. There would be no losing loved ones. Death could be avoided almost in totality, at least through natural ageing.'

'Right, yes. But if human beings are time-'

'According to one man. One possibly evil man who I am not saying was right.'

'Yes, sorry, if according to one definition, humans are limited time,' she said, 'and that natural ageing could be avoided through removing it, then maybe the conductor realised this and deliberately didn't bring time onto the train?' She paused. 'And that would explain the sky!'

Haradan watched her as she came to her epiphany.

'And so,' she said, turning to him as they walked, 'we're stuck in time.'

'Yes, possibly. Well, it's tricky. Stuck... Frozen. Perhaps it's not there at all. It's difficult to say. Again, these stem from myths. We cannot confirm the conductor. But I do believe that whoever or whatever designed this place did not bring time into it fully.'

He stopped, pursed his lips and stared down the length of the carriage.

'I believe that the train never stops, Daffodil—and it never has. And I know that the night sky we see out there has never once changed. Though of course—not in The City.'

Daffodil blinked. Her mind had been wandering, and she'd just been thinking about Adam.

'I'm sorry. What did you say? A city?'

Haradan smiled softly.

'Not a city,' he corrected. 'The City. Proper noun. There's only one.'

He hovered around another doorway, making some mental calculations before shaking his head and turning back to Daffodil. He seemed to realise her mind had been elsewhere throughout their long journey down the compartment, but he didn't blame her for losing focus—not under the circumstances. 'We'll go there soon enough. You'll like it,' he said. 'There are birds.'

'Birds?' she asked, noticing the smile on his face.

Daffodil didn't intend to smile, yet the corners of her mouth involuntarily flickered even though her eyebrows remained furled. She thought about this. Her anger. Her confusion. Her want to understand and not laugh and just find a way out and not have to deal with this crazy situation anymore that simply should not be happening in normal everyday life.

And then she decided to do something she had no reason to. She decided to not hold it back. She let it happen.

Daffodil smiled. Realising he was simply trying his best to lighten the mood and shock that she was going through, she let go of the immense weight she was holding in her mind and her heart, and smiled—for what felt like the first time in years. And it felt like a wash of relief. If Haradan noticed this, he didn't waste any time pointing it out, but rather, continued on to studying his next door.

His eyes were focused on one particular door as they made their way to it.

Could I hear its sounds? she thought.

Daffodil listened intently, trying to work out if there was anything distinct or noticeably different about this one compared to the hundred others they'd walked past. As she listened, she thought she could make out the faintest of humming noises, but then she decided that she must be imagining it, as it could very much have been part of the omnipresent rumbling of the train. She wondered if the train ran on tracks. Whatever was in front or behind the train was not visible from her outward view of the passing scenery.

'Okay. Now we've found something interesting,' said Haradan quietly, running his hands around the smooth edges of the doorway where the frame met the wall. Crouching, he squinted at the thin gap which bled the faintest of white light, as though taking in its inner workings.

'Every door has potential, Daffodil. Some of them will lead to nowhere, some of them will lead to places we have been to before. Some of them may end up where we have never been before. The trick is to try and retrace the paths you already know. We used to use markers, leaving little telltale signs near entry points.'

'Like gingerbread crumbs,' whispered Daffodil.

'Hmm?'

'Nothing,' Daffodil replied quickly, not wanting to interrupt his flow.

'Yes, so we used to try and track the different pathways of the train. But, and this is going to sound crazy, it was as though the train knew what we were doing. Before we knew it, our markers would disappear. Our paths would vanish, and doors that we were sure led somewhere, led there no more. We would instead find ourselves pitched into the void.'

Methodically, he gleaned around the door, keeping his left hand on the doorknob at all times. He shifted his grip ever so slightly with each glance at the frame, as though each centimetre of the frame provided him another clue to the puzzle of how to open the door.

'Now, what I do is just try to remember which doorway leads where, and learn the different doorways. They will often lead to more or less the same place.' He paused. 'Or at least to the same vicinity.'

When he seemed to have worked something out, he devoted his attention to the doorknob itself; soon there was an audible click. Smiling, he turned around.

'Let's see what we've found.'

She didn't know whether she should be excited or worried. He pulled on the doorknob, then pushed down on it and swung the door open in what felt like slow motion. Time slowed down, and she could just see the gap largening and white light pouring out. Then suddenly the door was open and everything sped up.

She felt the wind before she heard it.

Her eardrums instantly felt like they had collapsed in on themselves as her head filled with an all-engulfing screeching. Daffodil had never heard such an overpowering sound—such a visceral heart-wrenchingly loud roar. It was unnatural. Chaotic. Along with the sound, she saw a scene the likes of which she had never encountered before. In front of them was a grey, empty wasteland. In it was nothing but rocks—rocks of immense size. These rocks, or boulders, some as large as buses, scattered the vast open greyness.

Her hair flew back as a blast of crackling wind whipped at it, despite her standing a metre away from the door and this new land.

Her hands, her throat, eyes and every part of exposed skin felt as though it was under attack by microscopic shards of ice. But worst of all was that sound. That howl of the wind in the distance. It punctured through her eardrums and made her want to curl up into a ball.

'Is this the right place?' she shouted, hands over her ears.

Haradan looked at the empty landscape without answering her. He scanned the distance as though looking for something. The wind continued howling around them and then—

Thud.

He closed the door.

'No', he said, frowning at her. 'This isn't it.' He motioned for them to keep going. Daffodil hesitated for a moment before following.

There was silence between them for a while as they continued examining the doors. After some time, Haradan broke the silence.

'That, Daffodil, was an example of one of the many lands you do not want to venture through on the train. I'm sorry about that, Daffodil. I really am. That door did not lead where I expected. They often don't. Unfortunately however, I must break it to you that I have heard of this happening before. And, there are a lot more of those kinds of compartments on this train. We do not try to go to such places, but sometimes there is a lot of trial and error. You will hopefully not have to go into or experience any of those kinds of compartments or lands—but do they exist? Yes. Might you have to venture into one? I truly hope not. But it is a possibility.'

'Okay,' she said, a million questions racing through her mind. 'But I can't understand that wind. I felt like my eardrums were being torn apart—I've never heard anything like it. It was almost as though there was ... communication.'

He nodded somberly, though Daffodil thought she could sense a twinkle in his eyes.

'Those were your senses playing up,' he said, walking slowly on. 'In all honesty, Daffodil, your senses will not be the same now that you are where you are. Your sense of hearing will attack you, knowing you are not in the place you are used to.'

Daffodil didn't speak for a while, watching him scrutinise the various door frames and pathways and doorknobs that all looked the same to her. 'But why is it like that?'

Haradan raised an eyebrow. 'The wind, you mean? Those rocks?'

Daffodil shook her head. 'No. Why did it—that room... that place... affect me so much, and not you?'

Haradan thought about this.

'Experience, I presume. I've been here as long as I can remember; you have not. You have not yet witnessed the true breadth of these lands. We don't understand it all, but we do think that it comes from the transmutation of emotion. Those who come from other lands, like yourself, find things to be very different here. Their senses. Their emotions at times. Their memories.'

They walked over to the next door.

'What do you mean—memories?'

'I'll explain, but first I want to check this door.'

He walked through his usual routine: checking the frame, analysing the sides, manipulating the doorknob, and opening the door.

It swished open.

The first thing she felt was the cold. Even before she realised the water cascading, plunging, punching in and onto her. Water. Water everywhere. It was in her mouth, ears, nose—every orifice of her body. In an instant, she was taken aback. Waves of perfect blue tore her from her spot near Haradan and catapulted her back into the carriage. She tried to level herself, but the water ripped her from where she was. Her instinct took over, and she tried to twist her body into some kind of swimming position, or at least bring her head above the cascade.

I just need some air.

She tried looking around, but the deluge was impossibly strong. She could not even tell which way up she was. Just a blue mess of bubbles and blurriness.

Thrashing and flailing, Daffodil simply could not orientate herself. Energy was leaving her as she struggled with her remaining oxygen reserves. Now the water was entering her throat and her sight was darkening. She could feel herself being thrashed and thrown into different seats , into walls, into … wait. Seats.

With what little ounce of strength she could muster, she grasped with both hands onto the corner of the only seat she could see through her blurry vision. She felt the squelch of the wet padding around her fingers and held on for dear life. The waves continued thrashing and pouring around her. Then, as she strained to look up, there was a gap.

Gasp.

A gulp of air.

More currents of water attacked her as she held on.

Another lull. Another gasp for oxygen.

Every opportunity she had, she gained a little air.

And then, almost as quickly as it had come, the pressure seemed to dissipate; it was easier to get her head above the water and keep it there. The water was stemming now.

As she watched the current recede, she looked around, trying to locate where she must have been when this had all begun. There was water everywhere, and she found a soaked Haradan, perhaps forty metres away near the same door, panting, pushing against it as though it might reopen at any moment.

***

Silence. All except the steady thrumming of the train and the plodding of their feet to the next doorway. Daffodil was still soaked even though they had been walking for a while. At least she thought it was a while. How was she meant to know what a while was in a place where time did not exist? She decided to count in steps.

For some reason, they had not tried any new doors. It seemed that after being battered by that water, Haradan had become exceptionally cautious with the doors he was willing to open. The water-soaked area was far behind them, though it had affected quite a few seats and the wooden floor. Her feet had been squelching for a while, and she counted seventy-six more steps before the squeaks disappeared. Perhaps it had been a few minutes then? Now though, with the last squeaks of her shoes and an absence of conversation, Daffodil realised he wanted to say something. And it must have been important, for the silence was like a thick fog surrounding them, waiting to be lifted. Finally, Haradan spoke.

'You asked me about how memories work here, Daffodil.'

'Yes.'

'One thing I've noticed is that for all newcomers, their memories can get affected.'

She thought the fog had been lifted, but it came crashing back down with the weight of storms and hurricanes along with it.

'I'm sorry—what?' she cried, turning to him.

Haradan took a deep breath and sighed. It was the sigh of someone who knew they had to break tragic news to another person. He looked at her intently for a few moments, not saying a word, but then carried on walking. There were creases in his brows, she noticed.

'When people arrive in this place, Daffodil, they will often have a past they come with. Their history, right?'

Daffodil nodded quickly.

'Some of them are part of families, some of them working their day-to-day jobs. Whatever it is, everyone has a past. When they arrive here, and their arrival is a complicated matter itself, I must add, something we still have not fully worked out–but we'll come to that. Anyway, when they arrive, they're naturally distraught and upset. How did they arrive? How do we leave and go back to our lives? They're emotional and angry and upset. As they should be.'

He paused, looking at her, and his voice dropped a little. 'However,' he said. 'Very quickly, people seem to forget this. They forget how angry and confused and upset they were to be ripped from their lives. They continue their journey to escape the train, but as they do, their emotions seem numbed. They start to plod along, a little in limbo, and they start to forget. Eventually a sort of … fading happens, and finally—they forget their old lives.'

Daffodil was silent. He stopped and turned to her.

'Daffodil?'

But Daffodil was a million miles away.

'Daffodil?' he repeated.

Daffodil was rooted to the spot, her eyes glazed. 'They … forget their families?' She breathed slowly.

He chewed his lip for a moment. 'Yes. They forget where they came from—they can forget everything. They can end up thinking that this,' he gestured around, 'is all there is.'

Her mind raced through thoughts of Adam, Dad, Mum; Adam with his ridiculous puzzles; Mum and Dad laughing and joking with her in the garden during the summer heat of last July; Adam and her splashing water at each other, tickling each other until they couldn't breathe; Dad recording them on his old-school phone. How could she ever forget her family? The family she loved? The same family who loved her?

Neither of them moved, but instead looked on at the infinite series of doors that led on to an infinite series of locations. Eventually, Daffodil wiped away a solitary tear and looked him directly in his eyes.

'Haradan—how do people arrive here? How did I, and others, get here? Where did they go?'

He didn't walk off. He didn't turn away and continue inspecting doors. He looked at her pleading eyes with the same intensity she gave him: genuine concern and soberness, both in equal measure.

'I'm so sorry, Daffodil. Those are three very important and powerful questions. Sadly, all three have very unsatisfying answers. As for how they get here, it's safe to say we don't exactly know. There is no one way. People have arrived in different areas, and from different areas. You ended up on the train, but others have ended up in areas like the land in which you heard great winds earlier. Such people remember their last encounter of their world being out in the Arizona desert—whatever that is. People have ended up in our forests, through what they claimed to be a bedroom wardrobe. Others have ended up directly in The City, from libraries in their world. There is never one way.

'The problem is, people who arrive start to quickly forget themselves. Some will have a strong recollection to begin with, others less so, but after a little while, all they know is this world, as though there is nothing else. I mean, if you cannot remember what is outside, would you ever believe in it?'

Daffodil didn't know how to respond. People forget themselves? Her throat became dry, and she clenched her hands into involuntary fists. That sounded like the worst possible thing that could happen.

'Again, I am really sorry to tell you this,' he continued, now walking again, as though sensing her silent rage and moving on. 'You asked what we do with them — well, we help try to reconnect them back to the world they came from. Your world. Of course, not everybody wants to return, or believes in that return. We have something called The City. We try to house them, bring them into community on their journey, give them a better life than that of simply being alone and stumbling around the train or wherever they end up.'

Haradan continued speaking but started to sound a million miles away. Looking around, Daffodil thought about the situation she was in. What was going on? Where was she? What was this crazy place where people couldn't remember how they arrived, and forgot about their pasts? Her head span. What about her? She remembered the station. Moor Street Station. She remembered the man in the suit and the argument. Gosh, it seemed like a lifetime ago by now. But what about before that? Why had she come out anyway? Well, before that, of course, she had... she had what? Ah yes, school, she was going to school. The new school that Adam and her had spoken about. That was it—school. But why had she gone on the train and not gone with her parents? Why hadn't she... Didn't mum and dad normally drop her off?

Daffodil winced. Motion sickness. Her head hurt. She needed to sit down. But before she could open her mouth, Haradan had begun opening another door. And that's when she felt it.

Heat. Oppressively hot, blistering, scorching heat.

Daffodil instantly felt like all the moisture had been removed from her throat, though she was still in the corridor.

The door had barely been cracked ajar, yet she was internally screaming for water. She squinted through the gap and found the area beyond the door blindingly bright—some kind of yellow, parched, arid land of pure unadulterated hotness that filled the entire carriage with a golden white light and unfathomable heat. Daffodil felt the sweat soak her forehead and clothing as Haradan closed the door.

'Okay,' he said, turning to her. 'I tried just peeking into that one.'

The heat seemed not to have bothered him whatsoever, but Daffodil was hoping he'd have something to quench her immense thirst. She was about to ask, or motion for water, but Haradan already started rummaging around in his trenchcoat. From deep within one of the inner pockets, he pulled out a small metal flask.

'Here, have some of this,' he said, gently offering the silver flask with a discernible slosh.

She took it and unscrewed the cap. It was a brushed silver, and the metal was cool to the touch. As she peered in, she found the lightly swirling liquid inside to be some kind of water. She kept looking in hesitantly, unsure if she should drink this foreign liquid. The water, if it was that, was a light blue, even in the darkness of the flask she could make that out; and there appeared to be a slight shimmering quality, a twinkling from the water as it swirled around.

'This is a very special type of liquid. My own invention, actually,' Haradan explained.

'What is it?' Daffodil queried, frowning at the flask.

'Infused alchemic restoration balm,' replied Haradan pointedly. 'It'll help with the heat and thirst.'

'Infused alchemic restoration balm,' Daffodil repeated. 'I thought as much.'

Haradan smiled.

'What was that compartment you opened the door to? How did it have such heat?' She continued swirling the liquid around, her throat throbbing from thirst.

'That, Daffodil, was a sort of desert that I've only visited maybe three times. I never venture there unless necessary. As you've seen, the heat is unbearable.'

'Why did you go?'

He thought about that for a moment. 'I suppose I was looking for answers. But there are dangers in that desert, aside from the incredible heat. There are creatures that I've not encountered before.'

Daffodil didn't respond but simply looked on down the endless corridor. He continued talking about the desert, but Daffodil was only half listening. How had she gotten to this point? Her mind was reeling. Sitting there, with this flask in her hands, she realised she had absolutely no idea what to do. She was on a train that moved endlessly, with compartments that either led to nowhere, or seemed to want to kill her. *How was she going to get home? It was all a bad dream. One endless, bad dream.*

She closed her eyes and breathed in. She kept her eyes closed. She breathed out. Slowly. Where on earth were all these other people Haradan spoke about? She breathed in again. He hadn't let her down so far. And out. Perhaps she didn't have all the answers yet, or even some. In fact, the more she discovered, the more questions appeared. But she could at least carry on and keep trying her best.

Daffodil opened her eyes.

Haradan was staring at her, unsure of what to say.

She brought the flask up to her lips and took a big gulp.

'I want to open the next door,' Daffodil said.

Chapter 10

Looking

The door creaked open. She wasn't sure if she should enter, but she'd opened it now.

'Yes? No, please come in,' said a voice from within, seemingly having spotted her.

'Sorry, I wasn't sure if you wanted me,' she said.

'No, of course, please come. I was just showing your husband the files,' the voice encouraged.

Clarice walked in and shut the door behind her. Zakariyya was standing over a large wooden desk, next to a man in a shirt and trousers. They were finishing their conversation, looking at some pictures and videos on the computer. Zakariyya spotted her, realised the time, shook hands with the man and turned to her.

'My apologies, Clarice! I didn't realise how long I was there for.'

'Well, it is the third time you went back in,' she said, smiling, rolling her eyes. Joining her, they walked out of the back room of administration at Moor Street Station.

'Anything new?' she asked, half-hopefully.

'No,' he said, walking back onto the main road. 'They can't seem to find her on any of the footage at all. The police are still looking, of course, but so far, not much, no. There was this, though.' He handed her a manilla folder as they approached the traffic lights.

Buses honked, cars beeped, and people jostled around them. The buzz of Birmingham. The Bull Ring, as the town centre was known by many, was one of the busiest parts of their city, and they'd lived here their whole lives; they could traverse through the Bull Ring blindfolded at this stage.

Looking up at the lights, Clarice opened the folder and found a large A4 picture within. As the traffic lights changed colour and the pedestrians prepared their mini-sprints, she studied the photo.

A pavement. Circular silver dots on a dark blue building. Pedestrians walking along. She squinted further, letting the waiting pedestrians rush off around her, remaining motionless at the lights. There were the usual signs of a busy morning rush in the picture; dreary looking shift-workers, coffee cups, a faint brightness of the sky. In fact, it seemed similar to where they now stood. Then, something at the very edge of the picture caught Clarice's eye.

There was a man in a suit looking flustered, amongst many people milling about. He seemed to be talking to someone just off the image. All she could see was the corner of someone's red coat.

'What do you think?' asked Zakariyya.

'I don't know,' she murmured.

People were walking around them, looking disapprovingly at the couple who were standing stationery at the beginning of a busy walkway; one man in particular caught Zakariyya's eye—he was on the corner of the street, but Zakariyya could have sworn he was watching them. As Zakariyya squinted to study the man, he turned and walked away.

Before he could mention anything, Clarice turned to him.

'It could be Daffodil, actually! The tiny bit of jacket I can see looks like it may be her coat—her favourite red jacket. Chances are slim of, course. How did Moor Street Station have a picture of this?'

'Erm, they pulled it from their CCTV footage of the outside of the station,' replied Zakariyya, thoughts of the man from the corner rapidly scattering.

'That would mean it can't be that far from here.'

She looked around.

The blue backing of the building in the image was the Bull Ring main building, she was sure of that.

She squinted into the distance. There.

She took off, not caring about who saw or what traffic she got in the way of. She knew Daffodil wouldn't be there anymore, but she had to go and see.

Zakariyya sprinted after her across the busy road, barely any more careful. A car whizzed past inches away and horned for an eternity.

'Wait, Clarice! Go carefully!'

But Clarice was barely cognizant of his existence at this point.

She knew he'd be in step.

***

Bartholomew watched Zakariyya and Clarice from his hiding spot. He watched Clarice run across the road with the picture in hand. He watched Zakariyya chase after her.

Has it finally happened?

He followed.

***

When Clarice arrived at the spot in the picture, there was almost nothing to be seen. A pavement. Some people walking about. An old coffee cup stuck between the gutter and the curb. A few metres away, someone had left a pile of old clothes, an assortment of different colours, and a dirty red patchwork quilt on top.

'That's it,' she said, deflated. 'Nothing. Daffodil isn't here.'

Clarice had known she wouldn't be. But something deep inside her had yearned—longed for the tiniest glimmer of a chance that there may be something. Some clue. She knew it was ridiculous. The red corner of a jacket was nothing to go off of. It could have been anyone's. What would Daffodil have even been doing, talking to a man in a suit at that time in the morning?

Suddenly, just as Zakariyya crossed the final road and was jogging over to her, the quilt near her moved. A head poked out from underneath the pile of clothing. It was the head of a scruffy looking man with a frown on his face. He looked as though he had been sleeping, or something akin to sleeping, and had the slightly bewildered, confused look of someone who wasn't sure if they'd be dreaming or not.

'Did you say Daffodil?'

Chapter 11

Detective Work

Hoffman could almost hear the roaring of trains rushing by in his head, though he was only looking at a model. He'd been a little interested in trains when was a boy—he'd never thought, however, that he'd be in a museum researching them like he was now, facing this large model of Moor Street Station.

The Tyseley Locomotives Museum was a huge and sprawling building with life-size replicas and real vintage trains dotted around the vast interconnecting halls. Hoffman watched as a curator or tour guide directed a large crowd of children through the museum, explaining different elements of the various steam locomotives of the 20th century.

'The brakes of such trains are particularly interesting,' the man said, huffing as though it were the least interesting thing in the world. He turned to the class. 'When a freight train passes by, does anyone know why some of the wheels make a banging noise?'

'Oooh, oooh, ooh!' An excited schoolchild waved emphatically at the curator.

The curator pretended not to see his flailing hand and peered at the other twenty-eight children, who were seemingly mute.

The singular hand flapped faster in front of his face.

The man sighed, exasperated, and gestured slowly to the hand, now swinging in large arcs inches from his nose.

'Yes?'

'Is it because that's a flat spot? When a train is braking, the wheels are sometimes brought to a complete standstill even though the train is still moving, which means they will then slide over the rail and be flattened in a spot.'

'Perfect,' the curator said in the most monotone voice Hoffman had ever heard.

This man really doesn't seem to like children, Hoffman thought, turning back to his model. But Hoffman was only half paying attention. He had detached from all other groups, drawn to the miniature scale model of Moor Street Station. It sat in a large glass case, and seemed to perfectly replicate the station itself, with its trains and accompaniments.

The engraving on the silver placard read 'Scale 1:70 gauge'. He peered at the model and scanned it thoroughly, meticulously noting every station entrance, exit, the railways lines and surrounding vicinities. All in hopes of some kind of clue... inspiration... something he could infer or deduce or extrapolate—but nothing.

He shook his head.

This is literally the job of a detective, he told himself—that which he had signed up for, and what he had worked his whole life to achieve. Surely, he could make some kind of connection or work something out now that it was so needed, in such a pivotal case. It wasn't every day a young girl went missing from a train.

He had ended up here on a whim, after days of searching through the station, including countless carriages and compartments with his team, and many long conversations with the staff who worked there. He had come back with nothing. In fact, the more he looked into it, the bleaker the outcome looked. Daffodil was nowhere to be found. At this point, he was not even sure about his lead, James, the gentleman who was sleeping rough in the city centre and had guided Daffodil's parents to the station, as he had encountered her on that fateful morning. 'She said she was going to Moor Street Station,' he had said confidently when interrogated.

He had felt bad interrogating a homeless man, but with the little in the way of clues that they had, he had to exhaust all avenues and extract as much as physically possible.

And so Hoffman was now here, trying to jog his mental faculties—trying to work out how she could have vanished from a large network railway with CCTV pointing in every direction without showing up on any footage; he had eventually decided that the best way to work out how she may have been taken (if she had been taken), was to take a step back.

But after hours of interviewing James, hours upon hours at Moor Street Station, and now after hours at this place, he had still gotten nowhere.

'Howdy mister,' came a voice from behind him.

It was a teenage boy dressed in a cowboy costume, with a white shirt and true-to-style black cowboy hat including chin strap, ridges and dips. On his pristine white shirt proudly sat a five-pointed silver sheriff's star, and, most impressive of all, squeaky-clean crisp tan leather boots, the soles of which click-clunked satisfyingly, echoing through the large hallway.

Hoffman whistled. 'Wow—you look cool,' he said to the young lad who approached with a winning smile and cool grey eyes.

'Thanks. My dad is the owner of this museum,' the boy said, as though sensing Detective Hoffman's hesitation. He was quite tall and well-built, all things considered. Only his face gave away his true age; though, Hoffman supposed, some faces did look much younger than they were.

'I hope you don't mind me seeing if there's anything I can help with?'

'Ah, that's really very kind of you, young man, but… I'm not sure you'll be able to help me with what I'm doing,' Hoffman said, smiling thinly. 'I'm looking for something…'

The boy observed Hoffman for a few moments, not saying a single word. He then broke into a slow, comprehending smile.

'You know, it's odd,' he said in a hushed voice, almost conspiratorially. 'I've seen so many people come here over the years saying the same thing. My father before me also.' He paused, contemplating Hoffman.

'You know what I think?' he went on. 'I think they're looking for someone. Someone that's lost. I don't know for sure—they never say it to me explicitly. I'm just a kid, right? But… I have a feeling.'

Hoffman's eyes grew wide, though attempting to remain expressionless. 'What do you mean?'

'I've seen people over the years come to this exhibit,' the boy said. 'To this section of our museum, and just stare for hours on end, looking carefully at this model.' He gestured at the model of Moor Street Station. 'I mean, they're different each time. The people, that is. I never see the same one twice. Men. Women. All dressed a little bit like you, though. A nice suit, cool jacket—detective clothes. All looking for something. For answers, maybe.'

'You've seen others do this too?' Hoffman said.

'Oh yeah,' the boy laughed. 'So many. My father even more. He doesn't think anything of it himself. But I do. I think there's something up with that station. Something that makes people come and investigate. Makes people like you come and stare and think and pull their hair out the entire day trying to figure things out which just don't seem to want to get figured out.'

He looked appealingly at Detective Hoffman. 'It seems like I might be onto something?'

'I... I can't say,' Hoffman replied faintly. 'But—you really believe that?' he asked. 'Everything you've told me?'

'Oh sure,' the boy said, waving his hands around. 'I like to think these things can happen. My dad's a genius, see—but he doesn't believe the things kids do. I think that's the best thing about being a kid,' he said proudly. 'You really see the world. Adults don't, haha! Adults don't believe anything that goes against what they think the world is. But kids... Kids know the truth.'

He nodded happily.

Hoffman stared at the model station, unblinking. 'Yeah. I think you're right,' he said, not taking his eyes off the station. 'Sometimes adults don't believe.'

***

The snow fell thick as feathers, muting the sounds of rushing cars and buses outside Moor Street Station. The black metal gates that separated the interior of the station from the road steadily began to scrape open inch by inch, and a lone figure slipped in, silently—as quiet as the night outside.

Hoffman was on the tracks, as he had been for the last few hours, inspecting the railway lines. There were no trains running at this time—he'd confirmed with the station staff before gaining access to run his inspections.

Unsure what he might find, he had gone through everything—the tracks to the carriages to the turnstiles to the shops that littered the concourse—for any clues that might present themselves. He still wasn't sure of much in terms of Daffodil's disappearance, in fact, all he was sure of at this point was that he was freezing, and, after checking his wristwatch—

Ah, midnight. Hoffman shook his head. *May as well get going at this poi-*

CREEAAK.

Hoffman lifted his head, eyebrows furrowed. Was someone there? Surely not. He squinted back to the gate. It looked more or less as he had left it, though it was difficult to discern in the darkness. The security guard had locked it up for him and left. But... did that gate seem a little more open than before?

There had to be someone. Hoffman had been a detective long enough to recognise the signs: the vaguest shadow of a shadow flitting across under the distant lamplight on the other side of the concourse. A sensation of inexplicable change. The very air itself giving off the impression of some indefinable difference.

No. There was definitely somebody there. Hoffman knew it.

'Hello?' Hoffman called out to the darkness, stepping up and out of the train tracks. He scanned the station as carefully as he could, top to bottom, edge to edge, yet he couldn't explicitly spot anyone.

'Detective. It's just me,' a gravelly voice echoed from across the platforms. Where it had originated from, Hoffman had a general idea, but still he could not locate the man to whom it belonged. The voice sounded awfully familiar. But Hoffman couldn't pin the owner, visually or aurally.

'I can't see you,' Hoffman cried out to the voice.

Who on earth would be trying to talk to him in this place and at this time? He certainly had enemies. A lifetime of fighting crime and locking up criminals had naturally led to many an enemy; it was part and parcel of his work—he'd accepted that a long time ago—when you take on the job, you take on the good, the bad and the ugly.

'It's just me, Detective,' said the voice again, still concealed. 'James—from the street?'

Hoffman breathed out slowly and ran his hands through his hair. 'My word, man! You gave me a fright! Why are you in here at this time? You're not allowed in.'

'Sorry, sir,' James called out, shrouded in darkness. 'I was just around, and the gate was open; I thought I'd see how you were getting along.' He stepped out of the gloom, a large grin plastered across his face now that he was in the light, cheerfulness playing behind his kindly grey eyes.

'This area is closed off for our investigation. You're not meant to be here.'

'Ah, my apologies, detective.'

Hoffman fanned at him lightly. 'Ah, forget it. Just don't let anyone see you here!'

James had perhaps been the sole lead of this whole case, and in that capacity, he had been a great help. Smirking, he nodded his thanks to the detective and asked, 'So, any leads?'

'No,' Hoffman said, shaking his head, turning back to the train lines. The whistles and rushing of a far off train could be heard in the distance, and the biting wind crept through the gaps in Hoffman's jacket. 'We followed your suggestions about her heading this way. I'm almost sure she did come towards the train station—possibly even entered it. But there's no proof. No evidence. And in all honesty, there's no way she could have gotten into a train and simply disappeared. All the CCTV footage at the end lines show her never coming off…'

They stood there, looking out at the empty dark tracks.

'It's just impossible,' Hoffman stated, shaking his head. 'Nothing makes sense.'

'I know,' James said with a sigh, fiddling with the patchwork blanket draped over him.

'1909, this station opened,' Hoffman explained, looking around, taking it in—more for himself than James. 'In 1914, the location of it moved to these lines we see here.' Hoffman gestured to the tracks. 'And in 1987, the terminus was relocated.'

Hoffman sighed. 'I don't know how it all connects, but I feel like the answer is somewhere here. I just can't seem to find the right piece of the puzzle.'

'Impressive knowledge,' James said, staring at Hoffman. He turned back to face the winding, endless tracks, and began coughing. 'Excuse me,' he continued through bouts of coughs.

'You okay?' Hoffman asked.

"Eh. It's been there for a while.' James paused. 'You know, I remember being a little boy, watching this documentary. It was a bit conspiracy-theory and crazy, but it sounded quite compelling as a kid. They spoke about how people went missing many times, through history, and at least in some cases, other people would turn up on the other side of the world, sometimes with vague memories of that person's life, like it was their old life. There was a story, if I remember correctly, of a boy who was skiing somewhere in the Alps on a family holiday, but then he disappeared, and woke up on the other side of the world. He had all the memories of his old family and holiday and the skiing, but they began to fade quickly.' James began putting his hand into the inside flap of his jacket.

Hoffman squinted, watching—then laughed. 'What are the chances?'

'Sorry?' James asked, his hand frozen in the inside of his jacket.

'Oh nothing. It's just, you're not the first person to say something like that today.'

'I'm not?' he replied, slowly removing his empty hand.

'No. There was a young boy in the museum I was at earlier, who had an interesting theory.'

'Did he now?' James stared at Hoffman intently.

'Yeah,' Hoffman said, scratching his chin. 'He mentioned how … well … let's just say this station might not be all it's cracked up to be. Perhaps there's more to this missing person situation than meets the eye.'

They looked out at the dark train tracks, moonlight shining down on them.

'I see. Perhaps,' James said, smiling thinly. 'Well. if there's anything else I can help with at all, do let me know, detective.' He turned and began walking away.

'Thanks. Seriously, thank you. We really appreciate it.'

'No problem,' James said, already near the gate. 'I'm sure we'll see each other again soon; and I really do hope Daffodil is okay.'

His voice faded away, and he was covered in darkness once more.

Chapter 12

History

As quiet as a feather falling, Clarice stepped into the office. She could see Zakariyya poring over emails, as expected—a plethora of messages to and from various different organisations: the police, Moor Street Station, lost children charities and helplines.

All to no avail.

It had been two days since Daffodil's disappearance. Naturally, they had both barely slept.

As Clarice watched him, she leant against the wall, and noticed the deep bags beneath his eyes. Exacerbated (she hoped to herself) by the dim yellow light of the study, his face seemed a vestige of its former self—sunken-in, yellowed, and… distant.

Perhaps he could mask it from his colleagues at the office, but to his wife it was as plain as day—an expression hidden beneath, crying out, 'help me'.

He frowned and turned to her, realising someone else was in the room.

'Clarice?'

Like a bad actor, he put on a smile. A barely passable, forced smile. It was not that it was not sincere or genuine—but it was forced. But what was wrong with that? He was simply trying his best.

She didn't smile back, however. Instead, she walked over, gently placed her arms around his shoulders, and squeezed.

Clarice was also trying her best.

For those few moments, nothing needed to be said. A quietness seeped through the room. A silence—as loud as day.

'So, what's the news with Hoffman?' she asked, looking at the computer screen for clues—some small signs of progress.

'Not much,' he said, swivelling around in his chair. 'They're trying their best. Last I heard, he and his team were scouring the CCTV files they could get access to… We need to just hold tight.'

'Yeah, I thought as much. I didn't know what else I was expecting,' she said, more to herself than him. They stared at the glaring monitor—not a sound save for the soft breathing of two parents wishing their daughter return.

Ring-ring-ring.

Clarice and Zakariyya looked at each other.

An update?

They couldn't risk the optimism, the blight of disbelief that would be inevitable if they got their hopes up and then found out the worst.

But still… What if?

Zakariyya hesitantly picked up the phone and put it on speaker.

'Hello? Is this Mr Winters?' a deep, resonant voice asked.

'Ye- yes, it is,' Zakariyya said, struggling to keep the hope out of his voice. He had been waiting so long.

'I'm afraid I have some bad news.'

The father of Daffodil immediately sagged, his body slumping in the chair.

Clarice's hand shot to cover her mouth. 'Oh no. Surely not.'

'The detective assigned to your case,' the voice continued, 'Detective Hoffman?'

'Yes?' Zakariyya answered, unsure now of where this was going. 'I remember.'

'Well, I'm afraid he's gone missing.' Silence. On both sides. 'I understand he was highly invested in your case. We are doing all we can to find him, and we will of course keep you informed. In the meantime, we will be assigning someone else to your case as soon as possible.'

Zakariyya looked at her.

Clarice raised an eyebrow.

'He's disappeared?' Clarice whispered.

What did this mean? Zakariyya thought.

They had been making actual progress. After looking so long for their daughter, they had found James from the picture.

They had given the picture to Detective Hoffman. They had actually made progress.

And now he had disappeared.

A loud rapping on the front door surprised them.

'What do you mean he's … missing?' Zakariyya asked the voice on the phone, gesturing to Clarice to see to the door. It was quite late. Odd to have someone knocking at this time. He peeked into the hallway so she knew he was in close vicinity, and so he could keep an eye on the visitor.

We had finally made some progress… We'dactually worked something out.

'I'm afraid we aren't at liberty to divulge all the details just yet, sir,' said the voice on the phone.

'You can't divulge details that you know? He was working on my case—he's looking for my little girl!'

As he spoke, Clarice opened the door. Zakariyya could just about see.

There was a man outside, waiting in the rain. Short. Brown-leather jacket. Grey hair—perhaps around fifty or sixty years old. He said something that made Clarice answer, her back turned. Zakariyya didn't recognise him.

'I'm really sorry, sir, but we will have another person assigned to the case as soon as we can,' the voice on the phone said.

Clarice turned towards Zakariyya from the other side of the hallway. The man at the door had said something that had drained all the blood from her face.

'Zakariyya,' she half-whispered, garnering his full attention.

'Clarice?'

But before she could finish-

'I think you should put that phone down,' said the man at the door, looking right at him.

***

'I'm so sorry to scare you and intrude on your evening like this,' the man said, who had introduced himself as Bartholomew; he explained that he knew about the disappearance, and that Detective Hoffman would go missing. He was now sitting on their sofa with a warm cup of coffee in his hands.

'No, no, not at all,' Clarice replied, joining her husband opposite on the sofa nearest the fireplace.

'I'm so sorry,' Zakariyya said, blowing the wisps of steam away from his mug of coffee. 'Can you just explain that again for me from the top?'

'Yes, of course,' Bartholomew replied, sitting up straight.

As suspicious as his appearance had been in and of itself, he had explained to them that he was genuinely concerned for them both and Daffodil, and intimated that he'd been through something similar, and that he wanted to help. He had been following them.

'I'm guessing you've had someone that has gone missing. And that all the leads point at or around Moor Street Station. However, I'm guessing nothing seems to add up; that maybe the CCTV footage is somehow absent?' Bartholomew raised an eyebrow knowingly. 'And I'm guessing the officer assigned to your case has also mysteriously, eventually, disappeared—which, from the sound of it, is actually a great loss for you as he was, as you say—a good man.'

They both nodded, amazed at the inexplicable accuracy. Bartholomew stared at them, as though sussing them out somehow.

The crackling of the fireplace was the only sound beyond their bated breaths.

He nodded to himself near imperceptibly, as though deciding the couple were trustworthy enough for him to continue. 'A similar thing happened to me many years ago. I lost my friend. And it was around the station too. I have a theory—but we'll get to that. So yes, as I was saying, nothing seemed to add up. His disappearance was absolutely random, and there were no leads. Nobody could explain a thing. Eventually, even the police gave up. However, there was one man who helped me at the time; he was a worker at the station, called Amelio. He was a humble cleaner, but he had big ideas, and my gosh was he a very good person,' he said, smiling reverentially. 'This was a long time ago. 1988. Anyway, Amelio believed there was something… about the station.'

Bartholomew laughed softly to himself.

'This is going to sound absolutely crazy, but he genuinely felt there was something about the station that led to … people going missing. Not often. Not enough to arouse suspicion… Every few years or every decade. But like they could be taken from there—like they could be… moved somehow. Anyway, needless to say, nobody believed him. I personally didn't know what to think. I certainly didn't outright believe him, not at the time. I was, as you might say, well, what I thought of as a very logical man. But then here's the crazier thing,' Bartholomew said, sipping his tea.

'One day,' he continued, 'Amelio vanished.'

He stared at them.

'And that's when I believed.' He paused. 'There's something about that station, Zakariyya, Clarice,' he said, looking them dead in their eyes. 'People can go missing. People *have* gone missing. Ever since then, I've been trying to work it out. I've been watching and waiting and researching. When I saw you two, I knew. I knew it had happened again. After all these years.'

They simply looked at him, mugs in hand, not knowing what to say nor how to respond to any of his claims.

'Look, I get it. I'm a wacky old man who just appears unannounced at your door, seems to know far too much, makes highly suspicious assertions, and has theories that seem impossible by all stretches of the imagination; it's like a badly-written book, I know,' he said, smiling. 'But hear me out. Historically, there have been all sorts of odd people around the station who just don't seem to be connected. Amelio went missing in 1990. And he told me in the two years before he disappeared, when I would continue trying to find the clues regarding my friend's disappearance, that he was absolutely sure that there was a man who would randomly appear in the middle of the night, when he would be watching over the station.

But he would say you'd never manage to catch or properly see this man—not really. It was as though he was covered in shadows. He'd disappear into the stationary carriages, in the dark of night, but wouldn't come out again. He'd be absolutely impossible to locate— as though he had teleported.

'Amelio believed he was somehow connected to another man who, through his research at the time, he thought existed around almost fifty years prior, when the original permanent building was constructed. A man who he believed did similar things; at least whispers of stories indicated toward his existence. He thought that's when this all started. He became infatuated with trying to work it out; who the men across the years were that could go into the train and never come out. There'd been sightings of them, of course, but never any real confirmed proof. Since Amelio went missing, I've been looking at this non-stop.'

Bartholomew cleaned his glasses methodically with a small cloth. 'Obsessed, in all honesty. Yes, I've tried to work it out, but I've never gone public with my findings, worried for my own safety, but also because no, there is not any conclusive proof. Though do know that this isn't new whatsoever. There is actually a history of losses through time,' he said conspiratorially. 'It's not just the station. If you look through history, documented evidence, you'll find there have been missing people. Absences. People who disappear totally from one part of the world from particular places. The Bermuda Triangle of course is a famous one, but there are others. Certain parts of the desert. The Arctic Circle. I believe there are more, but these three I'm certain of. All connected. And all systematised.'

Zakariyya had finished his tea and simply sat there, along with Clarice. The embers of the fireplace crackled softly.

'How did you find us?' Clarice said, shaking her head softly.

'A couple of reasons. Firstly, the station. Over the years, I've always kept a watch out for any clues, to, well, anything. When I saw you and the detective looking for clues near the station, I just knew. I knew it had happened again, for the third time.'

'So, what do you think has happened to our Daffodil?' Clarice asked. Then she frowned, realising something.

'I don't know for sure,' Bartholomew said, frowning. 'In all honesty, even after all these years, I'm not sure. I don't know where my friend went. I don't know where Amelio went. But I have some ideas. What I do know is that I am here to help however I can. They might be after me now—whoever tries to hide this and covers all these tracks. But when I saw the look on your face earlier today at the station, I knew I just had to help. I couldn't let one more person go through what I went through without trying my best. So yes, I'm here to help however I can.'

Zakariyya, who had been quiet this entire time, finally broke his silence.

'You'll help us find our daughter?' he said.

Looking deep into the crackling fireplace, Bartholomew slowly nodded—then turned and faced the couple. 'Yeah. I will—even if it kills me,' he said, standing up and heading towards the door. 'So,' he continued, 'what are we waiting for? Let's go find your daughter.'

Chapter 13

Doorways

Riyul turned around to look at the opening of the carriage, near where he had been earlier.

His eyes grew wide.

There, standing in front of the rushing trees and night sky, on the very spot he had been sitting half-asleep just minutes ago, stood a shadowed figure.

'Who are you?' he asked.

After so long alone, with just him and Eli in this compartment, something had finally changed.

There was nothing but empty space between him and this new individual—whoever it was—that had somehow gotten into his chamber. Into the one room nobody else had set foot in since he had somehow gotten onto this train.

Who on Earth was *this?*

Then, appearing as quickly and silently as the first, the shadowy figure was joined by another. This second figure, taller than the first, seemed to step through some kind of … doorway of light … except there was no doorway.

Riyul's mouth dropped.

One second, there had been nothing but the open air blur of trees and shrubbery rushing past his carriage, the next a man was stepping through, as though through a portal or doorway, and now, it was the open air wall once again.

He quickly looked between one and the other for an explanation. With both individuals standing next to each other, he was certain he was looking at a young girl and what could be her grandfather. It was difficult to make out in the darkness and gloom, but if his eyes were not failing him, she seemed quite young indeed. Long hair, a red jacket and trousers—she could have passed as a schoolgirl; the other man was wielding a black cane, though again barely perceptible in this darkness.

They began walking over, and Riyul watched them approach with a mixture of apprehension and a tiny sliver of something else. Excitement? He scolded himself. This pair could mean trouble, undoubtedly. They were the unknown. But there was also a tiny glimmer of hope, of change, for the first time since he could remember.

But no. He had to be careful. Steeling himself, Riyul repeated his question, this time to both of them.

'Who are you?' he asked again, firmly.

The man spoke first, raising his palms out. 'My name is Haradan. This is Daffodil. We've been looking for you.'

'You've been looking for me?' replied Riyul, his face a look of confusion, but also hurt. 'I've been here for God only knows how long. Where am I? How did I get here?'

If Riyul looked hurt, then Haradan only more so.

'I'm so sorry that you've been here alone for so long,' Haradan said. 'I received word that there may have been someone who had arrived. Believe me, I've been looking. But I just could not get through. Thankfully, with the help of Daffodil here, we managed to locate you.' He gestured to the young girl next to him, beaming.

Daffodil smiled softly. She could only imagine what this man must have been going through—she had some semblance of an idea, considering she had been through this herself recently (however long ago that was exactly), but here was a man that had clearly been alone for some length of time, and was only now meeting another person.

To her, Riyul looked … ageless—simultaneously thirty and sixty, though perhaps thirty would make more sense. He had a neat, trimmed black beard with shoulder-length jet black hair and a scar on his cheek which made him seem dangerous and formidable, like a warrior of bygone times. His carriage showed clear signs of habitation, of long-term living: there were a few clothes, what looked to be a box or crate, a simple bed. But mainly—and most worrying—there were the etchings. A collection of markings on the wall, which, as she leaned over slightly to examine them, must have easily numbered into the hundreds. She wanted to gasp, but stopped herself. They must be his attempts at demarcating some kind of time system, she thought to herself, in part awe, part serious concern. She realised suddenly they were still talking, and her staring at his wall was probably not the most polite thing in the world, and she quickly turned back to the two of them.

Riyul continued speaking, seemingly not entirely convinced. 'But who are you?' he asked Haradan.

'Yes. You'll have a lot of questions. You're probably also wondering what this place is, and so much more,' Haradan said.

'Yes. Though I think I may have worked a few things out,' said Riyul. 'I've had a lot of time to think.'

'Of course,' replied Haradan tenderly. 'Nonetheless, please allow me to explain. Let us go for a walk.'

***

As Haradan walked around the compartment and explained some of the workings of the train in great amounts of detail (Riyul had demanded some more answers before he had begun walking), Daffodil looked around the room more thoroughly.

It hadn't been particularly hard to find the 'newcomer', as Haradan had called him. Daffodil and Haradan had simply continued working the doors, Haradan had taught her to listen carefully to the sounds emanating from deep within, and Daffodil had let the sounds of the train wash over her. And there was one particular door she'd felt a strong affinity towards. It had seemed to almost hum, as though calling for entry. So she'd tried it. And they'd found this.

They'd found Riyul.

She looked over. Haradan was now showing him how he located doors that led to other lands on the other side of the small carriage.

It was sad, she thought. How he lived here, alone, for however long he'd been here. He didn't look particularly old, not as old as her dad anyway, but there was something about the way he looked at them. As though he hadn't seen people in millenia.

And then there was the mystery of this room.

One wall which was literally just open air. She could feel the gentle breeze brush past her skin when she put her fingertips out. Twilight bathed the evermoving night-forest with a magnificent pearlescent light; a gentle glimmer, as though covered by a wafer-thin layer of shining silky gossamer, painted the tops of the impossibly fast trees with a silver sheen.

And his bed! So close to the edge! Could he not have fallen out at any point? As Daffodil looked at the rushing outside, she realised she had not actually seen such scenes beyond the train before. The streaming night sky and shrubbery did not change much, yet this was a lot more revealing than anything she'd glimpsed previously in the other corridors or carriages. The trees and bushes and night sky were more or less the same, but she could make out each plant much more clearly in the nightlight. She noted how the scenery did not change much, presumably as a result of the conductor's planning—if he ever existed, Daffodil reminded herself.

But what was outside the train? Beyond the trees and bushes that kept on blurring past?

An idea sprang to mind … but … would it work?

She turned to Haradan and Riyul. Riyul had just manifested his first door and was about to open it with Haradan's help. That was fast. Nonetheless, she was happy for the newcomer. Smiling, she began walking over, around the crate, strewn clothes, and general mess of the compartment. She felt bad. Like they were intruding on someone else's private space.

Then she saw the markings on the wall again, which she'd spotted earlier. But also something else. She was halfway to them, and that's when she realised the ceiling wasn't the open-sky ceiling like in the other compartment. No. The ceiling here contained more markings. Others. Markings and etchings the likes of which she had never seen before. These were not just lines, or tally marks like on the wall, but swooshes and swirls and logos and hieroglyphs; crosses and shapes and patterns. They were everywhere, covering the ceiling.

'What is that?' she whispered to herself. She needed to show Haradan.

She reached the pair of them, and was about to proffer her idea and talk about what she'd seen, when Haradan gave her one of his warm smiles and began gently opening the door Riyul had manifested.

'Okay, now that everything is explained,' Haradan said, 'I can explain to you both how we are going to progress—and how we can get you both out of here.'

Then everything started to go horribly wrong.

Daffodil had just enthusiastically began, 'Sorry, Haradan, before that, could we not climb to the ceiling of this carriage and see what's—'

And the door ripped itself open.

SCREEEEEEEEEECH!

The impossible sound. This time even louder than before.

A black void beyond the doorway, darker than ink.

An all-engulfing suction, vacuum, intense and chaotic pull began instantly ripping everything out of the carriage.

The whole world crashed around her.

Crates flew and whooshed out.

Wood splintered and cracked from all around. The entire room groaned.

And in that very instant, Haradan was sucked straight through the doorway.

'No!' Daffodil screamed.

But it was too late. He had been cleanly plucked off his feet, effortlessly, like a dandelion plucked by the hand of a child and then flung into the black void.

And yet the wind was not stopping. As Daffodil tried to process what had just happened, the pull was consuming everything in the room. She realised Riyul was barely holding on to the wall as his body was also being sucked in.

A large crate whirled past Daffodil's head, missing her by inches, and flew straight through the doorway.

She had to move fast. The only reason she was alive was because of her distance from the door, where the magnetic pull must be slightly less strong.

'Shut the door!' she screamed at Riyul through the wind. She needed to cling on to something, for she could already feel herself sliding towards the gaping doorway. The entire compartment seemed to be tilting due to the velocity of the suction.

'Use your legs!' she yelled through the onslaught, trying to scramble backwards, looking for something to grab onto, her hair flying around her and her clothes violently flailing in the wind.

HISSSSSSSSSSSSSSSSSSSSSS.

The wood panels were splintering and flying out at a thousand different angles, all narrowly missing her and Riyul.

This is chaos, Daffodil thought. It was all happening so fast, and yet it was all happening in slow motion. She felt like the world was being destroyed and being ripped apart at half-speed.

Riyul, who was almost parallel with the floor at this point due to the ferocity of the pull, was somehow holding on to the internal ridges of the wall with his fingers.

He realised his feet were right at the point of the open door, which had opened outward, despite the whirling wind pulling inward. He mustered all his strength and kicked with both legs, making a brush of contact with the very edge of the metallic door.

But that's all it needed.

With the slightest of nudges, the door moved a barely perceptible amount in Daffodil's eyes, but the momentum was caught in full flow by the impossible wind, and it was sucked back into place.

SLAM.

The door shut perfectly.

As quickly as it had happened, everything stopped.

Hay from pillows and clothes that were mid-air began to float down. Riyul, who was no longer mid-air, fell onto his feet, immediately pushed against the closed door for good measure, and panted heavily. Daffodil collapsed onto the ground. She was drenched in sweat.

There was a tiny squeal from the far corner of the room, and a white mouse poked its nose out of a small hole in the wall.

Daffodil didn't even question the mouse, but instead looked at Riyul imploringly.

'What just happened?'

Chapter 14

Aftermath

'I had a clock once,' Riyul said gently, pacing around the carriage, Eli in hand. Daffodil raised her head from her knees and peered over from the spot in the corner which she had hunkered down into. She didn't really see how this was going to help them work out how to leave.

'The problem is, it disappeared when I got here.' He looked around the carriage. 'I've never been able to keep track of time in this place. I feel like if I just could, I'd be able to solve something. I always feel like I'm on the verge of being able to work something out, you know?'

Daffodil nodded. 'But you never do,' she finished for him.

'Yes,' he said, nodding in unison. 'I never do.'

She felt his confusion. So many unanswered questions. But there was more. So, so much more. So many feelings and emotions boiling inside her, all raging to be understood and acknowledged.

A solitary tear rolled quietly down Daffodil's cheek. It fell, making its long descent down to the wooden floor which she was sitting on.

She didn't really know why she was crying, she just… was.

Overwhelmed? Perhaps that was why, she thought.

Nothing made sense. As though this madness was not enough, now, without Haradan, escape seemed even less possible than before. And the one hope she had of explanation, of help, of support, had been sucked out of the very door that was to be her means of escape—or, perhaps, death.

Did she really believe Haradan had died? She didn't know. There was definitely the chance. But something in her, some deeply situated, inaudible glimmer of hope hidden within, told her no. That man was too hardy to be taken so easily. She couldn't explain it, but he'd still be there somewhere. The question was, where?

So many questions. Daffodil didn't know what to do or think, so placed her head back on her knees.

'Daffodil,' Riyul said softly. 'I know this is hard, but I think we need to keep going. We need to try and figure a way out. Otherwise, everything Haradan did for us would have been for nothing.'

Oh, this really is like a bad movie, Daffodil thought, not lifting her head. *When am I going to wake up?* In the darkness, she pinched herself. Well, she was definitely awake.

Chukka-chukka-chukka-chukka-chukka. The omnipresent sound of the never-ceasing, never-ending train thrummed all the louder. Her ears were full of the sound. It pushed through her eardrums, despite her attempts at blocking it out. And why try to drown it out? What was the point in fighting anymore? She let the sound take over her. Let it push through to her inner being and just be.

Chukka-chukka-chukka-chukka-chukka.

'I don't believe we can get out anymore…' Daffodil said, head still buried.

'I understand. You feel like you're in a black void, spiralling down endlessly. When does the pain stop, right? When does it end?'

Daffodil looked up slowly. And nodded.

'Yeah.'

'Well, that's when you have to remember what you're fighting for. The people that believe in you. That love you.'

She remembered Adam. Ah, he loved trains. *I don't know if he'd love this, though.* She smiled to herself. Knowing him, he'd probably be able to think of a way out—that clever boy. Daffodil frowned. And kept frowning.

Adam.

Her baby brother.

'And when nobody else is around,' Riyul continued with a face that betrayed no emotion, 'you have to believe in yourself.'

He was right.

She had to get out of here. For her baby brother. Her parents. They wouldn't just sit here moping, curled into a ball like a crumb. She knew for certain they'd try their hardest to do whatever they could, whether it was finding her or escaping this situation.

Daffodil looked up, tilting her head to the side and leaning against her arm. *I wonder if they're looking for me.* Something deep within her told her they were. If she wasn't going crazy and dreaming this whole place up.

She looked around. The rushing trees outside. The dark night sky. There was Riyul, kneeling down, looking at and clearly thinking about doors. Daffodil didn't know what was real anymore, but she knew she had to keep trying. For she knew that's what her parents would do.

Daffodil got up.

Riyul looked over, raising an eyebrow.

'You have to listen for the sounds,' Daffodil murmured, pursing her lips. 'Slight variations in sounds tell you a lot. Those were the exact words Haradan had said.'

Riyul pondered on this. 'But then why did Haradan not realise that door was going to lead to what it did? Surely, he listened to the sounds before opening, right?'

She staggered forward. Even hearing his name was painful; the memory of what happened was still raw.

'Yes, but the lands that each door leads to can change,' she said. 'So one second, this door,' she pointed at the door with four fingers, 'can lead to a land of terrible wind and tornadoes and cyclones. Or…' She kneeled down and listened carefully.

Riyul was silent. It was just the sound of the train, and something else. Something quiet but melodic. Like some distant, incredibly muffled, far-off tinkle. Daffodil closed her eyes. She couldn't hear it exactly—it was more a feeling, deep within. So far. As though time warped around her. That sound.

Beats.

Musical notes.

She thought back to her musical theory, how many beats to a line…

There was a beauty to it. Not just the beauty of sound—the tinkle, it wasn't a sound—but the beauty of rhythm, timings, of maths.

With her eyes closed, she realised it was all numerical. It was real. As though she could see the sound itself. In the darkness, she could sense it: it was lands away, calling her, telling her to come find it. She remembered her art lessons, where she wouldn't fit in. She knew it then and knew it more so now—shapes could conjure up sounds, and sounds could conjure up shapes and numbers in her mind.

She opened her eyes.

'This door is safe now,' she whispered.

Riyul lifted an eyebrow.

'Okay,' he said. 'Let's try it.'

'Let's,' she said, placing her hand on the silver knob. It was cool to the touch. But a pleasant coolness. Her body felt right.

She turned the doorknob before she could second-guess herself, before her nerves kicked in, before she could back out.

And she opened the door.

In front of them was the oddest thing. She certainly had not expected to see this.

There appeared to be an identical carriage with the same wooden flooring, strewn clothes, walls and open-air side. In fact, as Daffodil looked around, she realised it was the exact same carriage. And off in the distance—no way.

She looked back, turning away from the open door. At the back of her carriage was another open door, which had not been there before, and she was looking at the back of the head of a young girl wearing a red jacket.

'Riyul,' Daffodil whispered, 'I think that's me.'

Chapter 15

The Endless Compartment

A clump of trees whipped past as Daffodil looked out forlornly.

Her watchful, transfixed gaze was suddenly broken as she was violently jolted up in her seat. Her nose, which had been barely resting against the glass, created an audible squeak as she was rocked up and down the rear passenger window of her parents' car.

Pothole. Clarice's eyes bulged as she recovered from the sudden jerk and smiled thinly. She looked back at her daughter.

Daffodil had regained her composure and settled back into her position, chin resting on her arm, gazing out at the passing scenery: an expanse of mainly dry sand with some trees scattered around as far the eye could see. She enjoyed the American deserts. As to her mother's question, she pursed her lips and half-heartedly forced out a smile.

They had been watching her for the last few days, trying to get her mind off things, such as with this very holiday. Her eyes caught her father's in the rearview mirror. He didn't say anything.

Oh, when would they just end this game?

Daffodil didn't have it in her to be loud, outwardly outraged with her parents, or to shout and scream. Her anger, her upset, was a quiet one. It simmered. It shook her core deep within, but on the surface, there was little to be discerned.

'I know the move isn't something you wanted, sweetheart, but as we'll all come to realise—it'll be for the best. It'll be a fresh start for all of us.'

Ah, so she finally mentions it.

Daffodil didn't say anything—she didn't have energy or the words for it—but instead nodded imperceptibly.

Their car continued on its winding route through the scenic roads. Daffodil sat in the back, watching out.

Mum and Dad began talking quietly.

Their vehicle had three occupants—in many ways perhaps, it was quite full—and yet, for Daffodil, she had never felt more alone.

***

'This is so weird because when I move, it's like a reflection. But at a crazy angle,' Daffodil called out to Riyul as she watched the back of her head through the doorway. She watched a girl who looked exactly like her, albeit from behind, look out at what must have been another version of her very room, just out of view. She stepped sideways to get a better view through the further doorway, and onward it seemed to lead to another one, and through that a very distant other one. And on and on and on they went.

'Okay, this is trippy.'

She suddenly felt a strong sense of vertigo. Clearly, the human mind was not meant to process multiple versions of the same room.

Or am I looking at multiple versions of myself? All those other girls in red jackets. Just the thought of all this made her head spin. Nonetheless, she had to keep working this out.

She raised her hand.

And the other Daffodil did too.

She cocked her head.

The other Daffodil did too.

All this she saw through the doorway, but when she turned around and looked at the back of her room, it was the same thing. Open door. A Daffodil standing there. And again, that unnerving feeling of sickness. It was like motion sickness, that nauseating feeling of being in a car too long; just experimenting with moving her hands and head made her want to lie down. Yet this was also entrancing, watching the figure at the bottom of her carriage match her exact movements, at the precise moment she made them. A bit like looking in a mirror. The actions were instant—but from an impossible, paradoxical angle.

'This is so odd,' Riyul said, watching.

She turned to the one thing which she thought might pacify her motion sickness (paradoxically): looking out at the rushing scenery. For her, staring out into scenes and vistas always had the capacity to soothe. And so, she stopped with the experimenting and took a moment to stop and look; Daffodil gave up working out the inner-workings of the impossible doorway, identical carriages and multiple Daffodils, and concentrated simply on the passing trees.

The problem was, as she tried to concentrate on the beautiful rush outside her carriage, she felt a magnetic pull to see what this view might look like through the doorway in the next carriage with the other Daffodil. She shook her head. She knew she'd feel uneasy just trying.

'I think I've done something wrong,' said Daffodil, staring hard outside.

'What do you mean?' asked Riyul.

'Well, everytime I look through the door into the next carriage, or even try to look—I feel sick. Like I'm not meant to be able to see this. Like... the train itself is pushing me away, repelling me from looking.'

'Huh,' Riyul said. 'Motion sickness is our body's way of telling us we are poisoned. Do you know this?'

Daffodil shook her head vigorously. She was letting herself experience the soft coolness of the wind gently stroking her face and pacifying her churning insides.

'Often when people feel like they want to be sick, it is because their body thinks there are toxins within it. This is why you feel sick when you are dizzy. Dizziness is your body's way of saying that you are poisoned. So they feel a sense of dizziness; they want to throw up to get the ingested toxins out. When people are on boats, or even trains, actually, they can feel this way. Their body incorrectly thinks it is poisoned, and that's why things are moving so quickly around— because the body believes it is dizzy when really it is just unnaturally quick motion.'

'Hmm, that makes sense,' said Daffodil, impressed with Riyul's knowledge. 'I'm guessing it's the same with cars.'

'Cars?' Riyul said, thinking. 'Oh, like on a train? Yes, exactly.' He turned to look at the doorway.

Daffodil raised a brow. That's not what she had meant at all; she was about to explain this when Riyul spoke again.

'So,' Riyul said, looking through into the identical carriage, 'shall we go in?'

'I don't know,' she said slowly, feet firmly fixed in her present room. Here she was safe, which couldn't necessarily be said about her experiences of other carriages. Discovering new places had been constantly risky since her arrival, with seemingly minimal payoff.

'Well, I'm going to have a look inside,' he said, stepping in. And before she could say anything, he was gone.

Daffodil watched in disbelief, fighting the nausea she felt by simply looking in that direction. The room or doorway seemed to be wanting to repel her from going in. Yet, all thoughts of that disappeared when she watched Riyul enter the next carriage. Because Riyul disappeared. She tried calling out to him, but her voice collapsed in her very throat when he stepped in, and his leg simply vanished from view, followed quickly by the rest of his body.

She whirled around, looking to see if he had come out to the back of the room.

Nothing.

She walked towards the rear door and looked in. There she was. The back of her peering through at the other side, with her carriage in between. And yet it was devoid of any Riyul.

'What on Earth...' she whispered.

Well, maybe I'm not on Earth.

She turned around again, contemplating.

He had stepped in, she thought, pacing over to the first doorway she'd opened. As he went in, he disappeared. She squinted at the frame—like Haradan had done.

Ah. A twinge deep within her.

No. Now wasn't the time for that—she'd think about, and find, Haradan later.

She examined the door carefully, comparing it to the ones he'd shown her previously. Nope. The doorframe seemed normal.

She perused the space between the frame, the air that stood between her current room and the one on the other side.

Again, this seemed normal.

Daffodil shut her eyes, hoping an idea would come to her, concentrating as hard as she could. She tried to think of an idea or some explanation. Yet, nothing.

All she could hear in the darkness was the train. *Chukka-chukka-chukka-chukka-chukka.* She smiled to herself. Darn sound. Not helping.

She opened her eyes and looked around the room. Alone. She was completely alone.

'Well… I guess I'm stepping in,' she whispered to nobody.

***

On the other side, Riyul stood in the middle of the same compartment room, gazing out at the night sky. Not a thing in the room looked out of place—yet he seemed somehow different.

Realising she had entered, he turned to her and took a step back.

'Daffodil?' he said, seeming startled, which Daffodil did not understand. 'You came? I was pretty much not expecting you at this point.'

'Of course I came—you just disappeared!' she replied. 'And why were you not expecting me?'

'Daffodil, when I came in, I waited for you, but you didn't come. I looked back into the room, and you weren't there. To me, it seemed that you had disappeared. So I waited here for you until you came. It must have been like an hour since I last saw you. I really was thinking we'd gotten split up or you'd ended up somewhere else.'

'An hour?' she said in a small voice. 'I looked around a tiny bit, and thought about a few things before I came, but I don't think I was more than like a couple of minutes at the most.'

Riyul stared at her, seemingly unsure what to say. 'Well, this is new. I think we may just have experienced some kind of change in time.'

'Yeah…' she trailed off. 'What do you mean?'

'Well, if my theory is correct,' he said, scratching the sides of his chin, 'What felt like seconds or minutes to you, expanded to hours to me. Like a time warp.'

He walked back towards the rear door, or his entranceway. He looked around the sides carefully before he turned back to Daffodil, his eyes bright.

'Daffodil. I don't think this is the same room. I think this doorway is more like a portal to another identical room, where time is experienced differently to the previous.'

She looked around. Not the same room? Nothing else seemed to have changed. The night sky was the same shade it had always been. The doors, front and rear, still remained open. *What would that mean about the girl I saw at the end? The one who looked like me?*

She shuddered.

'Hey—I have an idea,' Riyul announced. 'Let's go in again through the door, but right after each other.'

Daffodil considered this, trying to shake off more negative or scary thoughts, and weighed up her options. She supposed there was nothing else they could really do. They could either stay and work out how to open another door, or they could try this one again and see what happens. Well, not exactly brimming with choices.

I guess of the two options, this is probably the least horrible. Also, though she didn't really admit it, she wasn't sure if she totally wanted to try any other option yet—not with the enigma that was this doorway.

'Let's do it,' she said, focusing on the doorway at the end of the room. She felt uneasy again. 'Just nerves,' Daffodil said under her breath.

Riyul nodded, heading towards the topmost doorway once more. Daffodil followed.

'Okay, so I'm going to step in,' he said. 'Be sure to be right in step with me, okay? Come in straight away—as fast as you can.'

'Got it,' she said, nodding and trying to match his enthusiasm. 'I'm right along with you.'

'Great. Let's have a go.'

He paused, looking at her.

Then Riyul stepped right through. As he did, each portion of his body past the doorway instantly disappeared.

And—he was gone again.

Daffodil found herself staring through the doorway at the empty carriage once more. She could see herself at the end, not moving. Hesitating. Like when she was anxious that she couldn't sleep, which deterred her sleep even more, her view of herself not moving only rooted her to the spot further.

Her heart pounded and her whole body shook—but she couldn't let herself remain fixed here.

Without allowing herself to think any more, she took a quick breath and stepped in.

As she came through, Riyul simply washed into view. He was there again, in the middle of the room, but this time, not standing as she had expected. Instead, he was on the ground, lying down on what must have been his old pillow.

She ran over. Before she could wake him, his eyelids shot open.

'How long?' she asked, exasperated.

'Hours and hours,' he said with a smile. 'I think eventually after waiting, I fell asleep. One thing I tried to do was measure time, or seconds,' he continued, sitting up. 'One Mississippi. Two Mississippi. And so on, to roughly measure seconds passing. I got past 15,000 before sleep took me.'

Daffodil felt like her throat had dried up. 'I'm so sorry,' she said almost inaudibly. 'I promise I followed in right after you, but I may have hesitated for like a second at most. But I swear I thought it was pretty much straight away.'

'I believe you,' he said with a smile. 'You did nothing wrong. The question is what is going on, and what we can do.' The words hung in the air as they both considered this. He chewed on his lip. 'Each time I go in, the timespan between my entry and your entry seems to expand.'

He looked out at the doorway in silence, as though it was the bane of his life.

'You know, it's funny. Until you entered my life, this doorway hadn't even existed. And now all I want to do is figure out how it works, and how to get somewhere with it.'

'I wonder if there's something else we could try,' Daffodil said hopefully. 'I know! I could go in first.'

'Hmm. I don't know. I feel like that might not help, and if anything, it may be more dangerous.'

She understood what he meant. Whilst he may have gotten used to being alone for months, or what felt like months, she didn't know if she could take hours of being alone, or dealing with whatever was to come—on her own.

'Maybe we can go look for another door,' he suggested, gesturing around the room.

'Yeah,' Daffodil said, a little disheartened, but not showing it.

'But before that,' he continued, 'I have one last idea.'

Daffodil looked up at him as he paced over to the door once more.

'This time,' he said, looking at her, 'we go in simultaneously.'

She got up and walked over. 'How do we do that?'

'First, I think we should make sure we are both technically in at the same exact second, so there is no time gap. Maybe we just put our hands in at the same time. We don't need to rush this. We can go in slowly, but at the very same second. This doorway has a clear point of entry,' he explained, showing her how the place where the metal met the metal right through the centre of the doorway must be the exact point where it led from one place to another. 'Then, as long as we feel it to be okay, we slowly enter both our legs, then our bodies, and then, if we are confident—if we feel like we are in the same place at the same time, we pull our heads in and see where we end up.'

'Okay,' she said slowly. 'I think that could work.'

'Alright, take a moment, and tell me when.'

They prepared themselves, and when Daffodil had taken a deep breath, she stepped forward and in line with Riyul.

'Ready?' he asked.

'Ready.'

'Okay then, just our fingers and hands enter first,' he said, hovering his hand just at the point of entry.

Daffodil did the same parallel to him.

'Okay,' he called, 'On one... Two... Three.'

They pushed their hands through the doorway. Daffodil gasped. His disappeared, and somehow hers did too. Her arm led to nothingness where her hand should have been: just a red sleeve leading to a clean cut of nothing, with the usual image of the compartment on the other side.

'That hasn't happened before,' she said, astonished. 'Normally, your body disappears but mine remains visible.'

'I see, yes. Well I can't see yours either.' He moved his arm forward, and as he did so, it continued to disappear from sight. Daffodil tried this too. It was disconcerting, but it seemed to work.

Oddly, Daffodil thought, the air on the other side of the doorway felt a bit different. *Perhaps cooler?* Before she could give this any more thought, Riyul spoke.

'Shall we try our legs now?' he asked.

'Let's do it.'

They both carefully finished taking their hands and arms in, and then stepped in with their legs. They did this slowly but meticulously, ensuring they were in line at all times. They worked slowly, angling and adjusting and pulling their bodies through until just their heads remained in their original compartment.

It is definitely colder on the other side, Daffodil thought, *though still impossible to see.*

'Okay,' Riyul's floating head said. 'Ready?'

'Ready,' Daffodil replied, smiling, attempting to stifle her giggle. With Riyul looking the way he did, she could only imagine what she must look like right now. He smiled with her.

'Okay. One,' he called.

She readied herself.

'Two,' she said with him. Daffodil took the tiniest of breaths.

'Three.'

They pulled their heads in at the same time. A wave of darkness. A shatter of cold that only lasted a moment but came with an immediate rush. Of air. Of temperature. Of colours.

For a split second, she felt weightless.

And then—as quickly as it had come—her vision and hearing and balance quickly reorientated themselves. And she opened her eyes.

She was facing the same silver-framed doorway, and she could see the compartment through it as normal. However, above and besides the frame, things were different. It was … white. Pure white.

She turned. Riyul was right next to her. That was good.

Then she saw where she was.

Her eyes grew wide.

'Oh my.'

She turned back quickly to check the doorway, and the previous compartment was still there. She spun back at what lay in front of them.

Before her was snow and ice as far as her eyes could see. Rolling hills of pure, unadulterated snow dipped and undulated into the distance. She took a tenderly step forward and heard the soft crunch of snow compressing beneath her feet.

'How beautiful,' Riyul said in awe.

Daffodil beamed, continuing to take it all in.

'Yes,' she agreed. 'We've finally gotten somewhere. I can't believe we actually made it off. Wherever this is.'

She basked in the glare of the midday sun and scanned the horizon with all its crests and peaks of mesmerising snow. Yet in the distance was something she could not quite make out. Her smile faltered. Two somethings. On the furthest hill of snow, far off in the distance, were two tiny black dots. She squinted, trying to get a better view.

'Daffodil,' Riyul said, seeing what she was seeing. 'I think those are people.'

'Yes,' she said, watching carefully. 'And ... I think they're coming towards us.'

PART II

Chapter 16

The Land of Snow

The wait felt like an eternity.

Not being able to do anything but watch as two dark figures grew larger and larger? Daffodil couldn't take it.

'What if they're blood-sucking killers?' she asked Riyul.

He frowned. 'Why would they be blood-sucking killers?'

Daffodil shrugged. 'Why are we in the middle of a snowy wasteland, after having gone through a doorway portal on a train we were somehow teleported to?' she asked, gesturing around at the landscape.

'Fair enough.'

Couldn't argue with that logic.

They continued to wait, outlooking the pristine white snow land, Daffodil twiddling her thumbs and chewing the inside of her mouth anxiously.

Riyul had surveyed the landscape, considering avenues for them to escape, should they need to. Not because the approaching figures were blood-sucking killers, but because he agreed that they didn't know for sure if the approaching individuals were hostile or friendly.

There wasn't really anywhere they could go.

He had suggested that if they really had to, they could consider going back through their entry doorway into the compartment they came from—or try to, for they didn't actually know if they could reenter despite being able to see through the door. Her hand had disappeared through well enough when she'd tested it, but until they stepped fully inside, they would not know where they'd end up this time.

Perhaps better not to go back that way, she thought.

Daffodil was worried.

Should they hide from the approaching people? They didn't even know where they had arrived from the train—or was this land full of snow still part of the train world?

Even if return was an option, something deep within her told her that she wasn't going to go back. No matter what would happen—now matter what new difficulties she may face out here, she was not returning back to those carriages.

And so she had made a choice, clearly, with Riyul's thoughts considered. They would meet with whoever these people were.

And so they waited. Mostly in silence. And with every passing moment, the dark specks grew. From the tiniest of specks to slightly less tiny dots. Then the dots began to grow, and ever so slowly morph into the outlines of two people—hazy and vague. And—

Huh, that was odd, Daffodil thought.

Squinting hard, she could have sworn there was a third tiny dot with them, now that they were around two-hundred steps away.

She inspected Riyul nervously, but he simply stood, hands clasped behind his back, unmoving and poised. Her back stiffened a little more.

If he can be confident, so can I.

But who or what was that approaching?

Three people? Two with an animal, perhaps?

One-hundred steps.

There were definitely two people, walking slowly across the vast white plain—accompanied by another, smaller outline.

Daffodil squinted even harder to make out the figure.

Was that... a child?

She immediately thought back to Adam, and just as immediately waved his image away. Not now, Daffodil. He'll be okay.

Fifty steps. They were close now. And it was definitely a kid with them.

The two adults had long black hair, and wore warm, wintry coats.

'Hello!' shouted a female voice across the white space. The compacted snow all around absorbed most of the sound, and there was no real wind to obstruct. It was the person on the left who had spoken. Or... had it been the one on the right?

Riyul hadn't responded yet. Daffodil wasn't sure she wanted to yet either.

The trio got closer, and Daffodil realised the voice could have been either of the two women standing before her.

They were sisters.

'Hello, dears,' said the woman on the left, smiling. She seemed slighter older, of slim build, with a kindly smile and gait. 'I'm Safa, and this is my sister Marwa, as well as my son, Seul.' She gestured to the other two in turn.

'Hello!' said Seul, delighted.

Marwa nodded at them, neither smiling nor frowning, nor saying a word.

The sisters were dressed well, considering the location. They seemed around thirty, according to Daffodil's world, wore long dresses and coats on top—the kind Daffodil had only seen in black-and-white pictures, but they seemed stylish here. The coats themselves seemed old, not burlap but of similar coarse material, yet warm and hard-wearing; as though they were dressed for their environment. Unlike Daffodil. She shivered slightly, looked down at her attire and pulled her own simple red jacket around her, ensuring the hood was on snug.

'You seem cold, my love!' Safa exclaimed, handing Daffodil a coat like the kind she had. It seemed to have come from nowhere.

'Oh… thank… thank you,' Daffodil said, completely befuddled as to where the coat had appeared from. She took it gratefully nonetheless, and wore it above her red jacket. Riyul seemed warm in his black leather.

'We're really pleased to meet you. I'm Riyul, and this is Daffodil. We're, erm, not exactly sure where we are.'

The young boy gasped, then, realising everyone was looking at him, quickly covered his mouth and spun around. Daffodil smiled at him. He looked about eight, with short brown hair and huge eyes.

'You're joking,' Safa said quietly.

'No…' replied Riyul.

'You're not from our lands at all?'

Riyul and Daffodil shook their heads.

Seul, the young boy, seemingly unable to withhold his dramatic tendencies, spun back around and ran forward, excited.

'It's people from the outside—actual real people!' he hollered, running up to Riyul, clasping him and shaking him, then turning to his mum with a humongous grin plastered to his face. 'I can't believe there are other people here!' he screamed again, giving the biggest smile Daffodil had ever seen, right in her face. From this close, she saw he was missing some teeth. She couldn't help but smile back.

'Seul, stop running around and screaming at our guests!' Safa said, dragging Seul away from Daffodil.

'It's okay,' Riyul said, laughing.

'So sorry,' Safa said. 'He's just never really seen people in the Land of Snow out here on our journey.'

'Land of Snow? sorry—your journey?' Daffodil asked.

'Yes,' Safa said. 'Gosh. I've barely met anyone with memories of just coming to the world. These are our lands.' She gestured widely around her. 'Everyone knows of this particular area, the Land of Snow. So, when you said you're not from here, I figured you must be from outside. Anyway, as for us, yes. We are on a bit of a journey; well, we are near the very end, actually. As you've probably realised, my sister here does not really speak.'

Marwa nodded again and smiled weakly.

'She has been iced,' Safa said mournfully, clearly saddened by whatever this term meant.

Daffodil looked at them. 'I'm so sorry, but what does iced mean?'

'Oh yes, you're not from here! My apologies! You need to tell us how you got here, by the way, but in answer to your question, iced means that there is ice within her, and this has taken away her capacity to talk. She is—I guess you could say—semi-frozen within, at all times, and it is seizing her up slowly, including her mouth, and thus affects her ability to speak.'

'That sounds horrible,' Daffodil said.

'And, pardon me,' Riyul said cautiously, considering the circumstances, 'how does one become iced?'

'That's a good question. Hmm, how do I explain it?' Safa said, thinking. 'Have you discovered alchemy yet?'

'I have a little bit. From a man called Haradan,' Daffodil said.

'Ah, Haradan! How is he?' Safa asked brightly.

'He, erm… He got sucked into a doorway by a strong wind.'

'Oh, I'm sorry to hear that. But don't worry. I'm sure Haradan will be fine. Hey, if you want to know if he's okay, we could try to run an alchemic trace on him if you'd like. Do you have any of his possessions?'

'No,' Daffodil said sadly.

'Ah, no problem. We'll find him. A lot of what we know is from him. If anyone is coming close to mastering alchemy, it is that man. Did you know they say he has worked out a way to change your physical appearance with a new blend of liquid he has mixed? But anyway—your question. Look, it's like when you take a vial of elixir and transmute one element to another.' She proceeded to withdraw a vial of clear liquid from her jacket and carefully pour a few drops onto the snow at her feet. Immediately, there was a flash and burst of smoke, which, upon clearing, revealed hardened earth with visible hard cracks, as though baked in the desert sun for years.

'Fascinating,' Riyul said, tapping the crusted earth with his knuckle.

Seul grinned happily.

'So, we have four elements we work with in alchemy. Earth, Air, Fire and Water. Marwa had been trying to master her fourth element—Water, or its other form, Ice—but sadly, something went wrong when she was experimenting. She happened to be alone at the time. We found her on the floor all frozen up. Luckily, we got to her when we did. She had almost lost her ability to breathe from the ice crystals inside her. Anyway, we tried to fix it. I tried using Fire and

Earth therapy. Didn't work. I tried getting her to show me what she did exactly that day. But it's beyond my abilities. And so we've tried everything to reverse this. Doctors. Decanters. The court of Notra Gerrihend. Apothecaries even, like the Herbalore Centre. Nothing. We've worked out vaguely what happened, with her showing us how it occurred, but the ice is so far gone that nobody seems to really know how to really help. Sure, people were able to mitigate things a little—and honestly, we are forever grateful for what they've been able to do—she'd be a lot worse now otherwise. Even more frozen, that is. But we think there's only one solution now to truly reverse this and find the cause of the issue. And that is to find our old teacher.'

'I think you need to explain who that is, Mum,' said Seul, tugging on her long coat.

'Of course, dear. You're right.' She turned to them. 'There aren't many people in our lands. Well, we think there are, but from what I understand, for those who come from the outside, our numbers might not seem like an awful lot. Anyway, as for people of real knowledge, there are even fewer. To be fair, Haradan is one of them. Anyway, our old teacher, also called Professor, is someone that taught both me and Marwa when we were much younger. There aren't many schools in our world, but the one we went to was the best. Most people hate school, but we loved it. When the alternative is a life of the same day-in, day-out chores and duties for The City, school life is infinitely better.'

Seul looked at Safa with something akin to longing in his expression.

'Since the new government came into power in The City, and that Gerrihend,' she said with a scowl, 'we've not had the same kind of schooling for our children. Let's just say, I'm not the biggest fan of what the government wants to teach our kids.' As she said this, she put her arm around Seul and squeezed him. 'And so young Seul has not actually gotten to learn the things we did as kids. We're hoping if we can find our old professor, maybe he could mentor Seul also and teach him some things, as well as help us work out the best way to de-ice Marwa.'

'Is he far?' Daffodil asked.

'We don't think he's far, no, we're not too far at all. Just a bit more hiking, in fact. But what about you?' she continued. 'Tell us about yourselves. You're from the outside, you say?'

'Yes,' Riyul said, looking away. 'It's a bit of a long story, actually.'

'Mhmm,' Daffodil agreed. 'So you know Haradan? He found me first. I remember him mentioning Gerrihend also.'

'Haradan?' Safa said. 'Of course. He's been here as long as anyone. He's good like that, always searching for ways to help people. I don't know about Gerrihend, though; Haradan may think he's the only one with enough power and knowledge to help you escape, but I wouldn't be so sure. I've seen some questionable things happen in that palace. But no, I've heard that Haradan has always tried. Gosh, it's been a while since he said he was going to go looking for someone. My husband was good friends with him, actually. Sadly, he's passed away now.'

'I'm so sorry to hear that,' said Riyul.

'Me too,' said Daffodil. 'This is going to sound rude of me, but if I may—how did he pass? I only ask because Haradan said to me that people do not really age here. That there isn't the concept of time.'

'Hmm,' Safa said, chewing her lip whilst Seul rubbed his toe in the snow, and Marwa suddenly became interested in the distance. 'Before my husband, the ageing thing. I wouldn't say ageing is completely nonexistent: people do age up until a point—but yes, he was probably explaining ageing in the simplest way possible. We kind of age. Though it must presumably be much longer than anything you've experienced. Like, I remember when I was a young girl. Smaller than I am now. And as time went on, I obviously grew. So we do have a sense of growing up to a degree. But nobody gets to such an age that their bodies become weak and die, as I believe happens out in your world.'

Daffodil and Riyul nodded.

'Instead, the only way to die here is if you are killed.'

'Killed?' Daffodil asked.

'Yes. Sorry, you're young, but it's probably best you know. Unfortunately, my husband was killed in The Great War. It was us against The City, mainly. My husband, like me and my sister, believed there was a world outside. The City didn't—and still doesn't. And ... let's just say that things got bloody. It all started off peacefully enough. I mean—all protests do, I think. But yes, sadly, there were battles and skirmishes. And he died.' She said this with a glimmer in her eyes, as though she had come to terms with what had happened, and was proud of him. 'We try not to think about it too much,' she said, shaking her head. 'Anyway, sorry for all the information in one big go! I know that's a lot to take in at once!'

Daffodil smiled politely and looked around.

The Land of Snow…

She noticed Safa wore a silver tennis bracelet on her left wrist, which glittered in the midday sun.

Wait.

'Safa,' Daffodil said quickly. 'We were stuck on a train carriage, where outside it was nothing but night. Endless night.'

Riyul agreed. He knew better than anyone just how endless the night was there.

'And,' she continued, 'now we seem to be in this … Land of Snow as you say, where the sun is out. How do the days and nights work here?'

'Ah,' Safa said, 'I'm sorry, I don't fully know the answer to that, I'm afraid. But essentially, each land is different. In this land, it's always day-time. In The City, it's always sunset. On your… train, was it? On your train it was night. They're just fixed.'

'Makes sense,' said Riyul, chewing his lip. 'Based off of what Haradan told us, this may be because of the way it was designed.'

'Maybe,' Safa said, nodding, along with Marwa. 'I mean, I believe that. But that's because I am with Haradan in his belief on the outside. You should be careful who you go saying things like that to, however. Not everybody believes in The Conductor. Particularly in The City. Things have become better now, since The Great War, a lot more so, but sadly, a lot of people were persecuted for their beliefs. There's still animosity out there for people like us.'

'But we know there's an outside,' Daffodil said, baffled. 'I'm from there! I can tell you all about it!'

'I'm sure you can, my dear, and we definitely want to hear about it, most of all Seul, I'm sure,' said Safa. 'But people are … tricky. Humans are like that. If they believe something, nothing can change that. If people don't believe something, nothing you say can change that either.'

'So then how do we get out of here? If nobody believes there's an outside.'

'Nobody? Not nobody! I believe, of course! These two do also. But—' She paused. 'We are few and far between. It's complicated— but it will make sense soon, I hope.' Safa looked out across the snowy hills and pointed at some point far off. It just looked like endless snow to Daffodil. 'Well, you've got two options. Either you can go straight to The City to find someone there. I mean, your best bet probably is there. There's a… creature called Skutlish. I don't know if I'd call him a person, really. He's experimented with so much alchemy, his body has changed. Anyway, he believes in an outside world, and the whispers are that if you want to escape, he's the one to go to. Funny enough, The City doesn't really say anything to him. He keeps to himself mostly, I guess—maybe that's why. But they say he's the one to go to if you really want to leave. That's what they say, anyway.'

'What's the other option?' Daffodil asked.

'Join us, of course!' Seul cried happily.

Safa smirked. 'Yes, you can join us to meet our old teacher, and we can see what to do from there.'

'Hmm, what have others done?' Daffodil said.

'I am not too sure, I am afraid,' said Safa apologetically.

'Have others not tried to leave? Others who have ended up on the train?' Riyul asked.

'Well, I mean, you two are the first of your kind we've ever met,' Safa said, shrugging. 'That being said, we've heard of others, sure, but I understand eventually people stop … caring so much about leaving. I think they end up liking it here.'

'Haradan told me something like that,' Daffodil said quietly. 'That the train can affect your thinking, your personality.' She looked at Riyul, then Safa. 'Maybe they wanted to leave, but then the train got to them and made them lose their will to go.'

'Maybe,' Riyul said quietly.

'You keep saying *train*,' Safa said, cocking her head slightly and frowning. Seul copied her, seemingly wanting a part of the action, but his head went the wrong way. He quickly tilted it the other way. He also forgot to frown.

'Yes…' Riyul said slowly, pointing at the doorway they'd come through.. 'This is all… part of the train land, right?'

Safa looked into their entry doorway and smiled. Seul, seeing this, quickly smiled too. But his head was still tilted.

'You look scary,' Daffodil said to him.

Seul frowned—head still tilted the wrong way.

'Yes, I remember the train.' Safa said, 'This place you're in now is, I guess you could say, attached to it. Or led on from it, but we've been on this side for so long now that it feels like much more than just that train. Some of us live our whole lives and never step foot onto that train, actually.' She inspected the doorway they came through, picked up some snow, and threw it in. It vanished. She didn't place her hand in like Daffodil had.

Smart, Daffodil thought.

'You've probably realised the dangers of going through doorways, especially before you've really learnt about how to manipulate them. So I wouldn't even risk this one again. You just happened to start there. But to answer your question, no.' She pulled out another vial, this time much smaller and thinner, more like a test tube. Swirling within it was a dark blue iridescent liquid.

'Instead,' Safa said, carefully unplugging the vial and pouring out two drops onto the snowy path. 'There's this.'

The instant the first drop fell down and made contact with the snow, a blue-green light burst up from the very ground itself. As the second drop made contact, a streak of light raced in front of them like a flame ripping across poured gasoline. The light ascended impossibly fast, and doors began manifesting before their very eyes:

solid brown wooden doors with that same enchanting glow shifting around their frames.

'There are doors all throughout our land,' Safa said, seemingly just as awe-inspired as them. 'They're connected to all of Aethril. And one of these will be your door home.'

Chapter 17

Notra Gerrihend

Notra Gerrihend sighed.

He shut the door behind him and stepped into the bedroom, where his wife was waiting. The bedroom was smartly furnished, with red tapestries and a four-poster bed sitting contendly centre-field.

Pulling out the band holding back his hair, his long locks flowed down. He had just given a speech to his people, and was now back to confer with his wife.

'What we do is not easy. But it needs to be done.'

She stared back at him impassively.

'The memory elixir is almost ready,' he continued, rubbing his hands together compulsively. 'He's not back yet. Which means Skutlish has taken the step. We must do this now. The people don't always know what they need. That's why royalty exists. We are the ones they look up to—whether they like it or not. The exemplars that are aspired to. The decision makers. And we take the falls also. So we must do what must be done.'

She looked at him without saying a word, though he could spot her tears involuntarily welling up. They had had this conversation.

'Yes,' he said with more conviction, feigned or not. 'The potion will be made. And memories will be wiped.'

He turned away from her, concluding to look out through the large glass window upon his subjects in The City.

'For the people…' he whispered, his hands pressed firmly against the stone windowsill—such that his wife would not see the silent tear that rolled down his own cheek.

'For the people.'

Chapter 18

Walking

The five of them stared at the growing line of doors that stretched out into the horizon.

'Never ceases to amaze me,' Safa said, beginning their walk to a door far off in the distance. 'They're hidden from plain sight, but they all lead somewhere. And they're all connected. Just a little bit of alchemy reveals them. A master alchemist can control where their door leads to.'

'That's sure something,' Daffodil whispered, mesmerised by the changing hues. As she looked at the doors manifesting, she realised there were subtle symbols pulsating at the top of each door. Faintly. Extremely faintly. 'I can't believe you managed to do this…'

'Oh, you're flattering me. It's just some alchemy, my dear.'

'Yes,' Seul said, rolling his eyes, 'if you keep complimenting her, she'll end up showing her party trick.'

Daffodil grinned. 'What party trick?'

'Oh no,' Seul said, groaning.

'Oh, I mean, if you *insist*,' Safa said excitedly, with nobody around her really insisting at all. 'Please throw something into the air.'

Seul looked around. There was just snow.

'Except snow,' Safa added.

Seul sighed and proceeded to get some kind of rock out of one of their bags. He lobbed it high into the air.

Safa threw something at the ground a few metres away from them as the rock reached its peak, and a plume of purple smoke erupted in the snowy wasteland. She then, without missing a beat and with pinpoint accuracy, threw a tiny empty vial at the rock and hit it square-on midair. The rocky projectile seemed to pause for a moment, give the briefest of quivers, and then came hurtling to the spot Safa had thrown her purple smoke attraction device.

'Wow,' Daffodil breathed, in awe as the rock came to a smooth rolling stop right at her feet.

Even Seul had to smile at the reaction.

'Those symbols,' Riyul said, pointing to the top of one of the doors nearby. 'What do they mean? I've seen them before on the train.'

'We're not too sure,' Safa conceded, preparing their bags for their walk. 'I think the Professor might know.'

'We need to decide how we are going to progress,' Riyul said. 'We do need to find our way out, especially if our thoughts can change.'

Daffodil nodded. 'The Professor probably has some answers for us, but if what we've been told is correct, we may need to get out sooner rather than later.'

'No, we completely understand, and we wouldn't expect any such thing! We want you to get home in the quickest manner,' Safa said. 'We also would take you to The City ourselves, properly, but as you can appreciate, with Marwa in the state she is in, we need to find an antidote as quickly as we can, and so, we need to get to The

Professor as fast as possible. I think we can go together for a large portion of the journey regardless, and if you want to, you can then take the door straight to The City, or join us and speak to The Professor and consider his thoughts to point you in the right direction. Regardless, to get to where we are going, we'll both have to go the same way anyway.'

'Seems like we've got a walk ahead of us then,' Riyul said, looking out at the blanket of white that stretched as far as the eye could see, framed by a tunnel of parallel opposing doors, each set around five metres apart, that also ran the length of the land.

Safa agreed, slinging the final bag over her shoulder as everyone had gotten prepared with their things. Then, she looked at Daffodil and Riyul inquisitively. 'By the way, have you two eaten?'

***

Daffodil didn't know how long they'd been walking for. All she knew was each time she looked back, the trail of footsteps grew ever longer and longer. It reminded her of a snake game she used to play as a kid, sitting in front of the fire, on her mum's phone.

I'm going to make my way back to you somehow, Mum.

They'd had a hearty meal of carrots and sweetcorn, which Marwa had somehow pulled out nonstop from a pouch within her jacket. It wasn't the tastiest, but she was not going to complain. The meal was simple, tasted fine, and was filling. Daffodil hadn't realised how hungry she had been; she supposed she had been so busy since her arrival that she'd forgotten to even think about food; Riyul said he hadn't even been hungry during his time in his carriage. He had just slept without having to eat previously, which was odd. She also had no idea how people kept pulling things out of their jackets or how any of this alchemy worked—it felt like every time one question was answered, another ten cropped up.

'So, how did you end up here?' Seul asked her, attempting to make conversation whilst bounding over a nonexistent ball of snow. Their journey so far had been a bunch of snow, snow, the odd snow-covered rock, and more snow. Seul had been the only thing keeping her sane with his random topics of conversation, though his Mum seemed to think he spoke too much (he had started by asking Daffodil questions about how different things worked where she was from—and he seemed particularly enthralled when she told him about stairs). His conversation was a refreshing change from the bleakness of her situation.

'Remember the doorway where you found us?' Daffodil said.

'Yeah.'

'There was a train through there.'

'Oh no, I know that,' Seul said matter-of-factly, as though her stepping from a train into an expanse of snow was the most normal thing in the world. 'I meant, how did you get onto the train?'

Daffodil started to speak, but then caught herself.

'I- I-'

She blinked.

Hmm, how did I get onto the train?

She … couldn't remember.

Daffodil frowned. Thoughts of having an argument with Mum and Dad drifted into her mind. She closed her eyes and tried to think back, hard.

Where are my memories?

The night preceding. Adam. The dream.

She opened her eyes. There were gaps.

130

'It's okay if you don't want to tell me,' Seul said. 'I can understand it'd be difficult leaving your family, or not being able to find your family.'

Daffodil swallowed, her mind elsewhere.

Why can I not remember clearly? I remember speaking to Adam. I went to sleep. Morning. Mum and Dad. I left the house for... for what?

Seul was still looking at her.

'Sorry, my mind is elsewhere,' Daffodil said, shaking her head; she treaded carefully, eyes fixed on the snowy ground.

'It's okay. Hey, I know! Shall I talk about me?' he said chirpily, a contagious smile plastered to his face.

'Sure,' Daffodil said with a chuckle.

'Okay. How old do you think I am?'

'How old do I think you are?'

'Yep.'

'I thought you don't have time in this world.'

'We don't—but answer the question!'

'What? How can I answer the question if...' She stared at him. 'I- I don't know! You look like you're eight.'

'Nope. Not technically. I might look eight. I might even be eight. But I am a hundred.'

Daffodil didn't know what to say. Seul continued on happily.

'I spoke to a scientist once. She estimated according to the outside world—your world—I'd be like a hundred of your years. But she said the way ageing works is that our bodies and minds move slower—or something like that, and your body never gets that old, really, even when you've lived for a super long time. She said the worst age is between one and two hundred of the outside years; that's when kids get 'moody' or something, and like to grow super fast.

They get growth spurts, I think she said, and shoot up really quickly. I didn't fully understand.'

Daffodil nearly walked into a door.

'Are you okay?' Safa asked from the front of the group. She and Marwa were walking together, leading the way; Riyul was almost alongside, just in step; the two 'children' (though was Seul really a child?) made up the rear of their odd ensemble.

'She's just shocked at how old Miss Daisy said I was,' Seul called out proudly.

'Miss Daisy says a lot of things, Seul. It doesn't mean they're all true,' Safa said, unimpressed.

'Yes, but they might be.'

Safa rolled her eyes. 'According to Miss Daisy, I'd be like a thousand years old.'

Riyul looked at her. 'A thousand?' he said, whistling. 'That'd mean you were alive during the Viking invasions of Britain in our world.'

Daffodil tilted her head, thinking back to her history lessons at school. 'But Riyul ... didn't they start in like 793?'

'Yes. And went on until 1066.'

Oh, that would explain it then... Still odd that he'd connect the Vikings to being about a thousand years before our twenty-first century.

'Yeah. Well, I'm not sure what any of that means, but anyway,' Seul continued enthusiastically. 'History lessons aside, I'm trying to work out what element I want to study when I grow up. Have you decided yours yet?'

'Sorry—what element?'

'Yes, like Marwa studies water.'

'I didn't really understand that earlier. What do you mean, she studies water?'

'Yeah, so she tries to do things with water and see how it is part of the world. She can attune water into fire, or earth, and find doors.'

'Ah, I don't really think we have that where I'm from. People end up becoming more … one kind of job, like doctors or lawyers or astronauts.'

'Huh,' Seul said, 'that sounds kind of boring.'

'Yeah, I guess it is, actually, but where we've come from knowledge has become pretty widespread; most people kind of just do one thing and try to become the best at that.'

'But don't they want to continue learning?' Seul cocked his head.

'Some do. Scientists, maybe.'

'And what are astronauts?'

'Now that,' Daffodil said, 'might take some explaining.'

She decided she liked Seul. He was a good kid. Not as bright perhaps as her Adam, but she liked him nonetheless. Even if he was a million years old.

She felt that twinge again deep in the pit of her stomach as her mind wandered to thoughts of her younger brother. How must he be right now, without her? He always told her that he needed her; that's why she enjoyed speaking to him so much. Nobody else seemed to speak to him at all compared to her. Adam would work a way out of this with that mind of his. He'd remember all the clues he picked up, and put the pieces together, and not forget a thing.

Daffodil sighed.

She missed him.

'Okay folks,' Safa announced, 'I think it's time to stop for the night.'

Daffodil frowned. It was still the same mid-day sun they'd experienced since arriving in this land, so she was unsure of how it was night time. There also clearly wasn't anywhere to sleep, unless they just stopped out in the barren snow next to a door. But if she'd learnt anything thus far, it was that the best thing was to just wait and see what happened.

Safa opened a door that had a black cross left on the snow outside it, and stepped through.

'I'd kept a mark outside this door for future reference, just to see if it'd stay. It looks like it hasn't changed,' she said as they squeezed through the doorway.

Once through, Daffodil found they were in a simple white room with no obvious form of lighting, yet it was brilliantly lit. On the three walls around them were five doors. Directly in front of them, the wall had one solid white door. On their right were two others, and on their left, two more. The door they'd come through was behind them, still open.

A gust of the wintry breeze snapped at them from beyond the doorway. It was nice to be out of that.

'So—pick a room everyone!' Safa said, gesturing towards the various white doors.

When nobody seemed to move, Marwa smiled, realising the newcomers' hesitation, and walked over to a door, opening it to show Daffodil and Riyul what was inside.

The room it led to was smaller than their current, equally white, and adorned with a simple cloth bed. The bed lay on the white ground, with a pillow made out of some sacking and straw.

'So, all the rooms are the same. Each is for one person. We'll get some shut-eye and then meet up after some rest, I think. I'll knock on everyone's door when it's best to carry on moving, how does that sound?'

Everyone nodded in agreement.

'Okay, wonderful. Let's get some sleep. We'll be right outside, connected through these doors.'

'Thank you,' Daffodil said, smiling. She took a step in and looked out at the four of them waving at her through the doorway.

'You know,' Daffodil said, 'I know we are in a rush and all, but I feel like it'd be useful meeting your old teacher.'

'Yes, that'd be good—I'd like that too,' said Safa, with a solid nod from Riyul.

'Well, see you very very soon,' Safa said, with mingled goodbyes from Seul and Riyul. Marwa nodded warmly. Daffodil waved them off, and before she knew it, the door closed on her—and she was alone.

Chapter 19

Dreams

Daffodil couldn't sleep. Though this was really the first time since she had arrived here that she was even getting the chance to rest.

Her mind was swimming.

How did this room work? Where was the white light coming from without any light bulbs, or sun? How was there a bed here? Why did she feel hunger but Riyul didn't? Was everything in this place due to alchemy, and if so, how did it work?

So many unnerving questions. But hidden under them all, buried deep within her thoughts, was something else. Something that didn't grow so long as she didn't pay attention to it—or she didn't let it grow. Something bigger, greater, more sinister than all else.

She knew what it was. It hadn't gone since she'd arrived. A deep confusion, a sense that twisted her core.

What was it her parents said before she left the house?

No matter how much she tried to wrap her head around it, no matter how much she racked her brain and squeezed her eyes and tossed and turned in the bed, thinking back, the memory had gone.

White space. Nothing. Whatsoever.

The memory had slipped away as cleanly as a cloth into the wind.

And yet, there was more. Despite everything, despite the fear and the gaps, no matter what had happened between her and her parents, there was something else, always with her, even deeper than the troubling memory loss. Another feeling, along with the fear and the confusion and the questions: Daffodil missed her family. She missed them oh so much.

She rubbed her eyes and turned to her side. Knowing she needed to sleep made it all the harder; she sure felt tired, yet her mind was everywhere, and it did not want to obey.

She turned again.

As her thoughts trundled on and on, Daffodil eventually started to drift into sleep, eyelids steadily drooping, fluttering open, then drooping again.

She could sense the land around her. This Land of Snow. In the darkness of her closed eyelids, she could envisage herself. This dot on a barren icy, snowy wasteland. Trudging and trailing footsteps. And beneath that... a sort of...

Daffodil squeezed her eyes harder shut, and frowned.

A grid?

She could see a grid pulsating in her mind's eye, contrasting faintly against the crisp whiteness of her mental image.

She must be dreaming now...

In and out she went, seeing herself walking through the snow, seeing Riyul and Seul talking and a train and doors and snow...

***

Images. Flashing images.
Those woods.
The blinding light.
Adam.

***

Daffodil thrashed about. She was screaming. She breathed heavily as she looked around her, eyes wide.

Where was Adam? Where were those woods?

Walls. White walls.

Where was the glow, the cabin, the sounds?

Sweat covered every inch of her body. She raised her hands, looking at them, splaying them, turning them, grabbing her bed.

She was in bed.

A sigh of relief.

Was she ... not at home?

Looking around, it all came flooding back to her. She wasn't at home—she was lost in this place from the train.

Daffodil lied down once more.

Those dreams that always ended in screaming had come back.

As Daffodil began to control her breathing, she listened to the echoes of her very screams still ringing in her ears, but then she frowned.

The screams were still going on. They were real.

And they were coming from outside her room.

She ripped the blanket off and ran to the door, ready to tear it open to find who was screaming and why.

Hand on doorknob. Ready to pull it. But... Daffodil stopped.

Do I need to be careful with opening this?

She thought back to every door she'd opened up prior. The floods. The winds. The suction which took Haradan. Should she risk opening this door?

Daffodil looked around her barren bedroom as shouts and cries continued to pierce through the closed door. What choice did she have? Someone was screaming. She needed to help: the screams could belong to Safa, or... *wait, was that Seul?*

Daffodil had to move.

Without a moment more to think, she ripped the door open and braced herself for whatever might be outside.

It was Marwa, hand outstretched, as though she were about to open Daffodil's door.

She quickly gestured for her to follow towards the sounds of screaming. She pulled her by the arm, running towards the opposite open door.

'What's happening?' Daffodil said as they ran.

Marwa simply shook her head.

No time to explain.

The screaming could be heard from beyond the open door they were about to enter. Daffodil had no idea who was sleeping in this one, but from the sounds of it, it might have been Seul.

All the doors around were open, including the one they had entered through, so Riyul and Safa must have already gone in.

Marwa entered first, followed by Daffodil.

The room was identical to her own. But with one key difference. Seul was sitting up in his bed, with Riyul and Safa standing over him. He was shrieking, looking off into the distance; sweat covered his entire body, and his eyes appeared a bloodshot red.

'Seul, what happened?! What did you see?' Safa urged, shaking his leg.

He continued to scream, looking wide-eyed at the doorway they'd just entered through.

As soon as he saw Daffodil, he stopped. His eyes somehow grew wider.

'You,' he said, raising a shaking finger and pointing at her. 'The whirlwind. It's coming.'

Riyul and Safa spun around to look at her.

'Oh no,' Riyul whispered.

'Whirlwind?' Safa said. 'What whirlwind?'

'On- on the train,' Daffodil stumbled, bewildered at how Seul knew. 'When I was with Haradan, we would try different doors to escape, and sometimes we would come across a doorway with a horrible wind in it. We closed the door fast enough. But once with Riyul, I don't know if it's connected, we opened a door, and there was like a black portal behind it, and this powerful vacuum that took Haradan straight out. Just sucked him out of the room.'

'I see,' Safa said calculatedly, looking around the room. She seemed to make a decision. 'Okay. Everyone grab your things. Don't forget your alc sets, Marwa. Seul, come on, we need to go.'

Seul nodded and dutifully got up, coming back to his senses.

'The wind you spoke about is dangerous,' Safa explained, bundling Seul's things from the corner of the room. 'But I believe it does exist. I've not heard of it happening before, but it can be controlled. Sent even. In theory, it's possible.

She began heading towards the door, Seul and Marwa in tow.

'What do you mean 'sent'?' Daffodil asked, rooted to the spot near Seul's bed.

Safa turned at the open doorway.

'Daffodil, we really need to go.'

'What do you mean by 'sent'?' Daffodil asked, refusing to move. 'Did I cause this? Is someone sending this for me?'

Marwa placed her hand on her shoulder tenderly.

'Daffodil, please forget I said that,' Safa urged. 'That is so unlikely, it's basically not possible. More likely, it is just a runaway wind created by someone new to alchemy that is going around—or who knows? Maybe even the conductor himself! But as I can now actually hear it, we need to get out of here. Now.'

She did not wait, making a point of exiting. Seul smiled thinly and went out with her. Riyul nodded to Daffodil somberly.

'We need to go,' he said, and left, hoping she would follow.

Only Marwa lingered behind, hand on her shoulder. She smiled her silent, understanding smile. Daffodil looked at her.

'Okay, let's go,' she said.

As they joined the others in the corridor area, Daffodil found the wind had become louder, like she very well remembered. It was approaching fast.

'This way!' Safa said, struggling to raise her voice over the whooshing cacophony. She headed back to the door they'd entered from and took a peek out of the doorway.

Where was the whirlwind coming from?

'Come!' Safa screamed, going out, followed tentatively by Seul and then Riyul. Daffodil was just about to enter next when the doorway began to shimmer a deep black violet, with specks of flashing colour distorting her view through.

She looked back to see what Marwa thought they should do, and then realised where the whirlwind noises were coming from.

Behind them.

'Marwa! The room!' Daffodil exclaimed, running back to close the door of Seul's room. But suddenly, there was an almighty pop, and she could see the all too familiar vortex spinning spirals of destruction starting to eradicate what little furniture there was.

The wind was alive, and it was now truly here. Daffodil could feel the magnetic tug on her clothes as it neared ever closer.

Marwa grabbed Daffodil's hand and pulled her to the adjacent door—a door Daffodil hadn't been through before, but presumed must lead to Marwa's room. The whirlwind was screeching and ripping at her hair, her clothes, her hearing.

The rushing of wind became all-consuming as Marwa jimmied the doorknob violently. Daffodil didn't dare look back. She didn't have the time to look back. The whole world around her became a whirling catastrophe of sound and blur. Marwa tried to open the door, but it refused to.

Daffodil closed her eyes and felt sensations she'd never felt before pounding at her insides. Not just fear and worry but also something else. A sensation of place, like her sense of balance going awry. Like when you know someone is watching.

Daffodil turned to watch the whirlwind coming closer. There was something about it…

She closed her eyes. Blackness. Sounds of sucking and escaping wind pressure. But in that darkness, she sensed something else. The wind was familiar. She'd felt this before.

How could they get out?

What had Safa said?

A master alchemist can control where their door leads to.

Somewhere away from here. Away from the wind and whatever was associated with it.

Opening her eyes, no time to explain, Daffodil grabbed Marwa with one hand and the doorknob with the other. With one turn, she opened the door and stumbled in as fast as she could. Marwa half-leapt through to escape the tugging vortex and slammed the door shut behind.

Brightness. Yellow.

A soft landing, collapsing on golden sand.

Tall, swaying palm trees lush with vegetation. A crystal blue ocean that stretched as far as the eye could see. Gulls caulking in the distance, and the soft spray of the refreshing ocean mist against her skin.

And, pivotally, a door—the door they had just entered through—that was now ever so slowly vanishing, and then silently ceased to exist.

At this point, she wasn't even astonished anymore. She brushed herself off with what little dignity she had left after collapsing through a doorway, and surveyed the area. She turned to Marwa.

'I think … I think we're on an island.'

Chapter 20

Lookout

Hundreds of miles away, the man with the distorted body had been watching.

From his tower, he kept a lookout on the group. There had been the usual, but also some that he had not expected. Confounding variables. But alas, he had to follow the plan.

He sighed, taking a seat in front of his hologenic scrying pool. The tower was dark grey stone and mostly barren. He didn't need much in terms of decoration; his grey desk and inventions were all he cared about. And he was proud of one particular invention: his scrying pool. A piece of his own creation, allowing him to keep an eye on any and all experiments throughout the lands. Any progress could be seen right from his tower.

People thought scrying pools were only mythical whispers in story books—that it wasn't possible to see across lands in this manner, but Skutlish knew anything was possible if you worked hard enough. Didn't people once think humans would never reach the skies? Didn't people once think the moon was a place humans would never reach? Science had proven otherwise.

So he had done his due diligence, and through painstaking research and experiment after experiment, he had managed to alchemise a scrying pool. It had taken many years, but he had done it. His entire tower was littered with such inventions and creations—a testament to the power of alchemy, perseverance, and beautiful science.

Wait. Did that just happen? He watched the group through the shimmering purple pool, raised in the centre of his study on a pedestal.

The man with the distorted face didn't like anomalies. They ruined experiments. How could one run a fair test, a replicable test, when they were additions or atypicalities? But, he also conceded that this was all part of good science. Working out the kinks. He had to have patience—real science was art, after all, and patience was the canvas.

Something had happened. Something he had not completely expected. He frowned, tracking the progress of the group of five as they exited the young boy's room. Any minute now, the whirlwind was meant to appear and carefully split the group.

At least that was what he had presumed.

The whirlwind looked like it had come now. But … for some reason, the five were not together. Riyul and one of the sisters had left the white corridor, along with the boy. But Daffodil and the other twin were still lingering behind.

Yep, there it was. He clicked his fingers.

The whirlwind was in their instance.

Three of them had gotten out. Two of them, including Daffodil, were going another way. To … another door? Marwa seemed to be tampering with it. Oh, that was smart, he had to say.

She opened it.

The whirlwind was metres away.

Marwa collapsed in, followed by Daffodil.

And before Skutlish knew it, they'd gone, just as the whirlwind made its appearance and ripped apart the room.

He smiled. Oh, Marwa.

So many variables. But that was okay. Patience. What was good science except trial and error?

He walked back over to his desk and considered their work. He scoured the papers and promptly took in all the different notes, previous experimental reports and historical records. So much data. Yet each experiment, something a little different. Each time a little closer to the goal.

As long as he kept watching and observing and studying, he would make this work. That was fine. Patience.

Skutlish sat down, back to his drawing board.

'Okay,' he whispered to himself, imagining his brother had received news already of what had transpired. 'Now it gets interesting.'

Chapter 21

The Island

Who would have thought doors would be this important? Daffodil thought to herself, pacing up and down along a mostly barren beach, the soft wash of the tide echoing in her ears and lapping against her feet. Like most things in life, it was hard to appreciate doors until they were gone. And now, Daffodil surmised, was one of those times. Oh, how she could do with a door right now.

Yet as Marwa and Daffodil searched along the coast, Daffodil trying to manifest them as Haradan had taught her, and Marwa using her own much more advanced knowledge, skills and tricks, they found the oddest thing—nothing. No doors. No matter how hard they searched. Nothing near the sea. Nothing on the rocky crags. Nothing inland in or around the thick vegetation or colourful flora and fauna that littered the picturesque island. Nowhere.

Marwa seemed especially baffled. She had tried listening and searching (just like Haradan had, Daffodil noted), and she had tried some drops from one of her vials in a few different places, as Safa had, but nothing worked.

As they ascended the set of boulders for the hundredth time, she finally threw her arms up and shook her head.

Daffodil understood her pain. What kind of place was this? It was unlike anything she'd seen so far. Alas, it was beautiful. The pair of them stood atop their boulders and gazed out at the island. Rising sets of hills peaked in the distance, topped with lush greenery. Golden, silken sand bordered the cool waters around them; the chirping of birds orchestrated a synchronised melody, complementing the entire scene. It sure was beautiful. But that didn't help them get out.

'I think we're going to have to figure out a way of eating and sleeping here, at least for now,' Daffodil said tentatively.

Marwa nodded. She must have been thinking the same; without the ability to speak, she had resorted to head movements and hand-gestures for the majority of their communication. She pointed at Daffodil and then towards her stomach, rubbing it.

Daffodil laughed.

'Yes, I'm hungry. Are you?'

Marwa nodded, smiling.

'Okay, let's go look for some food.'

***

After searching through the forestry with their stomachs leading them this time, they found a whole world they'd never seen before.

There stood, somehow, a banana tree.

'How does this all work?' Daffodil said, staring up at the abundance of green bananas overhead. 'I just don't get it. Bananas grow here…'

Marwa frowned, considering the sun above, which had not moved an inch, and the luscious fruit and vegetables, plants and flowers that surrounded them. She was a scientist at heart, so Daffodil could see her computing this in her head, trying to work it out. Eventually, she shrugged, slightly defeated.

'It's okay—we just don't have enough data,' Daffodil said, smiling.

Marwa laughed her silent laugh, except as she made the motions, Daffodil could have sworn she heard the faintest of sounds emanate.

No. Impossible. You're hearing things, Daffodil.

'Okay, let's get some of these bananas.'

Daffodil climbed the tree without any prompting, as ready and eager as she had been when out with her father in their woodland days.

'You know, I used to climb trees like this with my dad last year. And the year before. And … the year before.'

The bananas began falling, and Marwa deftly caught them with surprisingly quick reflexes.

'We would have the best times,' Daffodil said, shaking the branches in a way that only the ripest bunches would fall. 'My younger brother, Adam, was always with us. We'd hike through the forests, always on a ridiculously steep incline for some reason. Dad seems to love hiking up difficult trails. Why never the easy ones? And Adam would struggle to keep up, haha. I wish we would still go on those trips. They've stopped in recent times.' Daffodil smiled sadly as she shook the branch.

Marwa listened without missing a beat, catching every word—and banana—in the process.

And then something unexpected happened.

Marwa coughed.

Daffodil looked down at her, unsure if she had heard her correctly.

Up until then, not a sound had managed to come from her throat. But there it was. Clear as day. A cough.

Even Marwa looked shocked.

'Marwa?' Daffodil asked, flabbergasted, still up a tree.

'Ieugh…' Marwa managed to croak out. She dropped her bananas as she tried to talk, realising she could finally, somehow, make sounds again.

'The island…' she steadily enunciated, looking around. 'It's … it's given me back my voice.'

Chapter 22

The Librarian

The Librarian hadn't expected a different day. Most days were the same: wake up, research, tea, coffees, look up at the sky and wonder how, research, wake up, sleep, tea, coffee, research and look up at the sky. Not always in that order.

So when three individuals appeared at his door, he didn't know what to expect at all.

Knock, knock, knock.

The Librarian stopped. His teacup was halfway to his mouth when he realised the door had made a sound. He also realised that his tea seemed to have no sugar, though he normally added seven tablespoons. He spat it out—or tried to—but then realised nothing was coming out of his mouth. He looked down at his cup. Ah—no wonder. There was no tea in the cup! He really did have to remember to add tea next time. And sugar!

Knock-knock-knock. Quicker this time.

Ah drat. That darn door again.

When was the last time the door had made that sound? It must have been a long time ago. Hmm, *time. Time.* TIME!

KNOCK KNOCK KNOCK.

'Will you keep your pants on!' The Librarian exclaimed, making his way to the door. Before he opened it, however, he noticed something was wrong. His bottom half was cold; he looked down and realised he had no pants on. He must have left them with the sugar. 'Be right back!' he shouted at the door.

***

When Safa, Riyul and Seul knocked on the professor's door, they did not know who or what they would find.

After losing track of Marwa and Daffodil, Safa had decided that the only way they'd be able to find them was to double down on their efforts of finding her old professor. Doors could lead anywhere, and there was no way of honing in on Marwa—not that she knew of. However, if there was one person who may have some semblance of a clue of how to find them, it would be her old professor. He always had the answer when she was young, and if they really wanted to find them, he would be able to help.

But would he still be around?

Eventually, it had been Riyul who had found him.

He had closed his eyes and apparently followed a technique Haradan had taught him to sense doors. Safa couldn't understand it personally. But through Riyul's unexpected skill, they'd taken just the right doors, trekked just the right way through the snowy nothingness and located a cabin cresting over a hill—the same log cabin the professor had run his schooling sessions from back when Safa and Marwa were children.

Just as Safa was about to knock again, the door flew open.

In front of them stood a tall, sinewy man with wild black curly hair. As he stood, gently rocking in front of them, his long khaki-coloured jacket fluttered in the wintry wind, and the stacks of books and inventions and furniture behind him, covering every inch of interior space, looked like they would topple over at any moment.

He looked at the three of them.

'Safa?' he croaked.

Safa breathed out a sigh of relief. It was him. And he did remember her.

'Yes,' she said, breaking into a large smile. 'Yes, professor, it's me!'

'Oh, I'm not a professor anymore. I'm a librarian now!' he said, gesturing to the library behind him.

Books covered every inch of space, lined the walls and rose from the ground like paper stalactites. 'Please, come in!'

'Thank you, professor,' Safa said as she entered with Riyul and Seul, both nodding their greetings and thanks.

'I'm not a professor! I'm a librarian now!' he repeated happily, somehow in exactly the same pitch and tone. 'Please, take a seat!' he exclaimed, pointing at a chair that looked suspiciously like it was made out of stacks of books.

'What's the difference?' asked Seul, walking over to one of the many vast shelves.

'The difference? Who said there's a difference? It's the medium, my boy. Surely, you aren't Safa's son?'

Seul nodded, slightly confused about how there was no difference.

'Amazing. Look, being a professor and a librarian is really the same thing. It's about knowledge. Mental or physical. Professors are also libraries of information: libraries of the mind. And libraries of the mind are temporal. But libraries of the page? Libraries of the page are permanent. I no longer teach, but I like to still study and learn,' he said, nodding to his swathes of books.

'You seem to be very proud of your books,' Riyul said.

The professor stopped in his tracks and squinted at him.

'Yes,' he positively yapped. 'What else do you want to know?'

'W.. want to know? I didn't ask a question. I was just making a statement.'

'Oh. That's true! Please, call me The Librarian,' The Librarian said, beaming all of a sudden.

Riyul and Safa looked at each other. She had told him that her old teacher was a little quirky.

'Profess— sorry, Librarian, are you okay?' Safa asked, frowning slightly.

He gazed off, facing the rear wall. He seemed to have forgotten they were in the room.

'In the world out there,' he said randomly, still facing the wall, 'there was a man.'

'The world out there?' Seul asked behind him, shocked that The Librarian had mentioned such a taboo thing.

'Do not interrupt,' The Librarian said, pressing his forefinger to Seul's lips to silence him. Riyul and Safa tried to suppress their smirks at the sight of Seul's lips being squashed by the finger of a man who was not even looking at him.

He continued in a soft voice, still turned to the wall, 'I can tell you all know of the outside world. Anywhom, there was a young man in this outside world who lived on Barrows Road. I do not know if he still lives there. Or if the road still exists. Or if roads are roads. Or,' he said, raising his finger into the air, 'if roads are things.'

Seul shielded his mouth and slowly backed away as The Librarian lowered his finger.

'Anyway, he was the simplest, humblest man you could ever ask for; he never hurt a soul.

'One day—nay, one night—nay! One... *night*,' he said, raising his finger again while Seul stepped backwards and collapsed behind a pile of books. 'Thieves broke into his house. They searched high and low for valuables to steal. But they could not find anything. In their vexation, they decided to do the worst thing possible to a man of knowledge, an action that was borne out of nought but spite. Can you guess what that thing was?'

The three of them did not know if they were to respond, nor who he was addressing exactly. The Librarian was still facing the wall. Seul was trying to get up.

'Well?' he said, exasperated, finally turning to them as Seul tripped over again. He gave up and just sat there, cross-legged, listening to the story.

'Did they hurt him?' Safa asked.

The Librarian whispered, almost inaudibly, 'Worse. They burnt his books. All his knowledge. All his notes. His life's accumulation. Gone. In one spiteful instant. One fire. All. Gone.' The Librarian collapsed onto the ground cross-legged, a mirror image of Seul.

Riyul blinked.

'Sorry,' Seul said, getting up before The Librarian could silence him again. 'I don't see how this story makes sense. You used to be a professor.'

'Teacher!' The Librarian corrected, shaking his head.

'But ... you said professor earlier—not teacher.'

'Ah, yes, true, professor. Look, why don't you just call me Trill?'

'Err, okay. Is Trill your name, then?'

'No. Why would it be my name? I just like the sound.' He raised his chin and bulged his eyes dramatically.

'Okay, so, Trill-'

'That's not my name,' The Librarian interrupted.

'Okay, then, professor-'

'Teacher!'

Seul stared at him.

'As a professor,' Seul said again, taking a deep breath. 'As a professor, you had knowledge in your mind, not in books.'

'That is correct,' he replied, eyes bulging wider than anything Safa had ever seen before. They looked like they were about to pop.

'So then... Why-'

'Hey, can you stop that?' The Librarian exclaimed, jumping to his feet with one fluid leap. 'That's not how this story goes! Do you want me to help you find your lost companion or not?'

The three of them started.

'We... didn't mention losing anyone...' Safa said.

'Of course you didn't!' The Librarian said. 'But it's here... In the books.'

'It's written in the books or you worked it out from your books?' Riyul asked.

The Librarian froze; his left eye began to twitch. His head snapped to the door.

'You have to be careful,' he said conspiratorially, not taking his eyes off the front door. 'You never know who can wipe you.'

Riyul and Safa looked at each other again.

'I'm sorry—wipe you?' said Safa.

'Do you think you're alone in Aethril, Safa?' The Librarian asked.

'I... What?'

'Alone. World. Thoughts!'

'I ... I'm not sure what you mean.'

'Uthy!' he exclaimed.

Riyul shook his head. This man had lost his mind.

'Professor, please,' Safa said, not caring about titles any longer. 'I don't know what's happened or even, gosh, how long it's been since you've been around people, but you remember Marwa, right? My sister? We came because she's lost, and we've tried everything; the only people left that may be able to help was yourself and possibly Sherlotte, but she can only delay the icing, not stop it—'

'I know this,' The Librarian said, waving her away, still watching the door. 'And I'm guessing there's another member of the party now, and there was an attack and you got lost and yada yada yada. Well, guess what, people? Loss is part and parcel of this world.'

'What's a parcel?' said Seul.

'Uthy!'

'Okay,' Riyul said. 'Listen, professor, or librarian, or teacher— or whatever you consider yourself to be. You are obviously extremely intelligent, but it seems you have gone at least a little bit mad.'

Seul gasped involuntarily. Everyone looked at him.

The Librarian turned to Riyul, finally peeling his eyes off the front door.

'How do I know you're not here to wipe me?' The Librarian asked.

'Because I do not know what on earth-'

'What on *Aethril*,' The Librarian corrected.

'What on EARTH you are talking about,' Riyul repeated pointedly. 'But you know what I do know? I know a few things about you. A few golden nuggets of goodness that Safa told us.'

'Did she tell you I can sniff my own nostrils?'

'Did she... What? No—'

'Did she tell you I once fell up the stairs?'

Riyul blinked. 'How do you f—'

'Then,' The Librarian interrupted, 'she has not told you anything useful. You see, these things are impossibilities. I love impossibilities. In fact, I'd go as far as to say I am an impossibility. But not because I care about me, but because once you do an impossible, you have changed your world. I am doing really important work here with my learning, I'm sorry,' he said, waving his eyebrows up and down at an unnatural speed.

Riyul hesitated, unsure of what to say.

'You don't learn everything by being inside,' Seul said, frowning. He was looking down at the ground.

The Librarian looked at him.

'I think the most important things you learn, the things we learn about people, we only learn through going out. Finding people, talking to them and being with them. When people teach you things you didn't know, or show you something even about yourself you never realised, that's when you're doing something new and useful, right?'

'I mean, that's … not untrue,' The Librarian said. 'You're a smart kid.'

'Thanks, but I'm like a hundred years old to the outside world.'

The Librarian raised an eyebrow.

'What?' Seul asked, glancing sideways. 'Miss Sophie said so.'

The Librarian snorted. 'I'm sorry to say, you're probably closer to ten than one hundred. Miss Sophie doesn't understand how time outside fully works. I should know. I've tried to teach her since she was just a child—younger than you, in fact.'

'What I told him was about your lessons. I told him how much you care,' Safa said, sensing an opportunity. 'I told Riyul and Seul how much you wanted to do for those who came to you.'

To this, The Librarian did not respond. His quick wit seemed to have deserted him.

'Yes,' Riyul said. 'She told me how much you did for your community when she was a girl. Your people. Why you started learning and teaching.'

'And who in your community,' Seul chirped in, 'is in more urgent need right now than Daffodil and Marwa? If you remember my mum, you'll remember Marwa. As for Daffodil—she says she's from the outside, and she's wanting to get back there.'

'The best way to better your community at this moment,' Safa said, 'is to help us find them.'

The Librarian stared at them without speaking.

Eventually, he turned slowly around his house, taking in the books, the sparse furniture—everything.

'All my books are here,' he said, more serious than he had been since they'd met him.

'And they'll be right here when we come back,' Safa said, smiling softly. 'They won't go anywhere.'

If he heard this, he did not respond. When nobody else said anything, he finally began to speak.

'You know, I built this place with my own two hands,' he said in a low voice. 'Every wall, log by log. Every book I collected, from far and wide, with my own hands. I've lost books too. Destroyed priceless knowledge, with my own hands.' He paused, looking down at his hands as though he were seeing them for the first time. 'But you're right... What is the point of doing all this if I'm not helping people?

'You know, people have come and visited me through the years,' he said. 'They've come, I've acted mad and wacky and shown them amazing things and impressed them, and that was it; they got what they were looking for, and they left and went on with their lives. Yes, they've asked for things, often communal, but I've always said no. And that's what it took. But you persisted. And that's maybe all I needed. Thank you. We all need a push sometimes.'

He walked over to a crowded table and pocketed a small black leather notebook. 'I'll help you. Okay, first thing, I think you're being watched,' The Librarian said to no one in particular. 'In fact, I think we all are.' He walked over to some nondescript cupboards and began collecting bits and bobs into a bag.

Everybody's eyes went wide.

'How do you know this?' Safa asked quietly.

'Oh, there's no need to whisper,' The Librarian said, pacing up the room. 'I'm losing my mind and my memory and a third thing with 'm' to create alliteration, but I am not losing my thinking!'

Seul frowned.

'No, I don't think anyone can hear us,' he continued. 'When you spend enough time on your own, you get into a state of depth and see things you never noticed before. There are shimmers in the sky that indicate—to me, at least—something has changed. Do you remember the boy with the oculus orbs, Safa?'

'Yes,' she replied after some thinking. Seul looked confused.

'Ah, you may not know this,' The Librarian said to Seul. 'Before I took your mum on as a student, I had others. In particular, there was a boy who would always ask me about observance and how to visualise distances. The oculusory orb is the best way of doing this. Some orbs can capture their environment in a sort of recording also. Now, whatever is following you also creates a similar sort of effect, albeit on a much, much smaller scale. Anyway, my point is, if my theory is correct, someone somewhere has worked out a way of keeping an eye on you. When you arrived at my door, above you quite far off in the distance, there was the smallest of shimmers in the sky.'

'You noticed that just from opening the door?'

'Mhm. I also noticed there was a lot of white snow outside.'

'So what do we do?' asked Riyul.

'Nothing yet. We carry on doing what we were going to do. Nobody knows I've worked it out, so let's not give it away. More importantly, what should you take on your journey? Would you like my book on eggs?'

'Why would you need to bring your book about eggs?' Seul asked.

'We might get hungry during the journey. What was your name again? Sylvia? Syntax? Saliva?'

'It's Seul.'

'Okay, Saliva, think about all the great adventures you've heard about-'

'My name's not Saliva,' said Seul quickly before the name could stick.

'Ah yes, sorry—I meant Seul. Anywhom, as I was saying. Everyone looks forward to an adventure until they realise they hadn't thought about food. In such adventures, everybody is all happy and jolly sure, but where is the sustenance? That's my question. That's why we need to be ready.'

'With a book on eggs?' Seul asked.

'With a book on eggs!' The Librarian said. 'Well done, Saliva.'

Seul smiled hesitantly, then frowned, reconsidering the compliment.

'So what do you suggest we do?'

'Well, I think you'll need to find Marwa first before you'll find this other girl, Daffodil. I remember Marwa. She was bright,' The Librarian said.

'Wait, will you not be coming with us?' Safa asked.

'No, my dear. I've realised that's what they're expecting. You're being watched, remember? The moment you walk back out of this house, they're expecting me to come with you. Also, my thoughts are, if you want to fix Marwa, if you want to get out of here. You know who to look for.'

Safa paced up and down the room. 'Gerrihend…' she muttered.

'Indubitably.' The Librarian agreed.

'Notra?' asked Riyul. 'How is Notra Gerrihend connected to this?'

Safa looked at him. 'Marwa used to work for him, in his lab… Our whole family did. But eventually… Well, let's just say we became disillusioned with his antics. There was a rumour going around that he was tampering with the memory of the people.'

'Oh my…'

'Yep.'

They all stood silently for a moment.

'But I suppose you kept tabs on the palace?' The Librarian asked Safa.

She smirked. 'You still know me very well.'

'You didn't!' Seul exclaimed.

'I did,' she said triumphantly to her son.

'What's this?' Riyul asked.

'Mum alchemised a route to the palace!' Seul shouted in awe.

'Yes,' The Librarian said chuckling, 'that sounds like Safa. As soon as she learnt how to alchemise doors, she'd keep a route to everywhere she could until she was caught.'

'So we'll start off at the palace,' Safa said, 'and we'll look for Gerrihend.'

'And you want to … speak to him about Marwa?' Riyul asked.

'There's no other way. Weird things are happening in this land, Riyul. And mark my words, Notra Gerrihend is behind it. Like I said, we used to work for him. He'll hopefully at least listen to us. The problem is accessing him is extremely difficult. Most people can't get into the castle.'

'I would have to concur,' said The Librarian, thumbing a particular corner of his shelves, where the books appeared most aged. 'You'll need to get into his palace without detection. Thankfully, I can help with that, if you still remember your connection traits.'

'I do,' said Safa.

'So to find Marwa,' Riyul said, 'we are going to infiltrate Notra Gerrihend's palace quarters? Am I the only one who thinks this sounds like a bad idea?'

'I think it's a great idea!' exclaimed Seul.

'You can't come,' said Safa sternly.

'Aw.'

'Don't worry, we can stay together and ensure the doorway portals are kept active during the infiltration. Also, the other girl?' asked The Librarian

'Daffodil. Her name is Daffodil. If we can get to Marwa, they'll be together,' Riyul said.

'She's from the outside world,' Seul said.

'That is amazing,' The Librarian said slowly, picking out a volume. 'These books are filled with excerpts from people who have come from the outside world, all from different years. It would be spectacular to meet this Daffodil and learn from her. What about you?' he said, eyeing Riyul, pointing at him with his heavy tome.

'I'm from the outside world too, yes.'

'I know that,' The Librarian said, waving a hand. 'I can see it in you. I mean from when?'

'From when?'

'Yes. From when? By my estimation, the world outside will be somewhere, roughly, in the twenty-first century. What year was it in the world when you came here?'

'I don't know how much time has passed since I arrived,' Riyul said. 'But the last I remember, it was 1930.'

Chapter 23

Alchemy

'My throat is hurting again,' Marwa croaked.

Daffodil and Marwa had collected a dozen or so bananas and were now walking back to their makeshift camp mid-beach. They had discovered that Marwa could in fact speak again; something had happened that had started to reverse her icing, but she wasn't able to do this for long before the pain set in.

So they conversed sporadically, Daffodil just learning a few tidbits about Marwa's life, but otherwise doing most of the talking and questioning.

It felt like days had passed since the incident with the whirlwind separating them; at the same time it felt like just hours had passed. Daffodil couldn't decide which one felt more probable. How could it both feel like days had gone by, and just hours had gone by? Clearly, the passage of time was now completely warped.

Daffodil didn't talk much throughout their walk back. For once, there was no urgency to rush the conversation. Things were interesting with Marwa. When someone had no choice but to be silent most of the time, they became the best listener ever. And when someone was the best listener ever, there seemed less of a need to talk relentlessly, articulating every point that comes to mind. You just felt... at ease.

'Marwa,' Daffodil said, poking at the sand with her toes near their makeshift camp, 'how does this place work? I mean, there is no clear change in time. None of this should be real. But... is it not real?' She picked up a few grains of sand and rubbed them between her fingers, holding them up to the gleaming sun. She could not spot a single flaw. 'I've been to beaches in the real world. This is identical.' Daffodil sighed. 'I don't get it.'

Marwa looked at her passively, and then gestured towards her vials. 'Alchemy,' she said, conserving her words.

'Hmm, I guess you're right,' Daffodil said, thinking. 'Alchemy can do a lot. I suppose alchemy can even change what is real and not. But gosh, Marwa, this is all just so crazy. A day ago—was it even a day ago? I don't even know. A day ago—maybe two, maybe more— I was trying to get on a simple train... And now here I am. On a beach. After walking through a land full of snow. Like ... how? How did this all just happen?' She gestured wildly around.

Marwa cocked her head, frowned and made a hand gesture which involved twisting her wrist, palm facing up—as though she was asking her own question.

Daffodil paused, trying to work out what she meant.

'Ooh. Why was I getting on a train in the first place?' Daffodil asked.

Marwa nodded.

Daffodil did not respond straight away, trying to think of the right answer.

Marwa waited.

With no means of speaking, she did not eventually get bored and move the conversation. She knew Daffodil would respond. And, for once, Daffodil felt the grinding sense of needing to commit, to fully explain and to go through her train of thought.

'I got on because... Well...'

Her mind did not seem to want to comply. Every time she attempted to recall the reason for her journey, there was a blockade. A sort of fuzzy brain-fog.

'I remember being on a bus.'

If Marwa was confused, she barely showed it; she continued to smile politely, with hardly a vague frown indicating any lack of transport knowledge.

'Then... I went and... walked through town.' Daffodil kept stopping and starting.

Marwa waited patiently, interested. She probably realised if they could work out how Daffodil had arrived on the train, they could solve a lot of problems—and perhaps answer a lot of questions.

'I remember a man,' Daffodil said, squinting out to the horizon, visualising him. Remembering.

'There was a homeless man. It was odd. I'd never seen him there before, but he seemed appreciative. Someone had been shouting at him. Another man—in a suit. I decided to step in because it was unfair—nobody else was helping.'

Marwa nodded along.

'Then I went ... to the station. Moor Street Station. I got on a train, and then I remember a blackness. Everything just ... went out. Then I woke up here.'

Marwa listened intently. Then she moved her fingers in a backward jumping arc.

'You want me to go back?'

Marwa nodded.

'Okay. Before the man?'

Marwa nodded.

'Right, so I was on a bus.'

Marwa pointed emphatically, as though saying this is important. She gestured *why?* again.

'Why was I on the bus?' Daffodil asked.

Marwa nodded energetically.

'Er…' Daffodil said, looking around, trying to remember. 'I don't know. I can't remember.' She wanted to stop thinking about it, but persevered. 'Aaah, my head.'

She rubbed her forehead, trying to recall why she had gotten on that bus through the stringing pain.

Massaging her temples, she said, 'I remember now.'

Marwa's eyes grew in anticipation. 'My new school. Rarley. But why didn't Mum or Dad take me? I can't work it out. Why did they not take me to my new school on the first day? How do I not know this, Marwa? What's wrong with my memories?'

She looked from Marwa out to the ocean, head still throbbing. There were seagulls squawking overhead. Paired with the gleaming sand, Daffodil suddenly remembered Adam and the day they had sat watching the ocean on the beach. The day they had spoken of their parents, and his beautiful, golden words.

I think they carry on. Continue on—for us. They care about us. I don't know if they're happy, but I think in their quiet, shut-up-inside-themselves kind of way, they want to see us happy. And that, by extension, is their happiness. Their kids.

Her parents did care about her. Adam had made sure she was always cognizant of that much. But then why could she not remember much before the bus?

'I can't remember why they didn't take me, but I feel like it may have something to do with the fact that… My parents and I have become quite distant recently. I can't explain it. I can't explain why. But something happened. And it changed our relationship.'

Adam would know. Adam would always have the answer.

Her head throbbed again. What was going on?

Daffodil wondered what they looked like right now. Two people alone on a deserted island. A young girl and a woman... The wind whipping at their hair, sun shining down on the bunches of bananas at their feet.

'I guess we should try and set up some kind of tent for sleeping,' Daffodil said, considering they didn't know how long they'd be here.

Marwa nodded. She knew when to stop asking questions.

'Do you know how to build a tent, Marwa? Or could you just alchemise it?'

Marwa smiled and then gestured for Daffodil to follow her.

They began traversing the island, looking for materials for their tent. Sweating, Daffodil decided to tie her jacket around her waist.

'You know, one thing I still don't get.'

Marwa laughed.

'Yes. Just one thing,' Daffodil said, laughing in turn. 'I don't get where Safa got this jacket from. One second, nothing. The next—jacket!'

Marwa was pulling at a frond, presumably to gather some rope-like items. It snapped off, and the other end of the large plant leaf flung backward.

She placed the frond on the ground and took out another vial from within the pockets of her own jacket. Carefully, she poured a single drop onto the frond, and the entire leaf became a hardened, blackened, leathery material.

'That is incredible,' Daffodil said, kneeling down to touch the leathery substance. The coarse material had a springy hardness to it, like a cow's snout. It reminded Daffodil of leather jackets.

'Alchemy created this place…' Daffodil said in awe. 'All this time I've just been swept along this journey, but alchemy is the answer. I don't need to keep on waiting for things to happen. If alchemy is what it takes to do anything here, alchemy will be my escape. I need to get out of here. If what Haradan said was correct, my memories depend on it. Marwa, can you show me how to use alchemy like you?'

Marwa bit her lip hesitantly.

'Please,' Daffodil said. 'Without understanding alchemy, I don't have a chance. I need to learn. I'll be safe with the liquids, I promise.'

Marwa considered this. Then, without a word, they began.

She showed Daffodil how to drop the liquids from different vials into a new mixture.

She showed her how to be careful that she did not add too much of any kind, lest some danger occur that Marwa could not articulate nor Daffodil completely understand.

As they experimented and worked, Daffodil realised their silent communication was the best kind of learning, and she began seeing some sense of logic behind the combinations of liquids.

She saw the patterns.

'So,' Daffodil said, kneeling down at their camp after what felt like hours of practice. She carefully added a drop of a cool icy liquid into a new vial while Marwa watched over her. 'It's kind of about bringing together different amounts of hot and cold liquids with … earth materials,' she said, adding another compound ever so subtly. There was a slight whiff of smoke and ash, but no visible reaction in the liquids.

Marwa nodded slowly.

'Hmm… You're hesitating. Ah, but I'm missing something. It's that fourth element, isn't it? How does the fourth element, wind, come into it…?'

Now, Marwa nodded more enthusiastically.

'That's the question…'

Marwa rolled her fingers in a tight circle.

'You've spent a long time trying to figure that one out?'

She nodded.

'I see,' Daffodil said, looking up at her friend and teacher. 'Wind is the final key. You've mastered the other three. And if you can already do as much as you can with the elements you've mastered… I can only imagine what is possible once you've learnt to control the wind.

'But,' she continued, 'how do you capture the wind? Well my brother might ask how you managed to harness the power of fire and water, and then go from there.'

Marwa raised an eyebrow and nodded slowly, her way of showing she was impressed. Well, Daffodil couldn't take credit. She'd got that idea from Adam. He really did love his science experiments. Was it not just a couple of months ago that his ridiculous bedroom science had resulted in Daffodil's curtain catching fire? Dad had to run in and extinguish it, shocked. He had then proceeded to talk sternly to Daffodil about being responsible; he had seemed fed up, though for some reason, he hadn't asked if it was Adam who had started the fire. Still, Daffodil couldn't be too angry at him—he was her little brother, and she loved him—and she definitely couldn't throw him under the bus. She'd understood that her parents might not fully *get* her or her brother, but she had to be there for him.

'I'm going to figure this out, Marwa. I remember something Riyul said once. He said you have to remember what you're fighting for. The people that believe in you. That love you. And when nobody else is around,' she continued with a face that betrayed no emotion, 'you have to believe in yourself.'

In that moment, silent save the soft lapping of waves and the tinkering of vials, Daffodil finally found some peace, some purpose. And her alchemy began to take shape.

Chapter 24

The Palace

'See, the trouble with doors is,' Safa said, placing her hand on a very particular doorknob in a very particular hidden part of The Librarian's library, 'they are really darn powerful.'

'They sound it,' Riyul said, handing Eli over to Seul for their journey.

'It just takes one person who knows how to manipulate the doorspace, and you've got that person coming for you. I suppose it's a gift and a curse.'

'One person like you?'

Safa smirked. 'Well, having worked for Gerrihend did leave me with one positive, I suppose,' she concurred, opening the door.

If Riyul had expected a flood of white light, this was far from it. The door opened to what instantly appeared to be a dark room. The dank smell of musty damp wafted through the doorframe, and some very well marked spiderwebs hung lazily in the corner of the barely lit room.

'The palace basement is one place I know how to access.'

***

'You can't just connect to any door anywhere,' she whispered matter-of-factly as they made their way carefully through the bowels of King Gerrihend's palace, Safa cautiously checking around each corner for guards. 'Most doors in The City have particular receders built in nowadays, to detect any unwanted tampering. Thankfully, I removed the receder to that cellar door when I was working here. I had every feeling that there may come a time in the future where I'd need some kind of exit, or entrance, without the possibility of it being known or tracked.'

Riyul nodded silently, pretending he knew what a receder was, as Safa led the way up a ladder into a checker-floored kitchen.

'If we can just get to the ventilation shaft,' she whispered breathlessly, clambering on to what appeared to a large range, 'we can access almost any part of the palace.'

As she started to open a ceiling tile, a door squeaked outside the kitchen. Then — the clanking of shoes.

Safa looked at Riyul, and quickly lifted herself up into the ceiling bay.

'Quickly,' she mouthed, gesturing for Riyul to get up into the ceiling bay and join her.

But the footsteps were fast approaching. They'd see him going in if he went now.

'Close it,' he said, waving his hand to her. He then looked around. Tables. Chairs. There–a cupboard underneath a work table. It'd have to do.

Opening it, he found it barely had enough space to fit anything, but perhaps if he contorted himself…

The sounds of footsteps loomed ever closer. Clanking on hard tiles.

Riyul climbed into the cupboard, twisting this way and that to just about fit. He was parallel to the ground at this point, and his foot was still sticking out. With another squeeze, he pulled the side of the door closed with his foot and gently cushioned it from slamming shut.

Just as the main kitchen door opened.

A light flooded into the room, which Riyul could see through the crack in the cupboard.

Black boots. Military-looking trousers.

And … a wooden stick.

The figure walked into the kitchen, though Riyul could only make out the bottom half, the staff in hand. And around the staff swirled a substance. It was as though something dark and gloomy almost writhed around the stick. Like shadows.

And suddenly, a sharp spike of pain.

Riyul struggled to hold in a gasp.

It was excruciating. His whole body pulsated with pure unadulterated white hot pain.

It took everything in his power to not scream.

The pain was mainly in his head. Riyul squeezed his eyes and oh so badly wanted to make some noise. The pain. Oh, this pain.

With one eye barely open, he watched the figure, thankfully, start to make their way out of the kitchen, seemingly content with whatever they had come for.

The kitchen door shut. And Riyul slowly kicked open the cupboard door, daring to let out a gasp.

A ceiling tile slid open above and Safa looked down at him. She looked very concerned.

Before she could say anything, however, Riyul motioned for her to not speak yet. He closed the cupboard door carefully behind him and tried to catch his breath, more from the white hot pain in his head than the lack of air in the cupboard.

But then he stopped—and looked at the door, frowning.

If I were a guard… and I'd just come into a room to check it…

Riyul rapidly spun, climbed up the ladder and slid into the ceiling bay just as the kitchen door opened once more, the guard stepping in.

There was no time to close the tile, so they silently watched as the figure once again peered around.

Please don't look up.

Safa moved her hand toward her jacket pockets, seemingly to retrieve a vial of some sort.

Riyul sure hoped she wouldn't have to use it.

The guard continued staring into the room.

He must know.

Staring.

Not a sound could be heard except the thrumming of Riyul's own heartbeat under bated breath.

One heartbeat.

Two.

Three.

Safa lifted a vial with a mysterious glowing liquid and took aim.

There was a shuffle outside.

The guard turned.

And walked away.

***

'You know I really do not enjoy the stress of doing this,' Riyul conceded as they navigated their way through the labyrinthine air vents that sprawled throughout the palace's ceiling.

'Eh, don't be such a complainer; Notra is our best bet of finding and reversing what has happened to Marwa. I can't remember the last I heard her voice. She has been iced for that long. And with Marwa, we can try to get you both out of here.'

Crawling on all fours, they twisted this way and that—around bends and turns and corners, until Riyul became dizzy with the vastness of it all.

Thankfully, his blistering headache had quickly dissipated, and he had all but forgotten about it.

'Okay,' Safa said, 'I think we've found him.'

They were approaching light. Some kind of distant grille looking into what must have been a room within the palace.

They approached carefully. The ventilation shaft grew wider until they reached the grille and could look out.

Subtle sounds below.

Hushed voices.

As they looked down very carefully, hiding in the darkness as best as possible, the conversation could just about be heard.

'The elixir is being sent over,' the man at the table said to the woman sitting beside him, whilst he cut into a piece of what appeared to be chicken.

They both certainly looked like royalty, Riyul thought. The man appeared tall, with shoulder-length flowing black hair. The woman, presumably the queen, sat there neatly, legs crossed, observing his statements with pursed lips. They wore matching red robes that were tasteful and exuded royalty, yet were not garish and overly ornate. Her golden locks contrasted deeply with his jet-black hair, and nestled deep within she had placed a white rose.

'You don't seem too happy,' he said knowingly. Interestingly, there wasn't a lot of food on the table. Simply three dishes, though seemingly high-quality foodstuffs. The queen's plate was neatly sitting in front of her, her meal finished some time ago.

She opened her mouth, seemed to reconsider, closed it again, and didn't respond. The expression on her face suggested, *you know how I feel.*

'You still want me to delay the administration 'til he comes back, don't you?'

She stared for a moment. Then she raised her hand to her hair, delicately extracted the white rose and intricately fastened it onto his breast pocket. Then she nodded.

The king sighed.

He laid his napkin primly on his plate, gently placed his knife and fork down in their proper places, and stood up.

'Okay,' he said. 'We'll wait. But for now, we have a speech to give.'

***

Riyul and Safa approached another grille. After King Notra had left the room, they realised he was going to address some people. About what, Safa was unsure. But it seemed important.

They crawled once more through the passageway, on all fours. The pain on his joints, whilst present, was nothing compared to the piercing agony of earlier.

'You know, something weird,' Riyul said, rubbing his temple absently.

'What's that?' Safa responded, crawling behind him.

'The queen didn't really seem to speak, did she?'

'You're right. I don't think she said a word.'

There were sounds emanating from the grille now, or just beyond. Sounds of a crowd … cheering.

As they continued crawling, the noise grew louder and louder.

They looked out. Beneath them was a huge rally stage, and an audience huger still. They were in front of the palace, stretching all the way out to what must have the city gates. Beyond this was an array of crested ice-capped mountains brushing the auburn sky far in the distance.

But most amazing was the people. For the first time in a long time, Riyul saw people. So many people. What must have been hundreds, if not thousands of citizens of The City, waved flags and banners he couldn't make out from above, barely hidden in the wall of the palace.

A sea of observers, chanting and crying and waiting for the man on the stage to begin speaking.

He walked forward ceremoniously, his red and gold robes billowing behind him. And speak, he did.

'Oh people of Aethril!' Notra boomed, raising his arms triumphantly. 'I stand here before you today—not as a *king*, but as a *friend!*'

Cheers erupted from the eager crowd.

'Skutlish has whispered his evils for as long as I can remember. Yet you have been strong through it all! Even when your family and friends have whispered against you also. When others conspired against you also. You remained strong!'

A wave of cheers swept through the audience.

'Even when those in our own city seek to dismantle everything we hold dear,' he said, lowering his voice—yet somehow his words still carried across masses. 'Even when those in our own city wish to disassemble all we hold dear. They want to destroy our morals, dissolve our families and dissuade our youth. Those who believe … certain *beliefs* in our own City—they wish to take husbands away from wives. Mothers away from daughters. Sons away from fathers. But we will not give in to the other. We stand strong in the face of adversity.'

He paused. And the whole crowd waited with bated breath.

A gleam. Notra raised a golden sceptre, which Riyul hadn't spotted previously. Like the guard's staff he had seen before, something was turning around the sceptre; light smoke wisps spiralled around it, barely noticeable but there nonetheless. In fact, to Riyul, these were more clear. More alive. Notra raised his rod high up to the sky and called out, such that his voice travelled as far as the mountains themselves.

'And so I laud you, my friends. We know how much The Great War affected us all. Our lives. Our families. Our memories have become blurry! And yet we survive! So remain firm in your trust for me, my people, no matter what the whisperers claim. Know that I do not wish to preach nor pander. I purely want PEACE FOR AETHRIL!'

Notra turned, and, under the cloak of a million cheers, looked directly up at them.

Riyul and Safa hastily scurried back on all fours. But it was too late; he must have seen someone hiding up here.

His sceptre glowed white at the top as he glared at them; in an orb of brilliant pure white only visible to those close by, he somehow sent a shot directly at them. The white light orb buzzed, and what appeared to be pure visceral energy whizzed toward them, blasting the grille into a trillion pieces. A cloud of smoke and rubble mushroomed where the grille had been as they narrowly avoided the attack. Safa proceeded to reach for a miniature vial, took aim from her cramped spot and launched at the king.

It struck him right on his chest, at exactly the place his white rose had been, momentarily stunning him as. Without watching any longer, they turned back into the ventilation system and began their hasty retreat.

'I don't think today's the best day to talk to him,' Safa said, crawling as fast as she could.

'You think?'

They turned right and left and left and right again, twisting this way and that, until they came back to the ceiling tile that connected to the kitchen.

Riyul paused for a moment, putting his ear to the tile in case the palace guard was still around. Surely, they would have been notified by now.

Not hearing a thing, he slowly prised the tile open. The room below was empty.

They hurried back down, replacing the tile perfectly, and slowly edged out of the kitchen, listening for an attack.

They could hear definite sounds of a search, with shouts and calls from some distant part of the palace. The chase was clearly on.

Luckily, they made it back to the basement without detection. The way looked clear, and all that remained was the final door to get back to the library.

Just as they approached it, a man wearing all black wrappings stepped out of the shadows. He was covered head to toe in a midnight wrapping, similar to that of a mummy. Not an inch of skin visible, except for a straight slit for his eyes and ebony skin.

'Now, you look cool,' Riyul said.

'No way…' Safa breathed. 'Zear…'

The guard turned to them, swirling his staff in hand.

'Zear?' Riyul asked as Safa flung a vial at him, and one at the far wall.

'Well, sorry Zear, but this one's going to hurt,' Riyul said as they set off at a run to the door back to the library. As soon as they began moving, the guard was pulled straight to the opposite wall, exponentially increasing in speed until he nearly slammed into the obsidian brickwork.

But then something odd happened.

He didn't slam into anything.

Hurtling towards the wall, just as he was about to collide, he suddenly spun his right leg and skidded to a halt, slamming his staff down on the ground in the exact same moment.

Darkness itself swirled ominously from the staff, apparently able to negate the effects of Safa's vial.

'Well, my party trick seems useless,' Safa said despondently, frozen metres from the door, as Zear spun his staff, readying for a new attack.

'I do not want to see what he's about to do,' said Riyul.

'Nor I.'

They glanced towards the door, to their exit. Zear followed their gaze and readied his attack–the shadows coalesced into an orb and shot towards Safa. However, she seized the moment and flung another vial in his direction, conjuring up a great plume of purple smoke.

As though he knew her move before she made it, Riyul exclaimed, 'Come Safa!' as he ran towards the exit and flung it open.

Safa dashed, leaving the plume of purple smoke to dissipate from the swirls of the guard as she dove through the doorway like a leaping sturgeon, gliding through the threshold. Riyul hurried into the library after her, and when turned to close the door, he noticed the purple smoke had truly gone.

Zear had an orb of shadow coalesced, ready to shoot from atop his staff.

Yet he faltered.

For the briefest, most fleeting of moments, the guard hesitated.

His eyes narrowed and then widened.

Riyul did not wait. He slammed the door shut just as the king entered the cellar, enraged. Notra caught sight of Riyul through the threshold—and the palace was gone.

Chapter 25

True Alchemy

Marwa spun a branch at inhuman speed in a rapid twirling motion, as though blocking attacks from incoming projectiles. She dodged, ducked and parried in the air. Moving forward, she thrust her branch at the air, dodged again, spun on the sand and thrust again.

Daffodil watched in awe at the spectacle. A whirlwind of dust was being kicked up by the endless dance; for what felt like hours to Daffodil. Marwa had simply said she had to train, and had begun.

'Marwa,' Daffodil said, carefully pouring molten red liquid into another vial as her friend spun and blocked nearby. 'Who made this island?'

Marwa finished her procedure and sat down next to Daffodil, sweat beading down her forehead. She thought about her answer for a moment.

The sea waters were spectacular in their shimmering grandeur, rippling in lustrous sheets of crystal blue, and stretching for eternity; periodic splashes from the water mingled with the light tingle in the ocean air and breeze. It was almost like Daffodil could hear—very subtly—the music of the island: a song, a symphony of water, air, peace and harmony.

'I don't know,' Marwa said slowly. 'But I think the key is in alchemy. Alchemy has many powers and effects. I mean, right now, on this island... my throat is not hurting. What caused that? I don't know. I mean, you somehow found the door for this place at the exact time we needed to escape. How did you do it?'

Daffodil didn't say anything, but continued listening to the sounds of the island.

'You know, it's funny,' Daffodil said eventually. 'I remember being diagnosed with something, back home. Synaesthesia. Have you ever heard of that before?'

Marwa shook her head.

'I don't know if it's connected, but it's the chance for two senses to combine and sometimes even amplify; it's supposedly very rare. I remember when I first came here, Haradan spoke to me about the sounds of the train. Understanding them. Attuning to them. Hearing them. Like it was alive. It made sense to me straight away.

'At times, I feel like I can hear the island,' she continued, squinting at the furthest distance of the horizon, the sun catching her eyes. 'Its melody. Its life. Like it is also ... alive—telling me something with words or numbers or beats or rhythms. Wanting to be understood. Waiting.'

Marwa raised an eyebrow.

'You can *hear* the island?' Marwa asked, her voice rising for the first time.

'Erm, I suppose—perhaps? Maybe?'

'What else can you hear?'

'I mean,' Daffodil said, laughing awkwardly, 'this is going to sound crazy, but my condition means sometimes I feel like I can hear colours... taste numbers...'

Marwa's eyes grew wide. She quickly rifled through her bag, extracting four fresh bottles of liquid, and placed the vials in a neat line, a hand-span apart from each other. One with beautiful ocean-blue water that bubbled ever so slightly from the bottom. One of red, thick, viscous-seeming liquid that appeared to smoke within the corked bottle. One with some sort of rocky, muddy composition, like earthen sediment. And one of swirling grey silvery gas, somehow contained within a bottle and turning, revolving within.

'Ever since we can remember, there have been expert alchemists. People who didn't necessarily do what they did because of the science itself—which is one method to better one's self in the field–but through what they called intuition. I've never fully understood it, being a woman of science myself, but what you are talking about sounds like a heightened level of their claims. Understanding the world around you at a visceral, deep, gut level.'

Kneeling down on the soft sand, facing the line of vials, Daffodil waited for her next instructions. But Marwa didn't give any. She just sat there, watching, waiting, her face betraying nothing.

'Okay. So what should I do now?'

'I want you to do whatever comes to you naturally. If you can do this, I'd be very impressed.'

'I … Okay,' Daffodil said, hovering over the four bottles.

Her hand started going towards the blue one—instinctually. She picked it up, inspected it, swirled it around a few times as she had seen Marwa do to ascertain the viscosity and see how well it moved. She then opened the stopper of an empty vial nearby and poured in a single drop.

Hmm, what next? She eyed the other three substances. Four elements. She started to reach out for the red liquid, but hesitated.

No. That doesn't feel right.

She closed her eyes. It was as though she could sense some kind of grid around her in the blackness; like green lines crisscrossing the entire face of the world.

This was nonsense, of course. She wasn't superhuman, but she liked to imagine she could feel the grids. And in this place of darkness, with the fictional grids of the world around her, everything was pointing to the earthen substance; some kind of magnetic attraction directing her to it. The vial was a pulsating luminescence in this black void. And the earthen one was pulsing harder than the rest.

Daffodil opened her eyes, picked up the vial with earth and tried to swirl it around in the same fashion. It didn't move in nearly the same way. It was ... liquid—yet there was an obvious hardness to it. Daffodil could feel it—the toughness. It had soul. It could be used to build. *It ... it wants to build.* There was a rhythm, a numerical base that she sensed was correct.

And it really just *felt* like the right one.

Opening the stopper, Daffodil considered how much to pour; but then she almost broke into a laugh—she knew.

Like an experienced scientist at work, she carefully poured out the tiniest sliver of earthiness, the amount that felt perfect. There were very few things Daffodil had ever felt certain about. But this was one.

The earthy substance connected. The reaction was instantaneous, but not rushed. The blue liquid at the base changed colour rapidly to a darker, brownier murkiness, and, as she poured, the stream of new and old substance combined together and solidified.

Daffodil's eyes widened.

The continued stream of earth she was pouring progressively hardened. The new solid rock climbed up towards the vial it was being poured from. It was like watching a plant shoot up—albeit a hard, rocky plant.

Before the earthiness could solidify all the way up and into the contents of the initial beaker, Daffodil flicked it upwards and stopped the pouring.

The moment she did, the entire hardened structure lost all rigidity and hardness, and instantly began to dissipate. It gently collapsed into dust back into the mixture vial.

And in front of her now sat a swirling mixture, composed of the same material, but suddenly of a completely different thickness and viscosity.

Daffodil stared at the vials.

Marwa gestured at her to try again, but showed the number *two* on her fingers.

Daffodil did it again, but doubled up the substances. This didn't seem to have any stronger effect.

Something needed to be done differently.

Daffodil mixed the same substance once more, but this time took a nearby rock and poured the new liquid over it gently.

Instantly, the liquid began to morph into an identical, albeit white copy of the rock, thinly attached by a line of white. Marwa gave Daffodil another vial of brown fluid, and she poured it on. The replica rock began to change colour, matching the first, and the white attaching line retracted into the new rock.

What remained were two identical rocks.

'Cool,' Daffodil said.

'Daffodil,' Marwa said, 'you know how to do True Alchemy...'

Chapter 26

Trace

'Have you ever considered hippopotami?' The Librarian asked Seul as they sat playing chess.

'Excuse me?' Seul said, moving his knight across the board.

'The plural of hippopotamus. As in, have you ever deeply pondered about them?'

'I don't think so.'

'That's the problem,' The Librarian said, sighing. 'Nobody does. Nobody cares about hippopotami. Do you?'

Seul nodded vehemently.

'Bah,' The Librarian spat, waving his hand. 'I don't believe you. Who walks around thinking about hippopotami? Nobody, that's who. And if nobody thinks about them, then they suffer— thoughtlessly.' He then proceeded to nonchalantly move his king piece and nearly win the game.

The pair sat on two stools in the middle of the library, contemplative. Suddenly, a crashing sound distracted them.

'Ah, darn it,' The Librarian said, turning to the source of the interruption, his knight piece still in hand. 'We're playing checkers!'

Safa collapsed through the doorway, followed by Riyul, who barely managed to shut the door behind him.

'Mum! Riyul! Are you okay?' Seul hurried over, the chess board abandoned.

'Fine,' Safa responded.

'Right as rain,' Riyul grunted.

They both stood up, checking for broken bones. 'We met Zear.'

'What?! Like *the* Zear?' Seul asked, incredulous.

'I think so,' Safa said, brushing herself off. 'It was a bit hard to tell when he was shooting at me with I don't even know what.'

'Who is Zear?' Riyul asked.

'Only the most powerful assassin under King Gerrihend's rule!' Seul exclaimed.

'Well, your mum seemed to be able to handle him,' Riyul said, brushing off the dust from his trousers. 'She near enough flung him into a wall with one potion.'

'Ah, not at all,' Safa said, cheeks reddening. 'We were lucky to get out as we did. He is impossibly fast. If it wasn't for the element of surprise, we might not have escaped. I would not want to meet him again.'

'I'm guessing then you didn't manage to ask the king about Marwa?' The Librarian said.

'Bit hard to do that,' Riyul said, 'when he can shoot light. Why did nobody tell me he could shoot light?'

'Wow,' Seul whistled. 'Light!'

'I mean, I didn't know,' Safa said, shrugging.

'I did,' The Librarian said happily.

They all stared at him.

'Anyway, I didn't get any information out of him,' Safa said before Riyul could jump on The Librarian. 'But I did manage to get this.' She pulled out a white rose from her pocket—the same pocket she kept her tiny vials in.

'The king's?' The Librarian asked.

'Yep. When he started shooting at us, I thought it might be the only opportunity to get something that might lead us right to Marwa.'

'How would his flower lead us to Marwa?' Seul asked.

'Well, it's not just the king's, you see. In fact, it's not really the king's at all. It's the queen's.'

'Queen Syrys?' The Librarian asked curiously, examining the flower with his fingers.

'You got it. It's something Riyul said in the vents. He realised the queen didn't speak at all in the palace, almost like she might also be iced. I mean, it's a long shot, but if she really were iced …'

'Then we could try run an alchemic trace on it!' The Librarian finished. 'Safa, you're a genius!'

'Thank you; I learnt from the best.'

The Librarian grinned. 'Hey, have you ever thought about becoming a librarian?'

Safa shifted, looking around.

'Sorry, how does tracing work?' Riyul asked, letting Safa evade The Librarian's question.

'Alchemy leaves traces,' The Librarian explained matter-of-factly. 'Come,' he said, leading them over to another part of the house which contained more vials and liquids but fewer books (albeit barely). 'For anyone to be iced in the first place is an unnatural, alchemically-induced phenomenon, right?'

'Sure,' Riyul agreed. 'It'd take alchemy to ice them in the first place, yep.'

'Well, after that, it's basic chemistry, really. A person who is in the chemical state of *being* iced, well, they will leave a mark on all their possessions. Anything they own will now also have this trace. To a very small degree. And that's why the flower is so important. It's got a trace of ice. That would then very possibly match with someone else who may be iced, as they'd share the ice trace,' he said, holding the rose up to the light.

'Like Marwa?' Riyul said.

'Like Marwa. If we're even correct about all these points.' The Librarian placed the flower on his workshop bench as he began decanting and concocting varying mixtures.

'So if all of our theories are correct,' Safa said, walking over to pick up the rose. She twirled it lightly around her fingers and handed it to Riyul. 'Then this could be the key to finding Marwa, finding Daffodil—and then getting you two out of here.'

Chapter 27

The Boy

Daffodil had just done alchemy. And according to Marwa, *True Alchemy*.

She still had a million questions, and more questions dawning every moment. She might not have done anything with as much ease as the likes of Haradan or Safa or Marwa, but it must be something—especially if Marwa was this impressed.

If alchemy was really about understanding the chemicals that made up the world around her, then she had just unlocked some understanding of how to get closer to home.

A warm glow of contentment flooded Daffodil's core. A pure moment of unadulterated, unfettered joy.

Marwa watched her silently, having used up her energy recently by talking too much, and smiled—fully, broadly.

'What is True Alchemy, Marwa?'

Marwa tried to speak but realised she was low on reserves once again. And so opted to sign around her and then at the vials.

'Is it… to do with hearing the world around?' Daffodil asked. 'And making potions?'

Marwa chewed her lip, deciding to risk her voice again. 'Hearing the world around...' she said slowly, 'and using it to inform your alchemic creation. It's rare that anyone can do this, but it seems like you have the gift.'

Daffodil looked out to the ocean, hearing the lapping of the waves once more.

'Do you think it's something to do with my synaesthesia?'

Marwa looked at her in question.

Daffodil took a deep breath. She closed her eyes and took the island all in.

'Darkness,' Daffodil said. 'Like everyone else, I guess. But also ... faint green squares—grids—overlapping everything around me. It's like I can see something creating the world... The lines that make up the island itself.'

Then something occurred to her.

'Marwa,' Daffodil said quickly, opening her eyes, 'ever since I've been small, I could ... hear colours. I could smell things that weren't there just from seeing certain shapes. It's like my senses were all mixed together like a great pile of spaghetti. Here, it's better. Cleaner. It's like my mind can actually make sense of the world. I feel like I can sense a door on the island now.'

Marwa's eyes widened. 'But we checked so many times,' she said raspily.

'Something has changed,' Daffodil said, standing up. Suddenly, her heartbeat started to quicken, and a darkness coalesced within her. Something felt very wrong.

'Marwa, I have this weird feeling. And I don't know why, I can't explain it, but I feel like when we get off this island... I don't think you should tell anyone that you managed to recover your voice.'

Marwa raised an eyebrow sceptically.

'I have a feeling someone did this to you.'

'What do you mean?' asked Marwa.

'Well, I mean, you can't speak for so long. And then suddenly, you get separated to this place where it's nobody but us, and your voice starts to come back.'

Marwa looked out at the expanses of sand.

'How? I mean, it's just been my own sister. My nephew. Nobody else has been with us for a while—nobody has even seen us until we met you and Riyul.'

'I dunno',' said Daffodil. 'Sorry. I just have a feeling. Call it a gut instinct.'

Then she heard a sound. A light rustling to the side. Leaves.

Daffodil turned instantly.

Who was that?

In the woods. Central island. Movement. The shape of … a boy in brown clothing. Looking at her. Peeking through the shrubs.

Daffodil stood motionless. *No way.*

Whatever it was had quickly rushed off back into the thick vegetation.

Impossible.

The figure was gone. Had she imagined it?

But it had only just happened. And it looked like…

Without a moment's hesitation, Daffodil scrambled up and belted after the person.

Trees and shrubs whizzed past her as she ran.

A quiet, slightly swaying palm-tree was violently shaken back as Daffodil jumped and grabbed it to look around. The figure had been next to this tree. Yet, looking around now, Daffodil found nobody.

A crunch up ahead. Snaps of twigs.

Daffodil darted after the sound. Like a blur, she crunched and trampled her way through straight into the centre of the island. Something in her mind—a crazy, nonsensical voice—told her it was someone she knew. It could be…

No, impossible. She shook the crazy thoughts away as she rushed past a large boulder.

She must be in deep now, for she didn't remember that boulder, or these trees around here. She glanced around as she ran after the source of the sound—shadows loomed overhead. Daffodil was in deeper than they'd ever gone before.

She stopped, skidding up a cloud of dust.

The foreign trees cast wild shadows in a thousand directions. Her adrenaline was dissipating, her rush giving way to doubt.

Was chasing this phantom person really the best idea? Was this a trap? Or was she just imagining what she wanted to imagine?

Movement. Up ahead, through some bushes. No. This had to be real.

There was no way there could be someone else on this island. But she had to know. Whatever it was, she had to find out, and so ran once more.

Past more bushes and trees and boulders and openings and fruit she'd never seen fallen on the ground. Clearing a log, she entered into the centre of a patch of empty space, and slowed down in the middle of some sort of glade. Daffodil spun around. The figure had led her here. But where was he in this forest?

Absolute silence. No sounds—save the sporadic click of a cricket. Daffodil thought back to what she had seen when she had been on the beach.

What had he looked like?

Tattered clothing? A small figure peeking behind some trees? Or was it normal clothes?

Mind's playing tricks on you, Daffodil, she thought to herself. But she couldn't help it. She tried to visualise him again. He had been peeking out and looking at them. A dirtied, muddy face; she was increasingly confident, the image focusing and gaining more detail in her head. He'd been curiously studying what they had been doing— what she had been trying to do with the vials. Daffodil was sure it was a young boy. She was sure of it now. It was clearer in her mind.

'Adam?' Daffodil said quietly.

Nothing responded. There was not a soul in sight. Whatever she had seen, or not, whoever she had seen, or not, had completely disappeared.

A shuffling from behind her. Daffodil turned, hoping.

Marwa ran over, worry written all over her. She joined Daffodil in the centre of the glade, looking around at the emptiness.

'I ... I thought I ... saw someone,' Daffodil whispered, looking around hopelessly. Still anticipating to hear another clue any second, or to see some sign. 'I could have sworn I saw my younger brother. Adam. Or ... someone. It looked like a person. Someone on this island.'

Marwa looked around more carefully. She walked the perimeter and diligently examined bushes and shrubs and trees and rocks. But there was, of course, nothing. She pursed her lips and shook her head.

Daffodil looked at her. 'Sorry,' she said quietly. 'I'm guessing I saw just what I wanted to s-'

Suddenly, leaves rustled behind them.

And voices.

They turned to see trees moving and shrubs being pushed, somewhat violently, out of the way.

'Ow!' a voice called out. A voice they recognised. It sounded like-

Out through the line of trees and bracken broke through three familiar faces, and one new face—a man with some crazy hair and a long black beard. This new person was the first to speak.

'Ah, I knew they'd be here; didn't I tell you to trust me, Saliva?'

Seul, who was right in step behind the newcomer, sighed and rubbed his brow, looking like he had enough exploring for a lifetime.

'Who's Saliva?' Daffodil asked, grinning.

PART III

Chapter 28

Names

To The Librarian, everything was possibilities. He'd thought about physics for so long he could almost see it etched into the world around him—or worlds, as he'd realised. He'd analysed and thought and fathomed and come up with more synonyms for who only knew how long. Now knowledge itself seemed near tangible, in all its synonymous fields.

He felt like he almost understood it all.

Oh, he knew he must be mad. Everyone was a little mad eventually. When he was a kid, he'd always say, who wanted to be normal? Being normal was overrated, he'd said. But then he realised everyone said that. Then he'd realised saying that everyone said that was also oversaid. How cliché. Now he didn't say anything. Except when he said things. But who was to say how often he said that?

'So, what is your real name?' the new girl with the black hair and two coats asked him, interrupting his train of thought.

'My name?' The Librarian responded, shaken.

Daffodil looked around the six of them as they walked along the beach, confused. 'Erm, yes,' she said. 'I still don't know your name.'

'I have a very normal name.'

'Okay... so what is it?'

He looked around quickly. There was sand, water, trees, the group of them walking...

'My name is ... Footstep!'

Daffodil looked at him. 'That sounds suspiciously like you just made it up.'

'Nope. I've always been Footstep. Ever since I took my first step. My parents were very much into feet. Connoisseurs even. I hope to continue the line one day with my own children. I plan to name them all as different toes.'

'Your parents named you after an action?'

'An action done by a body part,' The Librarian corrected. 'My sister was called Click-of-the-finger, my brother Snap-of-the-wrist—and you don't even want to know what our dog was called.'

'What was your dog called?'

'John.'

Daffodil fixed her eyes on him.

'Okay, Footstep, how do we get out, then?'

'Who's Footstep? Ah, yes, me! Forget I said that. As for your question, we get off this island by getting to another door, of course!'

'Okay, brilliant. So where are we headed?'

'I don't know,' he said to Daffodil, shrugging. 'I thought *you* were leading the way.'

The six of them stopped in their tracks.

'Haha, I'm only kidding. I know where we can find a door to get back.'

Yes, now he was weird again, because what was the point of trying to be normal? There was no normal. Ah, not a cliché now. Crazy how time changes thoughts but doesn't change the thought.

'Remind me again why we don't just leave the way you came?' Daffodil asked.

'I need to teach you to listen to the sounds around you so that when we get you to The City, you can find the doors for your escape.'

'Is this to do with being able to hear their frequencies and sounds?' Riyul asked.

'Exactly,' The Librarian said. He gestured around the beach as they walked along the coast. 'Can you sense any openings or doorways nearby?'

Daffodil and Riyul listened intently. They shook their heads.

'Ah, my dears, that's because THEY'RE NOT HERE,' The Librarian said. 'Doors are fickle creatures.'

'Excuse me?' asked Daffodil.

'They're *fickle creatures*,' he enunciated. 'Also, you are excused.'

'No—I heard what you said, but I didn't understand.'

'What's the difference?' The Librarian asked, tilting his head.

'Well, you can hear someone but not … understand them, I suppose.'

He chewed on this for a moment, seeming to genuinely look up at the sky and ponder midstride. Then he lifted his finger and said, 'Precisely, young Daffodil. Precisely.'

'Wha… what? That didn't answer my question.'

'But you've already answered your own question.'

Daffodil blinked.

'You're odd,' she said.

'And *you're* right. Doors are fickle. Why do we not leave the way we came? To answer your question, they firstly do not like to make themselves known, but also, and perhaps far more importantly, is the fact that I believe we are being watched, or observed, or both, and the door we came through was our means of escaping surveillance. We shan't be using that again. Or perhaps we shall, let's see. Also, people are fickle. Even pickles are fickle.'

Seul frowned. 'What does fickle mea-'

'Don't interrupt, Saliva!'

Daffodil smiled involuntarily but then quickly said, 'Please don't call him Saliva. I don't think he likes it.'

Seul beamed, nodding, and then tripped over some sand.

Daffodil tried to ignore this and continued, 'Besides, aren't you meant to be understanding of people's feelings, especially as a teacher?'

'I'm not a teacher. I'm a librarian now.'

'But you *were* a teacher.'

'Indubitably. But think of me now as a librarian, or a lawyer. Or better yet—a janitor.'

Riyul frowned.

'How is a janitor better?'

The Librarian gasped. 'What is the purpose of a janitor?'

There was a sharp intake of breath as Seul got ready to respond. He looked like he had a good answer.

'Tell me—what is THE PURPOSE OF A JANITOR?!' The Librarian demanded instantly before Seul could finish drawing his breath. He exhaled deflatedly.

'To clean after people,' Riyul said.

'And the job of a lawyer?'

'I don't know. To tell people things?'

'To clean up after people too. At least a janitor is not arrogant about what he does. He does his job dutifully, and is absolutely instrumental in society. Lawyers could not exist if people did no wrong. There are lawyers who fight for good. There are lawyers who fight for bad. But if there was no bad? Would we need either lawyer?'

'But if people always cleaned up after themselves, would we ever need a janitor?' Daffodil posited.

The Librarian blinked.

'I always thought about that, but I never said it,' he whispered, scratching his head. 'Young Daffodil, you have won this battle. But you have not won the war.' He slammed down a stick which he had alchemised out of nowhere. 'I will now no longer call Saliva, Saliva, for Daffodil has won my respect.' He turned to Seul. 'What is your name again, child?'

Daffodil observed happily.

'My name...' Seul said, raising his chin and, for some reason, bulging his eyes dramatically, 'is Trill.'

The Librarian and Seul high-fived, laughing.

'Why is my life so weird?' Daffodil muttered.

Chapter 29

Books

'So let me get this straight. You think magic is real?' Zakariyya asked Bartholomew as he turned a corner.

'Not magic. *Alchemy. Transmutation.* The changing of one matter to another.'

Zakariyya sighed.

'Don't be rude, dear,' Clarice said.

'My apologies.'

Bartholomew smiled. He appreciated that while these two had been through hell, and were still going through hell, nonetheless they gave him the chance to explain himself. They were good people.

'So go on, tell us how alchemy works,' Clarice said.

'It's hard to say. I mean, I can't prove this, of course. But I imagine it like the states of matter we studied when we were younger. Typically, we learnt there were three states, right? Solid, liquid, and gas. There are actually more, and scientists are discovering even more every few decades and centuries.'

Zakariyya thought for a moment while weaving through traffic. 'You mean like superfluids?'

Bartholomew raised an eyebrow.

'I used to teach chemistry,' he said meekly.

"What do you know about the states of matter and superfluids?'

'I mean, I don't know how all of them interrelate, but I know these states of matter are not mutually exclusive. Substances can transition from solids to liquids to gases under different conditions, such as with a change in temperature or pressure. Ice might be a good example of this. Give it some heat and it becomes water. More heat and it turns into steam, a gas.'

'Absolutely,' Bartholomew concurred whilst flipping open to one of the dog-eared pages of a black notebook.

'I believe alchemy is the thing that we were made to believe was a myth—an ancient practice involving the unachievable goal of transmuting matter. But—as conspiracy-theory as this sounds of me—I think it's the answer to everything we are searching for. I think alchemy is real. And if we can work out how it works, then we can find Daffodil.'

'How?' asked Zakariyya.

Bartholomew looked up to answer the question, but then appeared to notice something. 'Oh, are we passing through Sparkbrook? Take a left just over there, please,' he said, pointing to a bend coming up once they had exited the roundabout.

'This,' he said once Zakariyya had taken the turn, 'is Barrows Road. Amelio used to live somewhere here. I've come here before to see if I can find any clues. But alas. Never any clues.'

'Sorry,' Clarice said, 'but did you mention that we can work out how alchemy works and that will help us find Daffodil?'

'There are places out there that people have disappeared to throughout history. These places are made using different states of matter, hidden in plain sight, but not as solids or liquids or even gases. Something else. Something unique.'

'But what proof is there for this?' Clarice asked.

'It simple. It's in this book.'

They looked at the black notebook in Bartholomew's hand. It was identical to other black notebooks he had been reading ever since they'd met him. He had a bag-full.

'Bartholomew…' Zakariyya hesitated, glancing from the road to the tattered notebook. 'Where did you find that notebook?'

'Oh,' Bartholomew said, waving the notebook nonchalantly, as though it were obvious. 'Amelio sends them to me.'

Chapter 30

Choices

'Okay, we don't have that long, so let's discuss the plan,' The Librarian said as they came to the end of the beach and approached a row of silvery boulders that faced the sea. Each stone seemed painted with a subtle sheen—clearly slick with ocean mist, and atop each was a small growth of perfect green algae moss. But one boulder stuck out. There was something about it.

'These boulders are the key to getting back to the library,' he explained to Daffodil and Marwa.

'This isn't how you came and found us, then?' Daffodil asked, running her hands over the wet boulder for any possibility of a door.

'No, it is.'

'Wait, what? You said we were not to leave the way you came.'

'I say a lot of things, Daffodil. Only about seven percent of them have ever been true. Did you know for instance that my name isn't really Footstep?'

'Why do you talk in riddles?' Daffodil asked dryly, walking around the boulder, trying to work out how it could possibly be their means of escape. Marwa also seemed unsure.

'People can't betray you if they don't know what you're saying... Right, Uthy?'

Daffodil looked around. 'Who's Uthy?'

'Nobody!'

Daffodil blinked. 'Okay, so how did you get to us again?'

'I managed to locate you through the prism technique. It's quite complicated, but I'm sure Riyul can explain it to you,' The Librarian said, gesturing randomly at Riyul.

'I—what?' Riyul said, looking at them, clearly never having heard of the prism technique in his life.

'Before we do anything else,' Seul said, 'do you think you could help Marwa?'

'Of course, young child. I mean, Riyul was about to give a detailed thesis on the inner workings of prismic locatory techniques, but alas. So, you say she has been iced?'

'Yes. Also, I'm not really a young child.'

'Ah, yes, you are correct, young child. Also, aren't we all young children, really? At heart? What even is age, really? Also! What even-'

'Professor,' Safa interjected, 'or, sorry, Librarian—about Marwa?'

'Ah yes! How could I forget! Yes, I have a theory to help her.'

Marwa looked at The Librarian. This was the moment she had been waiting for, Daffodil thought. Who knows for how long? Daffodil could sense the worry behind her unflinching, impassive demeanour. *Would she choose to now speak? To reveal that the island had begun to de-ice her for some reason?*

How would he 'fix' her? What if something went very badly wrong, considering the state she was in? What if he did not have the answer? Was their entire journey for nothing—would she make it anywhere else before her condition got worse?

'You just need a superfluid plasma water base with a slight fiery intake,' The Librarian said simply.

Safa stared at him.

Marwa's eyes widened. She broke into a huge smirk.

'That's ... so simple—yet makes so much sense,' Safa said incredulously.

Daffodil looked around. Even Seul seemed to be nodding along, smiling too. Clearly, this was totally doable. 'Sorry, is that not hard to fix, then?' Daffodil asked.

'Not at all, as long as the solution brews for long enough,' Safa said, already whipping out some vials of nameless liquids and swirling substances. 'I had just never considered the superfluid starting point. That's such an elegant, simple solution.'

'Simplicity is the key to good alchemy. It's like algebraic formulae. Or coding!' The Librarian exclaimed.

'Coding?' Safa asked.

'Forget I said that. Different place. Anyway, for the mixture— we'll have to let it all sit and infuse.'

'Of course,' Safa said, already pouring away from a plethora of different vials and bottles—many of which Daffodil had never seen before.

'In the meanwhile, the plan. So you both say you're not from this land,' The Librarian said, turning to Daffodil and Riyul.

They nodded.

'Firstly,' The Librarian said, breathing in deeply, 'I have many, many questions. But those can come later. More importantly, if the myths are true, from what I have understood, those who come to this land from the outside quickly forget about their origin. They doubt themselves, and before they know it, they completely question, then reject the existence of anything outside of this place.'

'That's similar to what Haradan told me,' Daffodil nodded.

'That is also terrifying,' Riyul said.

'Yes,' Safa added, still mixing liquids on the ground with Marwa. 'The fact that the government is so against our set of beliefs also does not help, as talking about such possible existences is essentially outlawed. We will have to go back to The City, I feel.'

'Yes,' continued The Librarian, 'Safa and Riyul went to try and speak to Notra, but that route isn't safe anymore. My point, however, was more so that if we are to try and get you back to whence you came, we will need to be fast. Very fast. Because the longer you stay here, the more you may forget yourself and your world outside. For instance, what can you tell me about the outside world?'

'What can I tell you?' Daffodil said. 'I mean, I don't know. There's a sky, and roads, and we have cars. I live on a street with buildings and houses.'

'We have all these things; we don't have cars, though—tell us more,' said The Librarian.

'Er, they have four wheels, and kind of ... take you to where you want to go while you sit on a seat.'

'That sounds like a flying sofa,' Seul said, staring at the sky, envisioning whatever he conceived a car to be. 'Cool!'

'Well, no, it's not a ... it's not a flying sofa. I mean, yes, sure you can go over a hundred miles per hour sitting in a seat, but ... you will stay connected to the ground, and just kind of glide along the road really fast,' Daffodil said.

'Sounds basically like a flying sofa to me,' Seul replied, folding his arms.

'I... No. Seul!' Daffodil said, exasperated, although a little unsure about definitions. She turned to Riyul for help. 'Tell him, Riyul!'

'I... I don't really know about these. Our understanding of cars is very different. In my time, cars don't mean what you say,' Riyul said slowly.

'What do you mean, *my time?*' Daffodil asked, realisation dawning.

'Daffodil, I think we're from very different times and years,' Riyul said.

'What… What year is it for you?'

'The last I remember, it was 1930.'

Daffodil's eyes bulged.

'I thought this would happen,' The Librarian said. 'From your reaction, it seems like you two are split by a large amount of … well, *time*.'

'I can't believe this,' whispered Daffodil slowly. 'We're split by basically a hundred years.'

Seul whispered to Marwa, also slowly, trying to copy Daffodil's speed. 'What's a year?'

She kicked him.

'I mean, things have been blurry since being on the train,' Riyul said, squinting and rubbing his forehead. But I didn't know it'd been that long.'

If Daffodil even wanted to say anything, she couldn't vocalise it.

'We need to get to The City,' The Librarian continued. 'And fast. We have two options. Either we aim to find a way back for you through Notra, or through Skutlish.'

'Notra did try to shoot us,' Riyul said, shaking himself, realising just how urgent the escape was. 'And he seems to push the idea that the outside world is not there, right?'

'We did also steal from him somewhat, and used the queen's flower to track down Marwa, meaning he was also behind the icing,' Safa said.

'Wait,' Daffodil said. 'If you could use the queen's flower to track down Marwa, why couldn't Notra? If he really iced her?'

They all thought about this. Safa shrugged. The Librarian stared at Daffodil intently.

'Unless there's someone else who iced them both,' Daffodil said cautiously. 'And Gerrihend is just…'

'A red herring?' The Librarian asked.

'Sure,' Daffodil concurred.

'Excuse me,' Seul said loudly, coughing three times. 'I must postulate greatly that I for one am not following thy along.'

Safa sighed. 'Seul, I know you want to be more adult, but nobody talks like that.'

'Ah, rats! I have been apprehended! Darn it woman, they weren't to have ever thy known!' he said, shaking his fist dramatically.

'A red herring is like a trick or a false lead,' Riyul explained. 'Also I don't think you're using the word *thy* correctly.'

The Librarian continued watching Daffodil.

She glanced up at him.

Did he realise about the island … and Marwa's voice? Was it connected?

'Daffodil…' The Librarian said slowly. 'Was everything okay on the island before we arrived? Did anything … change?'

Daffodil pursed her lips. He knew something. She glanced at Marwa quickly, whose eyes widened ever so slightly. She looked downward, as though to her throat, and gave the most imperceptible nod of her head. Her voice was still there.

'Yes. I mean no. All fine.'

'So. Do we move forward by going to Skutlish or Notra?' Riyul asked.

'Notra is known amongst the people. Not everyone agrees with the rumours that are spread about his supposed plans, but historically, we've seen he has always cared for his people and looked after them. Skutlish on the other hand is a bit of an unknown. We don't know what he's capable of,' The Librarian said with something akin to a shudder.

The group thought about this.

'So it's either a highly suspect king, or an unknown…' Daffodil stated.

'Skutlish?' Riyul asked.

'Yes, and for what it's worth,' added Safa, 'Notra almost certainly wants to imprison or kill us.'

'Why do you think you prefer trying to speak to Notra over Skutlish?' Riyul asked The Librarian.

'I don't know. I can't really name it. I just have a bad feeling about Skutlish. But it's your choice at the end of the day; we've found Marwa. We can help her. But your escape is your choice. You've heard both sides. What do you choose?'

Everyone looked silently at Riyul and Daffodil.

Daffodil spoke first.

'Based off everything we've seen and heard, I think Skutlish may give us our best chances.'

'I'd have to agree,' said Riyul.

'Okay,' said The Librarian. 'But I think the most important thing is that you polish up on your alchemic skills, so that when you get to Skutlish, you can use the right alc to open a doorway into your world. After you've studied up, we will take a door to The City and find Skutlish's castle; it's connected to the graveyard in the northwest division of The City. We'll create a diversion so you both can see him without the government or any of the police catching you or suspecting what you're up to.'

'You'd create a diversion for us?' Daffodil said, incredulous.

'Imagine no means yes and no means no. What's the answer to your query? Maybe.'

'How does that make se–'

'So, without further ado, let's initiate the first step of our plan. Training on how to find and make doorways to other places.'

Daffodil turned to the left; a wave crashed against the sand. She had grown used to the island's numerous sounds and ambiances… and she felt like she could sense something.

'We're … near one,' she said.

The Librarian raised an eyebrow.

'We're near an exit, aren't we?' she said again. 'I can sense a door nearby. This is how we escape, isn't it?'

'Very good,' he said, tracing an outline on the boulder beside him. A hairline black outline of a curved door began to form in the rock. The outline quickly formed into a pure black doorway, unlike any Daffodil had seen before. It was like looking at a tilted rectangular window directly into the blackness of space.

'This is the door. So, who wants to go first?'

Chapter 31

Doors

Bartholomew, Clarice and Zakariyya parked up and got out of the car. A building sat squat in front of them. It was a woodworkers' and hardware store.

'Please explain again how you think Amelio, all these decades, has been communicating with you,' Zakariyya said as they began walking.

'He sends me these books.'

Bartholomew pulled a small black notebook from his coat pocket.

'I have found them in the most obscure places over the years. It's like they just make their way to me. But they always lead on to the next clue, understanding how he got to where he did. But they're never fully clear. Ambiguous. Just little snippets. As though if he gives away too much about the way to get to where he is, something would happen—I dunno,' Bartholomew said, shrugging. 'I do know one thing, though.'

'What's that?' asked Zakariyya.

'Doors,' he said, flapping the book in front of them. 'That's how they took your Daffodil. Hidden in plain sight. That's the key. If we can understand alchemy, or at least replicate some workings of it, we can transmute a door, like mentioned in one of the notebooks … and bring her back.'

***

'As soon as we arrive at the door to the library,' The Librarian explained as they walked, 'we're one step closer to The City. And that means one step closer to danger.'

The snowy peaks and troughs around them looked just like the area Daffodil and Riyul had first come to when they had met Safa and Marwa, but this must have been somewhere else; the hills they traversed no longer sloped the mountainsides. Here was mainly flatness—a great expanse of nothing except snow and footprints and cold. The walk had been slow but steady. After leaving the island through the odd boulder doorway, they'd ended up a little way away in this very land. It wasn't directly in or around The Librarian's house—as he explained, he had made sure to build his home away from any close-by doorways or 'transmutation portals', as he called them.

'I think we should learn to defend ourselves,' said Riyul.

'Yes, I want to learn to fight. We don't know what might happen when we get to The City. Marwa, Safa, even Seul have alchemy control, which means they can look after themselves. I feel like we should be trained too,' said Daffodil.

'You want to learn alc fighting? Though, to be honest, we just call it fighting; once the weapons exist, they exist, and we don't really refer to them anymore. All fighting is alchemic fighting in this world,' said The Librarian. 'But yes, we can help with that, because once we hit The City, we have to be extremely fast before we are detected.'

'Can we not train them in the library rooms?' Safa asked.

'That could work. I must say, it's been a while since I've done anything there,' said The Librarian fondly.

'How do you have space to fight or train to fight in a library?' asked Daffodil.

'I always thought of you as a pacifist,' said Riyul.

'I do not *believe* in fighting,' said The Librarian. 'But sadly, we will only have one shot at getting you out of here, and those who do not want that to happen will have alchemic weapons at their disposal.

'Also, the weapons are cool. Some alchemists have managed to create orbs that contain little bursts of each element. Others have created battlestaves of fire. My favourite rumour, now confirmed by these two, is that the king has somehow created swords of shadows. I do not encourage fighting, but I can appreciate that a shadow sword would be pretty darn awesome.'

Daffodil kicked a clump of snow, imagining what a shadow sword would even be like, and remembering Marwa's practice on the beach—her onslaught of thrusts and parries. She wondered how her voice was.

During a slight lull in the conversation, Daffodil glanced back to check up on Marwa as they trudged through the snow. She hadn't spoken to anyone else, it seemed—nor made it clear that she'd been de-iced by the island.

Daffodil gave her a thumbs up and a smile, to which Marwa shook her head.

'You two have gotten a lot better at sensing doors, my love,' Safa said. 'Have you understood how their sounds work yet?'

'Their sounds?' Riyul asked.

'Everything has a sound,' Safa said. 'In your world, even people have sounds, right?'

'Do you mean like accents?' Riyul asked, petting Eli gently.

'Er...' Safa said, unsure.

'Yes, we still have accents here,' The Librarian continued. 'Accents, along with someone's voice and expressions, tell you all about a person—it's their unique sound print. In the same way, even the doorways in our land all have their own unique distinguishing features. And it all takes place in the realm of sound. If you listen extremely carefully, you can hear and make sense of these sounds. You know when a door just wants to be found. You know where it leads to. You become one with the land around it.'

'I guess it's a bit like forestry,' Daffodil said, thinking back to her dream of woodlands and the flickering light. Surely, there'd be signs in nature of what animals had been nearby and what trees were what species.

'Sure, forestry,' The Librarian said, nodding brightly, then looking at Seul and shaking his head.

'So what you're saying,' Riyul said, 'is if we can hear the doorways, or make sense of the sound patterns that make up this world around us...'

'Then you can learn to travel to different areas and go to different places,' Safa finished.

'Look, that's the house!' Seul exclaimed, pointing at a black speck that had just climbed over on the horizon.

'Yes, it is,' The Librarian said cheerily. 'I should probably make it clear now, Daffodil, that we are being watched.'

'What? We're being watched?' Daffodil asked, looking around quickly, thoughts of Marwa scattering momentarily.

'Yep. Look high above. Can you see those shimmers in the sky?'

She squinted up.

'I think so. What does that mean? Why didn't you tell us this before?'

'There wasn't really a need to tell you. Also, I did tell some of you. Also, we weren't being watched before. Also, how do you even know we're being watched?'

'You said it!'

'That's true. We are being watched. I was not wrong. Interestingly, this hadn't been the case on the island. Anyway, what it means is that we may have a very difficult period ahead. It means whoever is watching us may know our next move—one thing I cannot say, however, is if they have the ability to hear us; see us, sure—a scrying device is something I've long imagined could be created to see across distances–but *hear*? I don't know. We do know one thing, though.'

'What's that?'

'The City government, or someone, has their eyes on us, and any newcomers with us.'

Daffodil and Riyul looked at each other.

'What doesn't make sense to me, though,' The Librarian continued, 'is why the creator of the scrying pool would allow the shimmers of observation to be so easily visible.'

'You don't mean,' Safa said, 'that they want us to realise they're watching?'

'I don't know. Maybe.'

'Why would someone want to make it clear that they're watching us?'

The Librarian thought on this. 'It could be a triple trap.'

'A triple trap?' Seul asked.

'Yes, a triple trap, gosh darn it!' The Librarian said. 'Don't they teach you anything in school?'

'Sadly, he doesn't get to go to school anymore,' Safa explained.

'Well, that's ridiculous. If only you had a teacher who could teach you.'

Everyone looked at him. He seemed to not notice, or pretended to not notice, and continued.

'Anyway, a triple trap is just what it sounds like; in this instance, they might want to see us, but if they tried to see without making it obvious, or without us realising they could see us, then we would realise they could see us. But if they made it obvious they could see us, then we'd question if they could really see us, because it'd be too obvious that they could see us, so really ... Can they see us? And what is seeing anyway? And who IS SALIVA?'

'Not me,' said Seul.

'Okay,' The Librarian said to Seul. 'So the trap is that they want us to know they can see us, and for us to think that it's a ruse, but really it is not.'

'What is it then?' Riyul asked.

'A ruse, of course!'

Everyone seemed quite baffled.

'What's the solution, then?' Safa asked.

'There is no solution yet. We have to keep playing the game and be smart about it, whether they can see us or not, whether they know we know or not, and whether they know that we know that they might know about our knowing of the triple trap...'

'Or ... not?' finished Safa.

'Or not!' exclaimed The Librarian, clicking his fingers in joy at someone finally understanding his nonsensical train of thought.

Safa took a deep breath as they finally approached the door to the house. 'Okay, that was intellectually stimulating and utterly exhausting. Now, I think it's time to teach you two how to fight.'

Chapter 32

A Mission

Zear paced through the snow.

Swiftly.

Silently.

He had been searching for the thieves, trying all tracing methods possible—particularly after their little skirmish in the palace, this was personal now.

Yet to no avail. It seemed they had disappeared off the face of Aethril to some uncharted territory.

That was, of course, until Gerrihend had mentioned coming to the Land of Snow.

He continued trudging, staff in hand. Step after step after step.

Just a little longer. If there was one thing Zear prided himself in, it was conscientiousness. A job needed to be done. And it needed to be done well. It was an honour to do one's duty properly, and to uphold respect for Notra Gerrihend.

Zear walked with his back a little straighter, remembering his purpose.

The king had given commands. And they would be executed.

Chapter 33

Rooms

The library was spread across three open-plan rooms, half-walled into two squares and one longer rectangular shape. The living room of the cabin, which also contained a bed and small kitchen area consisting of a simple wash basin and shelves, made up half of the house in the long rectangular shape. Directly adjacent through the middle was a wall, separating the other half of the house: the library, which connected the three rooms together in a sort of horse-shoe shape, two box rooms and the adjacent longer central room.

Upon entering the library portion of the house, Daffodil took Marwa to the side.

'Your voice, what's happened?'

Marwa shook her head.

'It's gone again?'

She nodded.

'Oh no. It must have something to do with getting off the island, then. Do you think it's something to do with a trace?'

Marwa nodded slowly, indicating she wasn't sure yet, but now might not be the best time to speak, considering they didn't know the full situation, nor who may be listening.

'We'll figure it out,' Daffodil reassured her, clutching her shoulder briefly, then left to rejoin The Librarian on the tour.

The others—Safa, Marwa and Seul—busied themselves with odd jobs and tasks in the other half of the house; Safa and Marwa were still working delicately on Marwa's 'superfluid restoration balm', and Seul was trying his best to help, but apparently kept breaking things.

Daffodil's mind didn't leave Marwa, though, even when she found arrays of books she hadn't seen earlier; the living room had also contained many shelves and even random piles of books, but this half of the house was incredibly well-ordered. Books after books after books, all hardbound in varying kinds of coarse leather, lined the shelves. The first box room contained books with a lot of dark green as well as black leather spines. Most, however, had no markings, etchings or engravings on the covers.

'Firstly,' The Librarian said, 'I want you two to find the door to your training room.'

Daffodil walked amongst the shelves, listening carefully.

What was it about the island that gave Marwa her voice back?

She continued thumbing the books, and closed her eyes. There, in front of her in the darkness of her shut eyes, was a pulsating rectangle. She picked out a book with a particularly appealing crisp emerald green leather cover.

The moment she touched the book, it began to shake and quiver. The books around it also began to move subtly, until a perfect rectangle of books were vibrating.

'How did you do that?' Riyul asked.

'I … can just tell,' Daffodil said.

The Librarian pushed on the rectangle of books, which was conveniently the size of a traditional doorway, and it *opened*.

All the books moved as one solid door, and white light flooded the library room.

Chapter 34

A Log Cabin

White. White. White. White. White.

Endless white as far as the eye could see.

Zear slogged on and on. They couldn't be far now.

Yet this trek felt endless.

Maybe the trace was wrong.

Could the king have been wrong about where they were?

And just when he began doubting, as Zear plodded and plodded and plodded over one more snowy hill—something appeared in the furthest distance of the horizon.

There it was. It had to be. A log cabin.

Chapter 35

Training

'Alchemy started off innocently enough, but as you have probably realised, there is a lot of power when you can control the elements. As such, alchemists became more powerful, and weapons were created. I believe it's like how guns became popular in your world. And alchemic weapons are not outlawed in The City. So we may as well know how to use one.' The Librarian said this whilst standing in the middle of a beige training room. The walls were padded with a soft material that was not rubber or leather; Daffodil could not work out exactly what it was.

Around them were tables and holders and drawers full of wooden sticks and other weaponry.

The Librarian walked over and picked up a wooden sword.

'These are completely non-painful,' he said cheerily.

Daffodil frowned. 'Is non-painful a word?'

'I'm not sure, but I feel like anything can become a word if it is used often enough, or if you add a hyphen in it,' Riyul said, smiling.

The Librarian whacked him over the head with the sword.

'Ow!!'

'That's for calling Seul, Saliva!' The Librarian screamed.

'I... You... What???' Riyul replied, flabbergasted.

'I thought you said they're non-painful?' Daffodil asked.

'Oh, come on, people,' The Librarian said, exasperated. 'Non-painful isn't a word! Here, take this.' He threw a wooden staff with a red orb atop it to Riyul, who caught it in one hand and turned, slicing the air.

'Hit me with the staff.'

'I would love to,' said Riyul, turning to The Librarian while rubbing his head. 'But I wouldn't feel comfortable just RANDOMLY hitting you with a stick.'

'So you won't hit me with the staff. What about if I hit the staff with me?'

'Huh?'

The Librarian leapt at Riyul.

Riyul quickly raised the staff to protect himself, and The Librarian fell onto the staff, where it connected with his shoulder as he landed on the ground. Instantly, he was covered in an orange glow.

'Now, if I don't counteract this in the space of around ten Missisipis,' he said, the glow getting brighter every second, 'I will catch fire.'

He walked calmly to the table and picked up a blue orb. Lifting it alone diminished the orange glow around him. The Librarian then threw the orb at Riyul's chest.

Riyul reacted instantly. As though he could see the projectile in slow motion, he leaned back, and as it just flew over him, he used his staff like a hockey stick to hit the orb midair and fling it to the wall.

It crashed and caused a burst of ice to cascade upon contact.

'That would have frozen you in place at the feet,' The Librarian said. 'You have good reactions.'

He turned to Daffodil. 'Pick a weapon. We go again.'

They fought with projectiles and battlestaves and swords that shimmered in different colours; each time there was any chance of danger, The Librarian counteracted the element with another weapon of the opposite kind. Earth and Air worked in opposition; Fire and Water in opposition.

The Librarian moved with unbelievable poise and skill. He ducked and weaved and slid and rolled as smoothly as a ninja when Daffodil aimed, threw, thrust and parried. He never hurt her, yet she couldn't land a single blow.

What felt like hours went by in this manner, Daffodil sweating from the exertion.

'You need to be able to control your centre of gravity, and you will never lose. Your balance is everything. Balance physically. Balance mentally. It's all about sensing your surroundings and staying calm. Now, both of you,' he said.

Riyul raised an eyebrow, then went over and grabbed some orbs of differing elements.

Daffodil continued attacking with her staff, incredibly accurately, but failed to land a blow. At the same time, Riyul threw elemental orbs. Even with two onslaughts, The Librarian moved with inhuman speed, just about to be caught by an orb when he would spin or duck out of its range with lightning reflexes.

'Okay,' he said. 'Now that I've shown you what can be done with some practice and the right learning, let's get you both some training partners.'

Seul and Safa joined them whilst Marwa continued working on the restoration balm.

Why had she lost her ability to speak again?

They trained for what felt like hours. The Librarian coached and gave tips incessantly, and thankfully did not even speak in riddles—for the most part.

By the time it was over, Daffodil was exhausted, but she felt much more confident in her ability to defend herself. She could avoid most attacks, sense an alchemic projectile coming, and even land the right elemental orbs herself.

'Librarian,' Daffodil said once it was just her and him left in the room. 'Could we try one more run with the fire element?'

Chapter 36

Zear

Alchemic fighting is all about balance and poise.
Control your centre of gravity, and you
control every fight.

The Art of Alchemic Fighting

Once they were back in the first library room, The Librarian having equipped them both with tiny orbs of each element for their coming travels, he told them to have a look at one final section of the library before the last leg of their journey.

'This is the closing stage now. Your mental training is just as important as your physical training. This room is the lore room,' he said. 'I've collected in this room everything I have ever been able to get my hands on, forming this history and stories of our land.'

Through another winding doorway passage, they walked into a humongous cavernous open-plan library that seemed even bigger than what they had experienced previously.

'Sorry, the law room?' Riyul asked, astonished. The Librarian began perusing through the floor-to-ceiling shelves the opposite side of where they stood.

'No—*lore*,' the librarian said, enunciating the *r*, 'as in the knowledge of these lands, sometimes called Aethril.'

Daffodil opened a book to a page that had been dogeared previously.

The first thing that struck Daffodil instantly was that the text was written in English—or something akin to typical English handwriting; the words were a little foreign in their script compared to the typical flourishes and cursive style she had come to expect, but it was definitely the same English she'd grown up with and learnt in school. The present page was the start of a new chapter entitled *Time*.

Time is thought to not exist in this Aethril. As such, keeping compendiums of historical notes is a little like trying to listen for the signs of a door without having the sense of hearing. One may of course attempt to utilise their other senses, such as their sight, their sense of balance, their sense of bodily location—but without hearing, it is near impossible.

Because of the lack of time, there is little that noticeably grows. Growth, however, is not impossible to find. And in these instances, these minute clues, we find our first indications of time.

***

Zear gently opened the door. It had taken a while to disable the alarm mechanisms, but he wasn't trained for nothing.

Allowing the door to flitter open, he stepped back and flattened himself against the outside of the building, so the inhabitants might think the wind had somehow opened the door, and would come over to check or close it.

Eventually, lo and behold, no one else than the woman herself appeared. The one who had smartly lashed him to the wall and stunned him with her purple smoke. However, this time he was ready.

As she opened the door, puzzled, he built up the shadows and smoke needed to disarm her. She poked her head outside and looked around.

Left.

And then right.

Her eyes grew wide as she spotted him.

Not waiting another moment, he released the shot, and the smoke curled around her, wisping and knocking her unconscious.

Zear smiled beneath his obsidian wrappings.

He knew this woman. The woman that used to work in the palace. What was her name? Safa.

A traitor, it seemed.

'We'll see what the king thinks of you,' he whispered, and then peered into the cabin.

***

'Interesting, isn't it?' The Librarian said, looking over Daffodil's shoulder at the book.

'Yes. But I don't understand something. How is this in English?' Daffodil asked.

'Good question. Did you ever consider how we are all speaking English?'

'Erm, no, actually.'

'The origin of this world, as some authors have called Aethril, appears to have been from your world's England. And so the first inhabitants, if we believe this to be the correct narrative, would have been English, speaking English. Until now, English is still more or less all we know.'

'That's fascinating,' Riyul said. 'There are other languages out there, from our world, as you call it. But you clearly don't have other languages here... Do you have a name for our world, too?'

'Some call it Earth,' said The Librarian.

'Oh. right. Does that mean if we were to teach you, say, French or Arabic from our Earth, then that would introduce a whole new language to this ... Aethril?'

'Possibly, yes.'

'Oui bonjour.'

'I prefer the term *Librarian*.'

Daffodil walked over to another room which contained, again, many black covers, but also a variety of deep purple and indigo shades scattered throughout the shelves. This room was deeper into the library, and the soft hubbub of noise from Safa, Marwa and Seul quietened further. She picked out one of the indigo cover books and began reading around a third of the way through:

I wish I could work out how long I've been here now. All I know is that my old life is well and truly gone. There doesn't seem to be any tangible escape. And in all honesty, I have felt the effects of this land pull from my want to escape.

After some slumbers, I rouse and think, to what am I even attempting to leave to? On these painfully blissful occasions, I have to draw upon all the meagre strength within me to go on and keep pushing and remembering and trying to believe that my old life not only was, but is, and has meaning out there—for me to return to, and worth returning to.

***

Zear entered the house one careful step at a time. There didn't seem to be much here besides books.

He kept an ear out for conversation.

Inching forward, he turned corners deftly, waiting for the first sign of an ambush.

Then he heard the most unexpected sound. Was that … a child?

***

'Ah, the biographies section,' The Librarian said.

'Who wrote these books?'

'Good question. The simple answer is, I don't know. This is one of the most important reasons for bringing you here. If you read others' lives, you won't make the same mistakes or fall in the same pitfalls. Your memory will be as strong as your knowledge. Most authors stay anonymous. Of course, the government tries to wipe them and remove them from existence as soon as they are found in The City. That's why, as soon as I discover one, I bring it here, where nobody comes in.' He glared towards the kitchen.

'Because the authors are anonymous, who's to say that the same person didn't write many of these books? The black notebooks are the most interesting. I would pay attention to their writings most of all.'

As he spoke, a soft thud came from some distant part of the library. Shrugging, he led them on to the final room. This third room, as Daffodil slowly looked around, was very different to the first two. It was similar in size to the first, however, unlike the first or second, the books were not uniform in colouring. They appeared instead in a smattering of four distinct colours: blue, red, brown, and white or cream. The white covers were certainly off, with most resembling a more ivory shade, but the general thought behind these covers was ascertainable. There were also other colours scattered throughout.

'I'm guessing these are the different elements for alchemy, then?' Riyul said, walking around, taking in the different books.

'Mhmm.' The Librarian nodded. 'Water, Fire, Earth and Air. Interestingly, others have written about hotness, coldness, dryness and moistness as elements to be studied also. This concept of four pervades the sciences for some reason. Now pay attention to this, it's important:

'There have been some who have actually posited a fifth element in alchemy. *Space.*'

He gave Riyul and Daffodil a beaker of fluid each and gestured to a doorway nearby. 'When we learn to *include* space in our alchemy, we can *connect* space.'

He told Riyul to pour his fluid onto the nearest door. As soon as he did so, they saw a shimmer from beyond. The Librarian opened the door.

They were now looking into the front of the house, and could see Safa and Marwa and Seul in the kitchen. He closed the door.

'Space, connected. Once you're in Skutlish's castle, he'll possibly send you back to your world; if not, then use this same alc—I call it gateway fluid—on the doorway you sense is the right one. I'll give you throwing vials to make it easier. If he *has been* experimenting with travelling between here and Earth, then these vials will latch on to that connection and open the doorway for you to escape.'

He walked back towards the depth of the library.

'This part of the library is cut off from the rest. It'll be quiet and perfect for study—no sounds will penetrate, unless there's an Aethrilquake.'

'So,' Daffodil said, 'escaping...'

'Yes. Space may be the most important element to understanding this land and escaping it. With it, we may be able to dismantle the power structures that confine us, and perhaps finally see the truth manifest.'

He paused, turned and looked directly at them.

'Why the library? Why all this? Because we are all stuck here. I'm sure of it. The answer to making everyone understand the truth is in these books and the knowledge within. I know escape is possible. But I worry that's not everything. That there's a larger game at play.'

'I'm looking for something in these books,' he said, touching the spines fondly. 'Something to not just get *you two* out. But to get all of us out.'

Daffodil watched The Librarian and Riyul.

Riyul was taking it all in, seeming to grasp so much, so quickly. To Daffodil, it was all interesting and, of course, absolutely important. But there was one thing she could not get out of her head.

His age...

Daffodil hadn't spoken about it—but it did not stop playing around in her head. Riyul really had lived lifetimes here in confinement. He still didn't know what year it was outside where she was from—when she was from.

'What do you think, Daffodil?' The Librarian asked expectantly, staring at her.

'Sorry, what was that?'

'The City. I don't think there is much use in you reading up on a lot of alchemy with the time you have, nor am I sure how useful it'll be. We'll study alchemy, but given the rush, it's perhaps most salient if you look through some biographies before we go, to accustom yourself to some of the hurdles to expect. After that, we can finalise the details of our plan.'

As he spoke, he waltzed around the library, picking books out without looking.

'A little alchemy, some biographies, a sprinkle of lore.'

He collected around five or six books and dropped them into Daffodil and Riyul's arms.

'Put them all together, and then we'll have an egg. My egg books are in the kitchen, actually; would you like to read those?'

'No,' Daffodil and Riyul said at the same time.

'Great,' The Librarian said, beaming. 'I didn't want to share those secrets anyway. Now, something absolutely vital. We need to talk about your memories.'

***

Zear approached the young boy.

It must only be him and Safa here. Now that he thought back, she may have indeed had a child. Was this him? Who knew?

He looked incredibly young. Though, looks could be deceiving.

The boy looked up and cocked his head. 'You're not my mummy,' he said, lip quivering.

'No, I'm not, but don't worry—'

'I'm not worrying,' the boy said, losing all innocence of youth. 'But you should be.'

Instantly, Zear cursed himself for falling into a trap. He reflexively stepped diagonally—not forward, not backwards, not sideways—anyone aiming at him would have anticipated that. By only a hair's breadth did a vial fly past him.

An explosion of ice shattered near his right shoulder.

He spun on himself, staff in hand, and flicked up a wave of darkness, blocking the flurry of incoming projectiles which collided harmlessly in front of him.

Who's shooting these?

He squinted through the shadowed tint of his shield. It could only hold for so long.

There, in the corner of the room.

Was that Safa again?

It was indeed. He aimed another orb of shadow at her, this time ensuring it would be strong enough to truly knock her out–when it felt like a boulder rocked him sideways.

He looked down at his side and realised an actual huge rock had collided with him and sent him sprawling into a stack of books.

The young boy picked up another vial from the nearby shelf and took aim.

Winded, Zear rolled and sprang up, using his staff to further his momentum, and stood, getting a clear view of the room.

Safa hid behind a workstation in a corner. Who knew what other orbs and projectiles she had hidden away?

This boy had somehow mastered the art of earth manipulation. And he was flinging boulders for fun. Impressive.

Nonetheless, Safa and the boy would be manageable, now that they were in full view. He flicked up another shield of darkness to block an incoming boulder and ice shard in speedy succession.

Dropping the shield, he prepared another orb of darkness.

But there was a nagging at the back of his mind.

Safa... in the corner... hiding.

That was normal—why put yourself in harm's way?

But this boy. Why was he in the open? Did he think Zear wouldn't harm him?

He had already gone through the trap...

Unless this was more than just a trap. Was there something more than a double-cross?

For the briefest of moments, Zear thought back to what he knew of Safa.

And he remembered Marwa.

Of course, by then it was too late.

As his eyes widened in realisation, Marwa blasted through the wall between Safa and the boy. A large vial in hand, she aimed and flung it with impossible precision right at his torso. There was no time to extinguish the shadow orb and build a shield, so Zear simply sidestepped just before the vial collided with the wall behind him, producing a dense cloud of black smoke.

Zear flashed a wicked smile.

These sisters were good. And the boy too.

Let's see how they dealt with this...

Zear spun around as fast as the whirlwinds themselves and brought the shadows together. Aiming a dagger of pure darkness at the corner of the room, he stepped forward into the onslaught. The shadows flew like an arrow—straight and true—and crashed into the corner of the room, bringing down rubble and debris almost directly on to Marwa.

In this manner, Zear shot shadow after shadow until the sisters had no choice but to retreat into another room, Seul having run in before them.

Let's not forget why we've been sent, Zear reminded himself as he scanned the building. He continued shooting small orbs at Marwa and Safa and Seul—one after the other, each ducking and sidestepping just in time. He sped up the pace, continually shooting, until he hit Marwa with a small orb on the arm, spinning her in place. He shot another orb at the books beside Safa, causing them to collapse over her, and, capitalising on the momentary lull, he turned and scanned the room once more.

'Where is he?' Zear bellowed.

No response.

A sharp pain struck his arm. Like a million daggers, the intensity grew and grew.

It built to a crescendo as he looked down at the ice shards that had struck him. Marwa stood in the distance with a ghost of a smirk dancing on her lips.

If they were here, then surely The Librarian would not be far... And if he were indeed here...

Zear roared, wielding his staff. Turning once more to gather his energies, he prepared one final attack.

They must be preparing for The City.

He dodged and ducked his way to the entrance, clutching both staff and arm in one hand as blood began seeping through his tunic sleeve.

Well, may as well speed them up on their journey.

With one look back at the chaos and rubble around, he slipped out, but not before sending one last shot. One final shot that required everything he had and all the expertise he had mastered from his teacher and teacher's teacher. But this shot was a little different; for his final projectile, he sent a whirlwind.

***

'When you do meet others on Aethril—let's just use that term for simplicity's sake, though I have my misgivings—one of the biggest things to be careful of is your memory.'

'What do you mean?' asked Riyul.

'Because memories fade, when you start to speak to people, don't believe everything they say. Heck, maybe even don't believe everything I say! Actually no, never believe anything I say. I'm only right about three percent of the time.'

'I think you're going off track,' Daffodil said.

'Ah yes, sorry. Oooh, was that a pun?'

'N... yes?'

'Ah. I would have believed you if you had said y... no, but not n... yes. Seems like a quadruple trap to me. Anywhom, you may *misremember* the past because that is the nature of how the world works here. Your memories cannot be trusted. I have read about many people who have found themselves on Aethril from outside. They misremember conversations, and how are they to know their memory is deceiving them? Then this grows. They lapse in memories. They can't remember how they got here, and eventually, they begin to doubt themselves. And eventually ... they think they had a completely different life to what is on the outside.'

'Doesn't anyone try explaining the truth to such people?' Riyul asked.

'I'm not sure. Though I feel that for many, to explain the truth would be to take away the very existence they've conjured up. It would break their minds. Perhaps even they'd go insane.'

'So eventually they become people who have no recollection of the outside world?'

'Yes.' He nodded. 'Regarding this, I am almost positive. For instance, Riyul, what can you tell me about your past?'

'My past? I mean, what do you want to know? I have a wife. Kids.'

'How many?'

'How many?' Riyul laughed. But then he stopped laughing. 'I know how many kids I have.'

'Okay. Tell me about them. How many? What are their names?'

'I...' Riyul faltered.

The Librarian looked at them both. He gave Riyul the chance to speak, but nothing came out. Daffodil and The Librarian waited.

'My wife died,' Riyul said eventually. 'As for my children, I don't remember them now. They're starting to fade. But I know I had kids.' He took a deep breath.

'I'm sorry,' The Librarian said softly. 'But this is precisely my point. Your memory has already been affected. Do not fear, however—all is not lost. We are going to get you both out. And when we do, we can do something for the rest of us here.'

Riyul looked down at the desk, clearly wanting deeply to recall his family.

'We'll figure this out,' The Librarian said.

And Daffodil realised she might not have her family with her at this moment. She may not have her little brother or her parents, but she had their memories. She hadn't been here as long as Riyul. She was sure of that much. But she knew her past.

Looking around the library, she considered her position, and the journey she'd made thus far. She was surrounded by friends who had helped her beyond anything she could have ever asked. All she had left to do was to get to The City. Beside her, she could almost imagine her little brother cheering her on. He would have loved a library like this, with knowledge like this and books like this. She envisaged him sitting there, his head buried in a book, and smiled.

And so they began. They spent as long as they could, a time without time, quickly, briefly, cautiously learning, studying and planning their escape—discussing everything The Librarian had to offer.

They prepared the mixtures needed for all the steps of their plan, which hinged on getting to Skutlish's castle. They spoke about the path through The City; they considered the diversion required and how everyone was to play their part–if Marwa could make it in her condition before her balm was ready.

The final stretch of her journey was in sight.

Daffodil was getting back to her family. She'd make sure of that. She settled into her chair, deciding once and for all that she couldn't control everything, but she could control how prepared she was. In that, there was hope.

In the distance, soft murmuring sounds morphed into noticeable bubbling and crashing.

'Can you hear sounds?' Daffodil asked hesitantly.

Suddenly, Seul ran in, shouting, 'Zear's attacked!'

Chapter 37

Riddles

I don't actually think Aethril is as large as some presume. Oftentimes we simply believe the words of others and don't thereafter go and explore ourselves. But are there actually vast lands of snow and desert, or the same ones repeated? Discovering the existence of the Conductor, as some have whispered, has to be the key to true escape.

Unnamed Black Notebook #1, remembrance thirteen

Bartholomew, Clarice and Zakariyya stood in Bartholomew's living room, facing a single rectangular wooden frame.

Littered around them were around two hundred vials and beakers with various liquids and fluids within, each containing a varying shade, encompassing every colour of the rainbow and more.

Zakariyya's hair was singed. Clarice had burnt her fingertips multiple times. And Bartholomew hadn't slept in around three days.

They continued staring at the wooden frame, no door necessarily attached. It was still completely see-through.

Bartholomew flicked through the black notebook again, frustrated. 'We're missing something. We have to be missing something.'

As he stopped turning the pages, his eyes lit up and he began reading an excerpt aloud. 'The hidden key for alchemic restoration into planes without these properties usually seen, is superfluidity. Utilising all the previous techniques,' he said, eyes twinkling, 'an appreciation of superfluids will be the final piece of the puzzle.'

***

'I can't believe you were in a fight with Zear and we didn't even know,' Daffodil said. Her mouth opened to say more, but closed again, speechless, enraged. They hiked through the snow with their things. As soon as Seul had come and told them about the attack, they had gathered their belongings and left. The cabin wasn't safe right now.

'I told you the library was big,' said The Librarian.

She dismissed him with an impatient wave of her hand. 'We still did nothing,' she muttered, rigid with fury at herself.

'Also, I think you've literally never told us that,' said Riyul.

'And anyway, how is it so big that we couldn't hear a mini-war taking place and half of your rooms being demolished?' asked Daffodil.

'Hey, what can I say.' The Librarian shrugged.. 'It takes a lot of talent to be able to study as hard as we did all whilst missing the action. That requires a lot of discipline and talent if you ask me. It's like when you're preparing for an exam. All you want to do is go out and play in the garden or do something active, right? Well, the fun thing would have been to fight. But instead, we studied. We were reading instead of fighting! That requires serious self-control. You should be proud of yourselves.'

'But it wasn't deliberate,' said Daffodil, unconvinced.

'Speak for yourself!' The Librarian exclaimed.

'The main thing is that you three are okay,' said Riyul, ignoring The Librarian's nonsensical connections.

'We're fine,' Seul said chirpily. 'We thought Zear had us for a second, but Mum and Aunt Marwa owned him. It was an amazing plan, but really it was Aunt Marwa that got us out of it in the end. She shot him with straight ice shards. Like, how cool is that?'

Daffodil grinned. 'Pun?'

Seul grinned back at her, matching her energy. 'Yeah.'

As Daffodil walked over to speak more to The Librarian, Seul slowly turned to Safa and whispered, 'Mum, what's a pun?'

She shook her head.

'As you said,' The Librarian began, 'the main thing is we got out of there when we did. Who knows who might be coming for us now.'

'I really felt like we were making some progress,' said Daffodil, clenching her jaw.

'We are,' Riyul replied. 'We'll get home. It's just a minor setback. We'll get to The City and find a doorway out.'

Daffodil nodded and continued walking, her back hunched.

Safa had explained how they had indeed used a triple-trap the moment she suspected Zear at the door. Thankfully, nobody was particularly injured. Whatever Zear had come for, it hadn't been to kill.

'How did he manage to conjure a whirlwind?' The Librarian asked. 'It took out half the library. But how? That requires immense power. Clearly, he wasn't there to kill, otherwise he would have just done it.'

'Maybe he learnt it from someone,' Riyul said.

'There are very few people who have that level of knowledge and alchemic ability,' The Librarian responded. 'But I suppose it's possible...'

'So, how is the alchemic restoration balm coming along?' Riyul said as they trekked through the snow.

'Still needs a few more manipulations, I think,' Safa said, looking over at Marwa; she was walking slower now, wincing with every step.

'You know something I don't understand?' Daffodil said to Seul, who had diligently tended to both his mother and aunt after the attack, and now bounced around making jokes and comments that didn't always connect.

'My age?' Seul replied. 'How to make grumbugs become munjugs? The radius of a square? Why The Librarian started calling me Saliva? Why my mum keeps pretending she doesn't find it funny? How to-'

'No,' Daffodil interjected before he could take in a second deep breath. 'I don't understand how you knew the whirlwind was coming before we got separated.'

'Really?' he responded, raising an eyebrow. 'You're in a world different to your own, surrounded by strangers,' he said, now whispering, 'one of which is most certainly mad, whose name nobody seems to even know-'

'My name's Trill!!' The Librarian called out from the front of the group.

'HOW do you keep doing that?!' Seul exclaimed, waving his arms frantically.

'I don't keep doing that,' The Librarian said, striding calmly.

'You don't?' Seul said from the back.

'I *do not*.'

'No, I know what *don't* means. I mean, how do you not do that? Also, you do not even know what I was saying *how do you keep doing that* to.'

'Salivation,' The Librarian began, shaking his head like he was about to explain addition for the hundredth time.

'It's Saliva!' Seul exclaimed. 'I mean, it's Seul!'

'Hey, hey, I'm here to call you by the name you choose; I don't believe in calling you Saliva anymore. Isn't Salivation much more sophisticated?'

'But that's not my name.'

'What? It's not?!'

'My name is Seul,' Seul said, exasperated.

The Librarian pondered over this for the duration of three footsteps. 'Look, really, what is a name?'

'Oh no, please not this again.'

'Hey! You wanted to become all grown up. Time for some big thoughts, my friend! Now, aren't names just social constructs?'

'Sure, but you can't just call people by *not* their names.'

'Okay. You win. But I'd like to give you a fun nickname, to ensure we have our own bond.'

Seul considered this. 'Okay, sure.'

'Seline.'

'No. That's too long.'

'Sylvester.'

'What? No. And that's too similar to Saliva.'

'Okay, what about Sylvia?'

'Oh, come on, leave the poor boy alone. Does nobody ever challenge your craziness?' Riyul interjected, casting a disapproving glance at The Librarian. 'You say the most nonsensical things. You are the oddest mentor figure I've ever met.'

The Librarian stared at Riyul in mock horror.

'I mean, yes, you're helping us so profoundly—'

'You're welcome, by the way,' The Librarian said.

'You're helping us so profoundly,' Riyul continued without missing a beat, 'which is wonderful. But then you're also making fun of the youngest member of the group. I don't know how acceptable, or even normal, that is.'

The group slowed their hike through the snow, watching the new development. Safa and Marwa continued along, both watching and adjusting liquids in different tiny beakers—somehow without spilling a drop—even whilst walking.

'Sure, yes, I get it. You're mad. You've been cooped alone for who knows how long. That's still no reason to tease people—especially not young Seul.'

The Librarian opened his mouth to speak, but then shut it. Slowly, he broke into a smile.

'You're right. I hadn't realised. I'm sorry.'

The entire group stared at The Librarian.

'What? I know how to apologise. We don't always realise when we go too far.'

'Alright, awkwardness aside, I'm going to talk to *you* now,' Seul said, turning to Daffodil—pointedly trying not to look at The Librarian, nor Riyul. 'Where were we? Ah yes, sorry, yes, the dream.'

He thought for a moment, chewing his lip—then frowned. 'You know, to be perfectly honest with you, I can't totally explain it. I don't really know the science behind it, or if there even is any. All I know is sometimes, my dreams have actually come true. Sometimes I just get ideas, you know? I see things during a dream, then I may even forget about what I saw, but later it will come true or happen as—or close to—as I saw it.'

'You have visions?' Daffodil asked, somewhat dubious.

'I don't know if I'd call them visions, exactly. More like things I see which are almost directly what happens in the future.'

Daffodil blinked. 'So… visions?'

'I mean, if you want to call them that.'

'I think we're here,' said Safa, cutting the unfollowable train of half-sensical conversation.

Over the crest of distant snow capped hills and troughs shimmered distant rectangles that must have been doors. They were ringed by varying hues of ever-changing light, like an aurora miniaturised.

'And so we come to the three doors,' The Librarian said melodramatically.

'Why is your voice so deep all of a sudden?' said Seul.

The Librarian stared at him. Then looked away. 'I was trying to add a bit of suspense,' he mumbled.

'Sorry—the three doors?' asked Daffodil, although Riyul looked like he was thinking the same thing; he probably hadn't asked in case he was next in line to be teased.

'Yes,' The Librarian said, more serious now. 'Notice how throughout all of our lore, as well as throughout various aspects of your world, the number *three* seems to have profound importance in terms of riddles, logic and sequencing? The famed example of the bridge or boat riddles comes to mind.'

'Boat riddle?' Riyul said, abandoning any attempts at furtiveness.

'Oh, I remember reading this,' Daffodil said, falling into step with The Librarian. 'Imagine you have a fox, a chicken and a sack of grain. You need to take them across a bridge, though some versions of the riddle involve a boat, it's the same thing, really. The bridge can only hold you and one other thing at a time: either the fox, the chicken, or the grain. You need to transport all three across to the other side, one a time. The problem is, if you leave the fox with the chicken…'

'The fox will eat the chicken,' Seul said.

The Librarian nodded.

'And if you leave the chicken with the grain...'

'The chicken will eat the grain.'

'The question is then how do you take all three across whilst keeping all three intact,' said The Librarian.

'I guess we could take the fox first...' said Seul. 'Ah, but no... because that would mean the chicken eats the grain. So maybe cross with the chicken first? Then come back and get the grain—and take it over. Then get the fox?'

'Whilst you've gone to get the fox, the chicken has eaten the grain,' The Librarian corrected.

Nobody said anything. The only sound to be heard was the soft crunching of snow as the six of them ploughed onward to the three subtly shimmering doors.

'You take the chicken first. Then take the fox. Once you have taken the fox, bring back the chicken. Leave the chicken in its original place, take the grain instead to the other side, and leave it now with the fox. Go back to the start and now bring the chicken back, and you've got all three across,' Riyul said.

Everyone looked at him.

'Yes. That's correct,' The Librarian said. 'Perfect.'

'The doors, then,' Safa said, as they came up to them.

'Here we are, yes,' The Librarian said.

'Wait,' Daffodil said cautiously. 'Three doors. Three things in the riddle. Logical sequences. Do we need to do some kind of test or challenge to get to The City? To work out which door gets us there?'

'Yep,' The Librarian said jovially.

'And if we choose the wrong door?'

'Ooh, you don't want to know what happens then,' he said, shaking his head quickly. 'Let's just say lots of blood and flying heads.'

They looked at him, unsure if he was kidding, slowing as they approached the three doors. He briefly glanced up at the sky before looking at them.

'Lucky for you, they're inert. Someone has already come and crossed that bridge for you,' he said. 'The doors here should lead right to the south of The City, not too far from Skutish's castle.'

'I have a question,' said Daffodil.

'Yes?'

'Why don't we try go back through the train? That's how we entered, right?'

'I've not really seen the train myself,' Safa said. 'I'm not sure about that route. These routes are all part of the lands we know.'

'True,' Daffodil agreed. 'But do you think they may just be all within one part of the train?'

'Daffodil's right,' Riyul said. 'I feel like the train itself may be the key. And we're possibly going about this the longer way.'

'What would you like to do?' The Librarian asked.

They thought for a moment, the three doors standing like sentinels in front of them.

'Well, we are here now. If this doesn't work, we can always try the train,' Riyul said.

Daffodil nodded.

'Okay, onwards it is,' said The Librarian.

He turned the silver doorknob of the furthest door to the right. It opened easily, and within was darkness.

'Remember, once we pass through this doorway, we need to be fast. Everyone will be on to us before we know it. You need to get to Skutlish. We'll do what we need to do. And let's hope Marwa can make it,' he said quietly.

He nodded to them all—the nod of an appreciative general thanking his men as they prepared for battle; he lingered on Riyul as though especially thanking him, or perhaps considering him—and then stepped through the portal.

Chapter 38

The City

Escaping Aethril is not strictly difficult.
Escaping detection is difficult.
One must be games ahead, not mere steps.

Unnamed Black Notebook #1, remembrance forty-five

Daffodil had a rough idea of what to expect. Naturally, her reading in the library had prepared her somewhat for the sights she would see. She hadn't fathomed, however, that it would be just so different in person compared to on paper.

The moment they emerged, her jaw dropped, incredulous. In front of her was The City, and she was at least a little sad she couldn't stay for more than a dash to its west side.

Spires and monuments and buildings rose like sentinels, brushing clouds and sky—a sky unlike anything she had ever seen; it was burnished a deep rose gold, as though the sun was undecided if it was to fully relinquish its last rays of light or not—a sky in perpetual sunset, of the most mesmerising, gleaming kind she had ever witnessed.

Before them stood large gates that circled the entire metropolis; and within these guarded gates rose columns of blue, green and red buildings as far and wide as the eye could see: a vast city of colours from every corner of the rainbow, but not quiet and desolate like the lands she'd seen thus far.

Even at their distance, on the outskirts looking in, The City teemed with life: the coloured buildings consumed the corners of the vibrant, bustling metropolis, and swathes of little people (just pinpricks from this distance) milled about, with children discernible in far off, distant streets running around, playing.

Marwa turned to her, and looked around. Nobody else seemed to notice that Daffodil's mouth was gaping wide open. After a few seconds of uncertainly looking around, Marwa discreetly closed it for her, not sure if she would have otherwise closed it herself.

Daffodil blinked and nodded in thanks; she'd have liked to apologise, but was lost for words.

'I've never actually been so amazed,' breathed Daffodil, her voice but a whisper, laced and heavy with awe.

A deep grinding sound came from the border of The City.

The large, black gates had begun opening with an almighty groan, and children rushed out laughing, joking, playing. They were all wearing different colours, though upper and lower garments were always matching. Some wore bright blue shirts and tunics, whilst others wore red or something closer to white, and others yet dashed about in greenish browns. As soon as the children spotted Daffodil and Riyul, then ran towards her, faces agog with excitement.

'Hi! What's your name? I'm Pete!' one exclaimed.

'Don't listen to Pete! That's my little brother. I'm Sarah. We haven't seen you before! Do you want some eggs?'

'Hey lady, that's an awful nice coat. Why do you have two? Did you come from The Land of Snow?'

The Librarian pushed through the crowd of children, some of which were taller than Seul, gesturing the group forward. Adults now mixed into the crowd to see who the newcomers were.

'Remember what we spoke about in the library,' he shouted over the people as they made their way through the parting crowd. 'Out of the way!'

'Ow! You elbowed me!' said someone from the crowd. 'Your elbows are so pointy!'

The Librarian stopped. 'Thank you,' he said, rubbing his elbows like he was polishing glass, 'they're my pride and joy.'

He rushed onwards.

'Okay, we're coming to the first building,' he said. 'It's time to enact the plan. Out here, I will not be surprised if we're spotted pretty instantly. What we spoke about behind closed doors, however, should hopefully be safe.'

They made their way down the first road of the bustling city, past (or rather, *through*) the children-dominated crowd, and began rounding the corner of a tall earthen-coloured building, when a deep voice boomed through the streets, 'Hey, you! Stop right there!'

'Go, go,' The Librarian whispered. 'Daffodil, take this.' He thrust a tiny little black notebook into her outer jacket's pocket. 'This is what you need when you're out. Remember what we spoke about. The key to escape is just finding a powerful enough door. You're skillful, I can see that already. Find the right door, and you'll find your escape. I know you'll take it to where it needs to go.'

She nodded, and the group split off—she, Safa, Marwa and Riyul slipped into the crowd of city people going along their days, leaving The Librarian and Seul to face the guard running toward them.

***

'Okay, my love, turn your first jacket inside out,' Safa told Daffodil as they rushed north-west through the sprawling streets.

'Do you think they'll be okay?' Daffodil asked Safa.

'Yes,' she said. 'Those two can talk their way through anything. Also, the only good thing about this government is that they don't hurt children. The main thing is that you two don't get stopped.'

'Okay,' she said, still unsure.

They turned another corner.

A gurgling sound came from behind her.

Then a gasp.

Daffodil turned around.

Marwa had stopped on the corner of two roads, mid-stride, a look of fear etched on her face. Oddly, she was unmoving; nothing but short raspy breaths were emanating from her throat. People walked by and looked at her but continued on their paths as Safa smiled at them, holding on to Marwa's arm as though she were helping her somehow. As soon as there was a slight lull, she looked straight at Riyul and Daffodil.

'This is really bad,' she said to them. 'Marwa's freezing up.'

Chapter 39

Decisions

Cities not only contain, but also are hubs of useful people, organisations, and institutes. Information, sometimes more of a holistic nature, may be obtained from less cosmopolitan and populated places—for instance, in the little pockets of people living in the huts outside The City.

With the recent divisions of governmental power structures, however, these groups and villages are being slowly removed. Little by little. Silently but surely. Wiped—until only The City remains.

The City and Its Surroundings

'Who were those people just with you?' the man in the grey livery asked, marching toward Seul and The Librarian.

'Excuse me?' asked The Librarian in a highly offended tone. 'What's your name?'

'My name?' asked the guard.

'Yes, your name!' snapped The Librarian.

'I … do not see how that is relevant,' the guard said, unsure how *he* was now being questioned—so confidently too. 'Wait, I've seen you two before, but not those people who I'm sure you were just with. What are *your* names?'

'What is *your* name?' The Librarian demanded.

'You first,' the guard said.

'You second,' The Librarian responded.

The guard stared at him. 'My name is Bob.'

'Well, I'm absolutely appalled by this treatment, Bob. I have a question for you, who were these people you say were with us?'

The guard faltered. 'I don't know—that's why I'm asking you.' He turned to Seul. 'What is your name, son?'

'Oh, you want to know my name? I have a totally normal name.'

The Librarian looked at Seul, then tapped the guard on his shoulder. 'Excuse me, Mr Bob. He's not good with names—heck, he's not even used to speaking. Everything is a bit of a riddle with him. Process of elimination if you will. Did you know the other day he called himself Trill? Anyway, his name. What was it again? It's like Bob, but not Bob; it's like Rob, but not Rob. You know?'

The guard did not look like he knew a word of what was being said.

Then The Librarian whispered to him, 'it's Tob,' at which point the guard stared at him. 'Only kidding.'

The guard squinted at them quizzically, and made a note.

'Ah, I'll just spill the beans; this is my colleague, Mr Saliva,' he said, gesturing to Seul. 'He was once a soldier in The Great War, got stunted by a growth balm—never really grew older.'

'Colleague?' the guard said to The Librarian.

'Yes, colleague. Not cologne.'

'I … I didn't say cologne.'

'I didn't say you did,' The Librarian said, looking hurt.

'How are you two colleagues?'

'Well, we work together, of course. I mean, how are colognes, colognes? It's a definitional problem, really.'

The guard looked baffled. He turned to Seul hesitantly. 'Is Saliva really your name?'

'Yes, that is my name,' Seul said, his words coming out oddly forced. 'Not *Seul*. Saliva,' he said, glaring at The Librarian.

'That's a very odd thing to say,' said the guard.

'Yes, it really is, isn't it?' agreed The Librarian. 'Especially if your name wasn't Seul. I mean, who says, mid-conversation, that their name *isn't* something? I'd say that's awfully suspicious.'

'That's true,' said the guard, nodding.

'I don't know if we can trust Mr Saliva anymore—even if he is my colleague!' The Librarian said. 'We don't even know his real name, let alone his true intentions.'

Seul said nothing; he just looked up to the sky like he wanted to be any place but here.

This only made Bob nod in agreement even more vigorously. The Librarian also began nodding vigorously. They both nodded in sync.

'You know, Bill, I really feel like we're on the same side together,' The Librarian said.

'My name's not Bill,' interrupted Bob.

The Librarian ignored him and continued on, 'Against this fake! This phoney! This... This... Salivating soldier!'

'Is everything okay here, Bob?' asked a voice from beyond the crowd. It was another guard approaching.

'I don't know,' said Bob. 'It looks like we may have a code eagle sterilisation.'

'Ah, I see,' said the second guard calmly; he then turned back and walked away.

The Librarian and Seul looked at each other quickly.

Code eagle sterilisation?

'You know, I saw someone graffitiing earlier,' The Librarian said to Bob.

'Did you now?'

'Yes, oh definitely. I think it was just around that corner.' He pointed at a random building. 'At the Herblore Centre, I believe. That green one.'

'And what was the graffiti exactly?' said Bob, raising an eyebrow.

'It was a list, actually. Yes. A list of three things. A graffiti list. Quite inventive, I thought. It said "3 things I hate: 1) Graffiti, 2) lists, 3) irony."'

'Oh, did it really?'

'Yep. I can show you if you like. It's just this way.' The Librarian turned towards The Herblore Centre.

'Oh, I don't think that will be necessary,' said Bob, smirking.

Seul nudged The Librarian, but he either was not paying attention or pretending not to.

'Bob, I have a riddle for you,' said The Librarian.

'Of course,' Bob said. 'I'm good at these. I hope it's not the fox, grain and chicken one—I've studied that since basic alchemic logic training.'

Seul nudged The Librarian harder—to no avail.

The Librarian continued, 'If you could only save twenty-three children, or your daughter-'

Seul gripped The Librarian's elbow and poked him with it until he turned around.

'Ow!'

As he turned, a cluster of four more guards walked towards them. At the head marched a man in black wrappings, wielding a staff that seemed to emanate the shadows themselves. Zear stomped onward until he was standing face-to-face with The Librarian.

'You and your party are under arrest,' he said calmly.

'What are you arresting us for?' asked The Librarian in mock shock.

'I have been instructed under the orders of King Gerrihend,' Zear said. 'You are an elusive one. I almost thought we wouldn't find you this time. Please follow me, and do not make a scene,' he said, turning to make a path for them through the building army of guards and police that had congregated for The Librarian's arrest.

Seul began extracting a vial from his jacket. 'I can have a boulder on him in an instant. Just give the word,' he whispered to The Librarian.

'They haven't gotten very far away yet,' he breathed back. 'Alright, just follow my lead, get some distance, and don't do anything nonsensical.'

Seul sighed, extracting another vial from his back pocket. 'That is so offensive,' he muttered. 'I don't even know what nonsensical means…'

'I would really love to go quietly,' said The Librarian to Zear, 'but I've always been interested in a shadow staff, and secondly, I believe you destroyed half of my library.'

The Librarian whipped out five tiny orbs from his jacket and flung them at the police-force.

His aim was perfect. The five tiny orbs flew in five directions towards the guards. Upon collision, three of them flew back, encased in ice, another's clothes instantly combusted, and another barely dodged their orb.

Zear grunted as Seul dived off to the side and ran. 'Attaaaaack!' he yelled. 'And keep him alive!'

Without need for further instruction, the thirty guards suddenly rushed at The Librarian, shouting battle cries.

He split-stepped and prepared for the attack.

Out of nowhere, a vast boulder plummeted through the guards, taking out seven of them and flinging them onto the pavements. The Librarian turned to see Seul at a distance. 'You're welcome,' he said, blowing his fingers as groans came from from the men.

Zear slammed his staff into the ground as shadows twisted and writhed around it, seeming to charge it up.

A guard jumped at The Librarian, who ducked. Pivoting to his right, he took another guard's arm and slammed him into a third, taking them both down.

A punch flew at him from nowhere. He turned, found the first guard still mid-swing, blocked with his upper arm and turned again. He parried with an elbow to the shoulder and kicked him away. He weaved between two more guards, twisted and threw a knee into a gut. He ducked incoming high-kicks, and punched a guard in the stomach, sending him reeling.

Three more had run out from behind a corner and were rushing in at once.

Another boulder came hurtling into their side, causing them to groan as they flew out of view. Seul had run to higher ground and was manipulating his earth orbs without being attacked.

'Good lad,' The Librarian whispered, as he withdrew his own staff from his side, hidden beneath his jacket; a wooden pole with a soft blue orb fixed to the top.

There were still around fifteen guards left, who, having gathered their senses, were readying a synchronised onslaught.

Zear was building up a shadow orb at the top of his staff. The Librarian aimed and fired a shard of ice directly at the orb. Zear ducked, and the ice shards went straight through the shadows without diminishing them in the slightest.

'Huh. I really need to get myself one of those,' The Librarian said.

He turned and threw shards of ice at the approaching guards, one after the other—pinning each through their jackets into the walls and buildings behind them.

More rocks came raining down from the heavens upon the guards as The Librarian shot volley after volley of ice shards.

The remaining ten guards dodged and ducked through the incoming boulders and ice and jumped on top of The Librarian, taking him down and pinning him to the floor.

The pile of guards grew and grew until a mountain of guards was holding him, smothering him down onto the ground.

For a moment—nothing.

Seul watched from a distance as the bodies piled and piled.

'There's no way he can survive that...' he breathed.

Then a war cry cracked through the very air itself, as the guards were lifted up and flung away in a splaying orb. A blue expanding dome formed outward from the man standing in the middle, staff affixed to the ground.

The Librarian.

He looked up at the remaining attackers—of which there were none.

'Okay, playtime is over.' Zear stepped up behind The Librarian and aimed his staff, now ready and writhing shadows, at the back of his head. 'One more move, and that's it. Step down.'

The Librarian looked off into the distance to where the rest of his group had gone. He seemed to nod in acceptance, dropping his staff and letting it clatter on the ground. 'Okay,' he said, as raised his hands in the air for all to see.

Thirty guards groaned and moaned in the chaos around him.

He looked at Seul and nodded—the sign to leave. Seul nodded back and slipped away before the guards started to come to their senses.

'You've got me,' The Librarian said, turning to Zear. 'Take me in.'

***

'What can we do?' Riyul asked. 'Marwa's freezing up. They'll only be able to stall for so long before the government realises what has happened.'

They had managed to help get Marwa out of the main roadway and onto a side street with less foot traffic.

Safa didn't reply. She held the beaker with the restoration balm in her hand. 'We were afraid this might happen. The superfluid base has zero viscosity, so I don't know how she'll react to it, particularly without the Librarian here with us in case something happens. What if something goes wrong?'

Riyul and Daffodil looked at each other.

Marwa had closed her eyes and was lying on the ground, letting out raspy breaths. Daffodil placed the back of her hand on Marwa's forehead. It was ice-cold.

'I think you're going to have to try what you've made,' Riyul said slowly.

Safa raised the beaker shakily to Marwa's lips. The substance within was a pearlescent white and wavered between shining and not;

one moment it seemed to flow and the other it seemed like Daffodil was looking at unmoving marble.

Safa tilted the beaker, and the fluid slid out and into Marwa's mouth.

Her breathing slowed... and then suddenly became more ragged than before. Her eyes flew open. A sizzling sound seemed to come from within her.

Safa raised her hand to cover her mouth as her sister's eyes fluttered and her head turned from side to side on the hard ground.

Then, all of a sudden, she stopped moving.

The three of them watched with bated breath.

Marwa's lips twitched.

'Safa,' came a hoarse but soft, gentle voice. 'You need to get them out of here.'

'Marwa!' Safa exclaimed, hugging her sister and raising her tenderly into a sitting position. 'I will. I'll take them right away, but how are you feeling? I can't believe it worked.'

'I don't think it was fully ready. I still feel like there is ice within me.'

'I can't leave you here alone,' said Safa.

'It's okay. I'll go to The Herblore Centre. They must have something.'

'You can't. They'll figure it all out once I'm seen anywhere near Skutlish's castle, and then you'll be taken in for questioning.'

'What other choice do I have?' Marwa said, standing up weakly, voice croaking.

'What about Sherlotte?'

'Sherlotte? Sherlotte's not in The City.'

'Sorry, who's Sherlotte?' Riyul asked, slightly wincing.

'Sherlotte is an alchemist who works on remedial elixirs; she practises herblore and alchemy and knows a lot, but from what I understand, she's not in The City; we'd have to go north for quite a while to find her village.'

'Would it save Marwa from completely freezing?' Riyul said, a mask of determination hiding the pain that was surging through his body once more. A pain he could not explain nor wished to make known at this moment.

'Yes, but I couldn't let her go alone. And we need to get to Skutlish; I feel like the call will already be out looking for us; they may have even realised where we are heading.'

'Well, we can't leave her like this. I'll go with her,' he said.

'What?' Safa and Marwa both said.

'Look, if it's not safe in The City for Marwa after this, then I can go with her to Sherlotte. If Daffodil gets out, that's the main thing. Then I will leave. But you need to take her to Skutlish, Safa. You're the only one who knows the way. The Librarian and Seul have probably been taken to the Police Station and have diverted as much attention as possible. You know the plan. There will be as few guards out as possible right now—they'll all be interrogating The Librarian. We have to trust him. You have to take her now. And whilst the guards are all occupied, I'll go with Marwa to Sherlotte. After that, we can find each other and work out how I can get out.'

They all stood motionless for a moment, looking at Riyul.

'I don't know,' said Daffodil.

'Go, Daffodil,' Riyul said, smiling. 'Remember your brother. Your Mum. Your Dad. They are probably sick with worry.' He took a deep breath. 'I'm not sure how long I've been gone from my time, but from my calculations, and from what I'm thinking, it's been a lot longer than for you. You should go first. I know nobody has been talking about it, but I've been thinking about it. Do I go back to my time... or your time?' Riyul laughed emptily. 'I'm not sure how much benefit I'll be to the world in another century. But you? You're needed back with your family. Back in your time. Now. So go. We'll figure a way out for me.'

Daffodil opened her mouth to speak, but before she could utter a word, Safa raised her hand, looked at her, and nodded. The implication was clear. *Listen to him.*

Daffodil stared for a moment. 'Make sure you get out,' she then whispered to Riyul—to the man she had travelled with, planned with, and fought with.

'I will,' he said. 'As soon as Marwa is better, I'm escaping.'

'A wise man once told me something: believe in yourself,' Daffodil said gently, 'even if no one else does.'

Riyul smiled and nodded.

'Safa, go,' Marwa said.

'Thank you for everything,' Daffodil said as Safa tugged on her jacket.

'You're welcome,' he said. 'Now go find the graveyard above which Skutlish lives, and find the way out of here,' said Riyul,

And with no more to say, the two pairs parted ways, and Safa and Daffodil began their walk to Skutlish.

Chapter 40

The Castle

Skutlish's residence is a misnomer. Skutlish does not reside, for he almost certainly does not sleep. His home, his castle, is at the end of the graveyard. As though that is not suspicious and terrifying enough, it is quite conclusive that deaths are only possible through murder. His home thus looks out at all those killed in this land.

I do not understand why people think he should ever be the one to seek.

Tread carefully when seeking truth, for unless you can think the way an evil person thinks, then you've already lost; they will go places you can not even imagine.

Arrival at Aethril, an Autobiography

Thunder muttered aggressively.

Daffodil and Safa walked towards the graveyard and the castle beyond as dark clouds drifted over and blocked out sections of the impossible sky, the ocean of brushed auburn that was somehow simultaneously dotted with stars. Gazing up, Daffodil simply could not believe her eyes. She scanned the sky avidly for signs of fault, searching for some inconsistency or flaw. Yet there were none.

How? How can this seem so real?

Above, even through the cloud cover, there was a constellation that reminded her a little of Orion's Belt, when the stars would twinkle in the night sky out with Dad and his comically large telescope in Devon...

He always loved taking her out to see the stars, viewing constellations with his little girl.

He *had* always loved that.

Suddenly cognizant of her companion, Daffodil discreetly wiped the growing teardrop away. A powerful ache had begun to swell deep in her chest—half sadness, half grief, threatening to come gushing out and overwhelm her.

Nearly there.

'You seem mournful, Daffodil,' said Safa, face kindly as always. 'Are you okay?'

'Yes,' sniffed Daffodil, blinking profusely. How had she been lucky enough to be met by such a good soul, a woman who was helping her without gaining herself—the same woman who could now notice her emotions which she desperately tried to hide?

'I guess... I suppose... I just never saw this coming. I don't understand how it happened. The train I got on seemed normal. And yet it led to all this. Sometimes I genuinely don't know if I'm dreaming or awake.'

'I know,' Safa said consolingly. 'I'm with you though. All the way.' She did not rebuke her; she did not belittle her for her comment. It was not an accusation: it was understanding. 'You know, The Librarian used to say something when we were kids,' she went on slowly. 'Back before he started becoming so wacky... When things would go wrong, he'd say, "It is not for us to always know why things happen as they do—it is not for us to understand the *why* straight away". He used to say, "Know that questioning your path consumes happiness, and believe me, no good will come out of it. A day will come when things will become brighter, the sun will shine upon you and the path you were on makes sense.'"

Safa took a deep breath. 'Unfortunately, however, that day is not today. I think you have one more darkness to pass through, my love.'

Her head lifted ever so slightly towards the sky, towards the stars shining in a perpetual sunset.

'Remember what you read about this graveyard, Daffodil—and everything you've been taught. It's Skutlish's security mechanism, and he can use alchemy to control who sees what down its roads. It may very well be your test to see if he'll even let you in.' Safa gestured to the path ahead into the heart of the graveyard.

The plan had been set. Daffodil knew what to do. The thought of smiling briefly flickered across her mind, but she decided not to: it was not the time for smiling. Right now, she would not pretend to be something she wasn't—for now was not the time for façades.

Safa strode onward a little further.

Deciding to leave her thoughts at bay for the time being, Daffodil ran to keep up, the black behemoth looming over them, just beyond rows of graves. There must have been hundreds of graves scattered around. Tall sentinel trees seemed to have come from nowhere and shrouded the entire area with death-dark foliage. As they passed the first row of graves, Daffodil looked straight ahead at the castle, which seemed to grow larger and seemingly darker as they approached.

Movements.

The almost imperceptible rustling of leaves, dry and crisp as though animals scuttling through foliage: there were new sounds here that she had not noticed before. Whilst not distinguishable at first, the sounds of the gloomy, barely star-lit forest were growing louder.

Click.

She could hear pincers, barely audible, but altogether undeniable.

'Safa... I can hear things...'

Safa frowned. 'I've not heard of that before... But no matter what happens, Daffodil, do not pay heed to the sounds you hear. Alchemy can do many things—perhaps this is another tool.'

Daffodil's eyes grew wide. She felt them all around her. Animals? Monsters? She could sense their hundred stares—creatures of the dark watching her, writhing, waiting to pounce. As she scanned the vast darkness (where had the lights of The City gone?) for the source of the sound, she noticed something. Like a light reflected in a mirror, a glint of white flashed briefly in one of the castle windows, almost too quick to notice. Squinting, Daffodil tried to make out where it had come from, but it had disappeared as fast as it had come. Resolving that it was just a figment of imagination, another trick compounded by the nonhuman noises, she marched on.

Whispers approached her now; not metaphorical whispers of the mind or extensions of thoughts, but real, audible *whispers*.

They scuttled around her as she marched, hissing, peering, probing—growing into something substantial. Innumerable voices conjoining together... saying...

Leave usss.

Daffodil frantically spun, turning, glancing, swivelling around to the onslaught of ... nothingness. There was no one there.

But the sounds. The sounds must have been there. As though poltergeists come to life, awoken by her presence disturbing their slumber.

Boom! Whips of lightning forked in the distance, lighting up the world, roaring through the land with the accompanying thunder.

She turned back quickly, breathing heavily. The castle did not seem far now, though her estimations may have proven inaccurate in the darkness of night; as she squinted her eyes, she could just about make out the grey stairs leading up to the central doors of the ancient terminal.

And then she felt them.

In that instance, she felt the breath of oh so many souls, the innumerable forgotten waifs that were urging her not to enter—oh so many souls, but simultaneously none. Where were they?

'Do not search for the ghosts, Daffodil. If you search for them, you'll never find them,' said Safa tenderly, like a mother to a child.

'But I can... hear them,' stuttered Daffodil, heartbeat in her ears. She was making a concerted effort to not look around or behind her. Trying to keep up with Safa, she quickened her pace, wading through the impressions of death that surrounded her, all the while searching for the castle stairs. She had come to the slow realisation that there was an unnatural cold creeping under her sleeves,

Leave-usss.

Her teeth started chattering: her skin felt ice-cold while the whispers swam around her, weaving through the layers of her clothes as though tendrils of ice—searching, trying to get in.

Her vision began to waver.

The stone steps came into view. Three metres away. She could only perceive the five steps leading to a set of hazy, tall wooden doors; her sight was beginning to blur.

'Do not listen to the voices. Walk up to the door, and enter.'

Daffodil kept her unclear gaze fixed forward as she managed to stumble onto the first step.

Unbalanced, near-delirious, she swayed forward.

Second step.

The sound of pincers and the whispers and the excruciating cold began merging into one. The whispers grew into screeching, and her insides felt as though they were being wrung, rapidly changing between ferocious heat and blistering cold.

Third step.

'...The door, Daffodil.'

She was just a faint voice in another world now. Was that even Safa? She squinted through the pain—sounds and smells and tastes all mingled together: she could feel the pungent smells sweeping through her brain. Fainting was the only thing she wanted to do.

Fourth step.

Screams.

Overwhelmed by the shrieks of poltergeists, of people who'd been maimed, her vision began failing. Pictures flashed. A hundred images burst through her mind in a flurry, piercing through in the space of a moment. A girl crying, mourning. Graves. Lightning. A train.

Fifth step.

A million voices that were not hers cracked through her thoughts, shrieking, repelling her. Nearly collapsing, eyes rolling back, Daffodil floundered, searching with her fingers for hope— staggering for something solid. *There.* Coarseness—wood. She stumbled, pushing on the vast doors, grunting, exhausting what meagre energy remained, and slid into the depths of darkness.

Chapter 41

Family

Research is inconclusive in regards to Aethril's effects on memory.
Nonetheless, we recommend exercising caution and guarding one's
thoughts until a certainty of mind and spirit is attained.

Sciences of Alchemy

'Hello, Daffodil.'

The voice was the first thing she noticed. It was smooth—deep, but not unkind, and it was present even before her vision, for she was still bathed in darkness. Granted, she hadn't opened her eyes yet, her head hurt, and the—

Wait.

Safa.

The graveyard.

The castle.

Daffodil opened her eyes.

She was in a pristine white room, sitting down on some kind of chair. In front of her stood a man that was taller than anyone she had ever met. His hands, though spindly-fingered, were the size of her mother's china plates, and his feet, though presumably equally bony, were covered in leather shoes that would fit three or four of her own.

Paper-thin, his features bulged out, and whilst not unhandsome, there was something ever so slightly off about his appearance. Perhaps it was the stark contrast between his jet-black hair and his paper-white skin. Perhaps it was the fact his head nearly brushed the ceiling. Perhaps it was that he smiled at her without teeth.

Whatever it was, he terrified her.

'You must be Skutlish.'

'That I am.'

Daffodil looked around. The walls of the room were barren white, and there was a singular door behind her. It was open, but had blackness in its centre. A ... buzzing emanated from it. She shut her eyes. But the grids didn't manifest themselves here. Yet that buzzing... This was the strongest sensation she'd felt since arriving here.

That was the door she needed. She could sense the power. And ... something else... She felt like something was pushing to ... get in?

Turning away from her, Skutlish walked over to a desk facing the wall. Daffodil checked her pockets.

'You know there is only one reason people come to visit me,' he said, sitting down; this was quite the feat, as his legs seemed too long to be able to manoeuvre.

'I need to leave,' Daffodil said quickly. 'The City are after me and my friends, but if I can just get back to my family-'

'Then what?' asked Skutlish, tilting his head.

'I'll... What do you mean? Then I've escaped. The police are after me. I think the king knows. That's what all this is about. I need to escape. Then I'll try to come back and show the world what this place is, and how it's like a prison and ... And...' Daffodil stopped speaking.

Skutlish smiled.

'Will you tell the world about this place when you go?' he asked predatorily.

She looked at him. She looked at the room around her.

'You're not going to let me leave, are you?' she said slowly.

He frowned, and tilted his head again. 'Oh, Daffodil. I'm not the evil one. I want you to be free. I want you to ... know the truth. So tell me, what do you want to leave *to*?'

'To my family...' she said.

'Your family?' he said, enunciating each word. 'Ah yes, your family. The same family you left that fateful day, right? The ones you ran away from.'

'I ... I didn't know.'

He smiled again. A toothless smile.

'Daffodil, do you know how this place works? Have you figured it out yet?'

She shook her head.

'This place is your escape. Daffodil—you weren't abducted. You weren't taken. You chose to come here. You chose to leave your parents and flee their control and get out and disappear. You wanted escape. This is a world for those who chose to leave their old lives behind.'

She shook her head again, frowning, looking at him with eyes of fire. 'No. No, impossible. That can't be.'

'Can't it? Tell me, Daffodil, where did The Librarian come from? This mythical, magical man who just happens to know everything? Do you even know his real name? Well, I'll tell you. If you want to get out so badly, know the reality of this world. His name is Amelio. In the outside world, he was but a janitor who loved to read but could never amount to what he truly desired. Oh yes, and then he goes on to teach even the Conductor himself. Take away someone's disbelief in themselves, and they're capable of anything. What about Safa and Marwa? Ah yes, I do know about the sisters you adore. Safa never could have a child out there, on Earth. This world allowed her to have something she could never have outside. She may have forgotten her past now, but look how happy she is. Look how kind she is. Oh yes, I know you care about her—because, perhaps, she cares about you.'

Daffodil mouth opened, speechless.

'Marwa? Ah, she's a clever one. Yes, I've been watching. Incredible potential, that girl. But you see, it's hard with sisters, isn't it? Especially sisters that close to each other. One of them goes through trauma, and how does the other one help? Well, it takes a clever person to discover this world, to gain access to our doors, and to bring their traumatised twin sister over, whether she wanted it or not. But it was for the best. Given enough time, feelings change. But how do you speak of the traumas you went through—what you've done to your sister, perhaps, when you can't live with yourself? Maybe, consciously or not, you become mute. Oh well, I suppose they are happy enough now, on their adventure—on their journey.'

Her heart was beating in her throat. Sweaty palms gripped the edges of her pristine white seat until her knuckles pained.

'The question remains… You.'

'No. None of this is real. Time doesn't exist here. Please stop this. I just want to go home.'

He raised his hands, palms facing out.

'Hey, hey. I'm not the bad guy here. If you want to go home, I can give you whatever little I can to get you there. I won't stop you.

But let me ask you this. Let's just say I'm honest. Let's just say there's a chance that what I've said has a modicum of truth and not lies. Then doesn't that leave one question?'

Daffodil couldn't bear to speak. She was shaking. Tears fought each other to well up, but she fought them the harder. And she lost.

'How I got here...'

'How you got here,' he said, nodding. 'Ah, Daffodil. What is a memory? What do we really remember, and what do we really forget?

'You are special. Absolutely. You are chosen. Look, I can't tell you what is real and what isn't. That's for you to decide. But the one common string connecting all those you've met in this land? *Trauma.* People who need a better life. Oh, but not many people are ready until they've lost something. Or someone. The brink of despair, my dear Daffodil,' he said, gesturing at the room and world around. 'Isn't this the perfect escape? Where you do not grow old? What, oh Daffodil, was your trauma?'

Her heart dropped.

'You see, I looked into you. I researched your history with our contacts in the outside world, and I found out something about you, Daffodil. The reason Haradan chose you.'

'Please,' she whispered.

'If you want to leave, Daffodil, *know what you're leaving to.* Your files say you've had memory blocks for a long time. If you want to go, then you must know your past. Accept it.'

'Please.'

'Don't keep rejecting the truth, Daffodil. You've known for a long time, haven't you?'

She shut her eyes. Shut the world out. Shut out Skutlish and the white room and The City and the kindness she'd seen and the people she'd met and the world as a whole. With her eyes shut, she was in darkness. The one place where she need not face her life.

'How many people are in your family, Daffodil?'

She shook her head in that darkness. The darkness of that white room. 'Five. There are five of us,' she said shakily.

'That's interesting. Because from my research, it seems that there are four. The file showed that Daffodil Winters, daughter of Zakariyya Winters and Clarice Everwater, is an only child.'

Daffodil opened her eyes.

'But not always. She had a brother. He was called Adam. And the doctors write that Daffodil would see him even after he died, would talk to him, would believe he was still with her. That she still sees him—everywhere.'

'NO!' Daffodil screamed.

A million memories that felt like another person's flashed through her mind. The dreams—the non-stop dreams night in, night out. Adam. Puzzle pieces. Her parents openly reminding her that Adam died the morning she stormed out. Talking to him in the kitchen the night before she had run away. He hadn't been there at all. And further back. Memories of him for years throughout her life—none of them were real. He hadn't caused any fire. That had been her. He hadn't been the smart one. It was her—but she could never accept it. That's why her parents had always spoken under her breath about her.

Adam hadn't been alive for a long time.

Daffodil stared at Skutlish with tears in her eyes.

'I know why you sought this land, why Aethril was your escape,' Skutlish said softly.

She looked up at the ceiling of impossible light.

'You don't,' she breathed.

Skutlish raised an eyebrow.

'You don't know the truth!' she shouted.

Her face was blank now. She looked at him, but was not really looking at him, for her eyes were glazed, like she was looking straight through him. 'There's one thing my parents never told the police.'

He frowned.

'I was looking after him,' she whispered, hands trembling. 'That night. We were staying in the cabin. Mum and Dad trusted me … but I wasn't careful enough. Out in the woods. Oh—he was just a baby. A car hit him. I remember its lights… But I couldn't stop it.'

She was shaking now. 'ADAM IS DEAD BECAUSE OF ME!'

Shivers tore down her spine and racked her body. And in that moment of pain, of truth and clarity—in that perfect horrific moment, Daffodil knew what to do.

It was her best chance to escape.

Tears on her face, she stood up, eyes shut, sensing the time, sensing the place, sensing the moment.

She pulled out her two tiny vials of gateway fluid and duplication balm, and spun around, hoping her aim was better after her training.

Skutlish's eyes grew wide, like an electric shock had run through him—realising what she was about to do.

She hurled the gateway fluid vial at the only doorway in the room. In the darkness of her eyes, she knew. She could feel the power pushing from the door. Something wanted to get in.

It wanted to connect.

Immediately upon impact, she threw the duplication balm at the door, just as was the plan.

For a moment, nothing happened. She turned to Skutlish, shuddering.

Would it work? Did Skutlish really have the alchemy to connect back to her land?

As though on cue, a second door manifested itself next to the original white door.

Skutlish stood up.

Daffodil heard it before she saw it: the second door burst open with a deafening crack.

Instantly, a figure stepped through this new door—a man she very much recognised, eyes open or closed.

Skutlish's face was expressionless as the figure of Zakariyya Winters stepped into the room. He was followed by a short, plump man with grey hair.

Zakariyya surveyed the scene around him and immediately approached Daffodil.

'Dad!' Daffodil cried.

Zakariyya looked at Skutlish with death in eyes.

Skutlish did not say a word, but simply swept over the scene in front of him, lingering on the man Daffodil didn't recognise—his hand seemed to hover over a pocket for a moment, but then he got up and walked out of the original open doorway, through the black shimmering membrane. At the same time, Clarice stepped through the second door.

'Mum!' Daffodil screamed, jumping out of her chair and engulfing Clarice in a hug, smiling, laughing, crying all at once. 'How?'

'Daffodil,' Clarice said, hugging every bit of her daughter.

They embraced in silence for a moment, before Clarice pulled away, looking over her shoulder.

Near them, Bartholomew was hurrying them towards the doorway urgently.

'Honey, this is Bartholomew; he helped us get to you.'

Bartholomew nodded respectfully. 'Pleasure to meet you, my name is Bartholomew Uthman. I'm guessing you know Amelio; he used to have a nickname for me—Uthy. Listen, Daffodil, we know what this place is. But we need to go now, in case anything happens to the transmuted door—we don't have much time.'

'Mum, Dad...' Daffodil said, rooted to the spot, looking at them with tears streaming down her cheeks. 'Adam.'

They looked at each other, then at Daffodil.

'Was that what our argument was about on the day I went? The day I ran out and went to the train?'

They stared at her—still—and nodded.

Daffodil smiled at them. 'I couldn't remember. I couldn't even remember our conversation. Because you tried to tell me ... remind me of the truth.'

Clarice stepped towards her.

'He's dead, isn't he?' said Daffodil.

'Yes,' Clarice said gently, kissing Daffodil's forehead. 'And he has been for a long, long time, darling.'

'I've been seeing him. In the house... I remember on the beach... Other places. But he was never there.'

'You've come so far,' Clarice whispered. 'You've finally accepted the truth. Now you need to come with us, my darling. Out of this place.'

Zakariyya nodded as Bartholomew gestured frantically at the doorway. 'We can talk more outside. Let's go,' Zakariyya said.

Daffodil stepped towards the doorway, half-expecting Skutlish to come back with some trick or ruse or weapon.

'You go first, Daffodil,' Zakariyya said.

She nodded and stepped through. Just before she did, she took one quick look back at the room behind her.

Just a white chair. Near it was Bartholomew, who seemed to have helped her parents. Next to her was Mum, and Dad. But there was someone else. Barely a figure, really. The ghost of a figure. His proportions were unmistakable. Beside the white chair stood a silvery outline of a young boy. The boy who had been at her side her entire life, even after his death.

'Bye, bye, Adam.'

She blew her baby brother the faintest of kisses, turned and walked through the door.

Chapter 42

Restoration Balm

Nobody does anything thinking that they are wrong. I'm a
big believer in this; everyone has their reasons for things,
even if we do not see it, nor agree with it.

Unnamed Black Notebook #1,
remembrance seventy, footnote one in different font

Safa ran and ran and ran.

Where were Riyul and Marwa?

She had realised that something was wrong with this whole situation as soon as Daffodil had gone into the castle.

When Daffodil had been taken in, Safa had considered her next move, of course, her sister being the main priority. Marwa was now flaring up again, and therefore on her way to Sherlotte.

Safa panted as she ran along the outskirts of The City, due north, searching.

Why was it flaring up now though? That was the question. Just when they had almost made it to Skutlish. It was a convenient time for Marwa's icing to really kick in. Almost like it was controlled by something—or someone.

Safa looked left and right as she ran and ran. Still no sign of Marwa or Riyul.

In those moments of limbo, as she considered the true implications of the icing, she remembered the queen.

The queen was the only other known person to be iced. And she definitely *was* iced, from what they'd seen in the vents and confirmed through testing a duplicate trace for Marwa—using Syrys' flower.

And so, Safa thought to check the flower trace once more—to locate Marwa, but also perhaps the queen. The queen should theoretically have been in the palace, in the east of The City.

Yet she wasn't.

Her trace tests indicated Syrys was due north. Exactly where Safa had sent Riyul and Marwa. Due north. To Sherlotte.

Sherlotte controlled the icing. Sherlotte was Queen Syrys. And Marwa and Riyul were heading right to her.

Chapter 43

Reality

It is said the Conductor had two sons. Little is known about his other family. His mysteries are shrouded in further mystery, as though history has been constantly written and rewritten. One thing is for certain: you should ask where we came from, first and foremost, to find the answers sought.

On The Origins of Aethril

A seagull flew in the distance. And another. And yet another. Daffodil tried to listen to their cawing, but they made no sound.

Silence.

Positioning himself beside Daffodil, Adam sat on the sand and gazed out towards the endless blue expanse in front of them.

Daffodil stared at him, and then back at the sea sky; she looked around at the beach and playing children, and their parents off in the distance.

'You're not real, Adam.'

He smiled at her.

His beautiful, beautiful smile.

'No,' he said.

Mum and Dad were around a hundred yards down the beach, buying ice-cream for the family. The holiday was all it was meant to be: seaside resorts, great beaches, even a failed attempt at surfing. Daffodil could just make out Dad in his bright red shorts handing money over to the man in the stall, who swiftly disappeared inside to whip up some great ice-cream cones, and Mum standing beside him with her arms folded.

'Were these memories ever real?'

He smiled at her, and then looked on at the seagulls.

She stared at him, her baby brother, with his tousled brown hair and ridiculous suntan.

'I love you, you know that?' Daffodil whispered. 'I love you so much. Whether this is a dream or not, whatever is real, and whatever isn't real, doesn't matter. Know that I love you, forever.'

He looked at her, smiling. 'I love you too,' he said. And he began to fade again.

Daffodil smiled. She had a feeling this would be the last time she'd be seeing him.

Finally. The closure she needed. A poignant end was better than a lifetime of denial. She could now carry on.

But before he completely vanished, he opened his mouth.

Daffodil squinted. He was saying something. She could just about make it out from his lips—but it didn't make sense. She concentrated as hard as she could on this vanishing figure, the distant sound dissipating every second.

'There's more to Haradan than meets the eye...'

Laughter from the other children floated over from further down the beach. He faded away until beside her was nothing but empty sand, and her parents off in the distance.

Daffodil frowned. She could hear some kind of odd beeping sound.

Chukka-chukka-chukka-chukka-chukka.

'Daffodil,' said a distant voice. 'Daffodil, wake up.'

Daffodil looked around as the amorphous beach and sea and sky began to swirl and mix.

The entire scene was disintegrating.

'Daffodil,' a voice from everywhere seemed to call.

A dream?

Beep… beep… beep… beep… beep…

Daffodil opened her eyes.

She looked up at a blinding white light swaying gently on two thin metal wires. Around her were arrays of tubes, machines and what looked like hospital equipment.

Closing the door behind him was Haradan.

'Where am I?' Daffodil asked, sitting up in the bed, seeing him close the door. Just outside was a corridor, a reception desk, and above it, a clock.

'You're in a hospital,' Haradan said, shutting the door firmly, pulling down the blinds and walking over.

'What happened? Where are my parents? We… we got out.'

Haradan stopped, seemingly unsure of how to respond. He chewed his lip.

'I'm really sorry to tell you this, Daffodil, but you've been here since you passed out in the graveyard. Safa brought you right in. The police then took her in for questioning.'

'I… I could have sworn I met Skutlish. And … he told me crazy things about Safa and Marwa and… But… but he also told me… a truth. About my brother.'

Haradan frowned at her.

'My parents came,' she said.

'Daffodil,' Haradan said gently, 'do not trust Skutlish. Never go to his side...'

Daffodil stared at him in disbelief. 'What do you mean? He tried to tell me the truth.'

'Skutlish cannot be trusted,' he said with a sigh.

Daffodil stared at him.

'You've been here for a while. Your memories may have become even more muddled,' he said, shaking his head.

'Wh... what?'

'Daffodil, when was the last time you actually really remember speaking to your parents? Directly?'

'I...' she faltered.

'Aside from what you feel like happened after the graveyard incident.'

'I don't remember,' she said finally. 'The last memory I have is of leaving the house... but ... I don't remember speaking to them.' Things were getting fuzzy. She had vague memories with Dad in a forest, but when had that been?

Haradan pursed his lips.

What was real anymore? What if the entire train was a dream? She supposed heart rate monitors weren't too dissimilar to the *chukka-chukka* sound she'd been hearing. She looked back at Haradan, who seemed to be bruised in multiple places and was once again observing the door. *Was she still in Aethril?*

Was she on Earth?

Daffodil eyed the door; besides it was a glass window, mostly covered by blinds, but through the slits she could just about make out something.

The corridor beyond. With a reception and ... a small clock on the wall. Daffodil closed her eyes, and could faintly make out the sounds of ticking. Of hands moving. Of time.

She breathed out and turned back to Haradan quickly before he realised. She had made her decision.

'How did you get here? Why did you come here?' she asked.

He paused.

'Family,' he said after some time. 'Indeed, it was difficult. After being pulled through that doorway, I had to find myself back. Anyway, by that point I'd gotten wind of your plans to see Skutlish. As you've probably worked out, I'm not here just to say hello, Daffodil.

'The government has taken Safa, they're interrogating The Librarian, and I don't know what's going to happen to Seul. I want to get you out of here before they come for you. I've placed a temporary seal on the warp for that door.' He nodded towards the door that he kept looking at. 'Everyone is in grave danger. Including your parents. But we can leave through another one I have manifested next to it, only if and when you're ready.'

Daffodil looked up at the ceiling, and that blinding, swaying, ceaseless light.

He was lying to her. That much she was certain of. She looked into his kindly grey eyes...

Was he trying to say her parents were dead? She didn't remember speaking to them now... almost... ever.

When had she last spoken to her parents?

In the house?

Before she'd ran away?

According to Skutlish, that would have been when they'd mentioned Adam's death, and the reason she had run out upset.

Had they never been alive either, since as long as Adam had been gone?

'Your friends are in trouble, Daffodil.'

Why would he lie?

He smiled kindly, despite the gravity of his words. There was an urgency in his fleeting look. Obviously to get her back to Aethril before anyone discovered them in this room. Discovered *him* in this room.

What was the truth?

Daffodil had been through so much on Aethril. Was she really to leave her parents now, in this very hospital, after they'd worked so hard to find a way to get to her?

Skutlish… He had been truthful. Whoever he was, he had told her about Adam… and The Librarian. Safa and Marwa. Everyone but … Riyul.

Her eyes widened. She smiled at Haradan. If she didn't follow him and play along … What would he do to her? To her parents?

'You're right,' she said, gesturing him up. 'We should go quickly before anyone realises you've come. Can you check the doors before we go? I'm just getting my things ready,' she said to him, getting up.

He nodded happily, noticeably relieved by her compliance, and began looking at the door. 'You've been such a brave, young girl,' he said, checking the door itself.

Tears in her eyes, she pulled her jacket on, brushing the outside pocket for her notebook and vials whilst his back was turned. Daffodil looked between Haradan and the window to the outside lobby where she was *sure* her parents were. Just metres away. They'd undoubtedly fought so hard to get to her. But she had to keep them safe. And not following along with Haradan's lies could place them all into major danger.

She blew a kiss to the window beyond which her parents would be. 'I'm not leaving you on purpose this time… I'll find you, Mum and Dad. I'm saving you,' she whispered.

As he continued checking around the doorway seal, she stood beside the bed and faced him. She discreetly pulled out her vials and notebook and fumbled with them behind her back, still facing him.

Haradan turned back to Daffodil suddenly.

'Ready?'

'Yes,' she said, gently placing The Librarian's black notebook on the bed right behind her. 'Let's leave,' she said, stepping towards Haradan and the door.

***

Zakariyya and Clarice hadn't slept in days. When the doctors told them to leave Daffodil for a little while to rest, they had involuntarily knocked out on the sofas outside her hospital room, bodies happy to oblige.

Creak.

Clarice cracked open an eyelid.

Daffodil's hospital door. Open.

She looked up at the small clock on the wall near the receptionist's desk. 2AM. Had Daffodil gotten up and tried to call someone? The corridor seemed empty. Had a nurse gone into her room?

Looking around, seeing nobody, Clarice decided to step inside to check on her little girl.

Odd–the light was off.

She turned the switch on and glanced around.

The bed where they had left Daffodil was empty, with nothing on it save a small black notebook, just like the ones Bartholomew had said Amelio had been sending to him over the years.

Chapter 44

Amelio

Space cannot be created nor destroyed. Only controlled. Accessing one place from another place via transmutation portals requires the knowledge and control of space. A door can only ever lead to another place of space that already exists.

Doors are both physical feats of engineering and metaphysical windows to other worlds. Combine them with our work on alchemic transpondence and superfluid membranes, and one can access other areas, wherever another door is nearby.

Sciences of Alchemy

The Librarian was walked through the bowels of the palace, into a dark interrogation room, Zear pushing him from behind.

Seats and tables discarded, the king himself awaited until The Librarian was in front of him.

They stood face to face, not saying a word.

'Amelio…' the king said softly, finally breaking the silence. 'How many times do we have to do this?'

'What… What do you mean?' The Librarian asked.

'Thousands of iterations. Oh so many cycles. And yet your mind has still somehow just about held on.'

The Librarian stared at him. A pain shot through his head.

'I honour you,' the king said. 'We all do. All you've done for us. Without even knowing it…'

The king turned to the nearby table and picked up a vial of turquoise liquid; it bubbled and shimmered mysteriously.

'We really thought this time would be different, with Daffodil and all. I mean, there is still a chance. But not if Skutlish gets his way.'

'What are you talking about? How do you know about Daffodil? And who's Amelio?' The Librarian asked hesitantly.

The king pursed his lips and looked at The Librarian's face sadly.

'I know you are loyal. I know you won't tell me. But I need to ask. Where have Safa, Marwa and Riyul gone?'

'I … I will never tell you,' The Librarian spat, wincing in pain. 'As long as my name is Footstep!'

The king smiled. 'Forever the humourist. Well, I thought as much. Don't worry, we'll find them. And one day we will get you out of this torture. I'm sorry for this, friend.' Notra sighed and looked at Zear.

Zear stared impassively at the door.

'Haradan still has not completed the mission,' Zear said. 'We have no choice. We will have to wipe him once more, Your Highness.'

The king nodded somberly.

'Wipe me? You can't… My books…' The Librarian said shakily, all semblances of humour evaporating as the prospect of being mentally wiped truly struck him.

The king smiled kindly. 'Amelio… Do you ever think it odd that all your books contain the same style of writing? That they are black-leather bound until you change them up with coloured covers? That they are all connected to escaping and understanding Aethril, alchemy and the Conductor?'

The Librarian's eyes widened as the king's word sunk in and realisation dawned.

'My dear Amelio—all those books in your library,' the king said methodically, 'are written by you.'

The Librarian let out an uncharacteristic grunt as the words triggered flashbacks to time gone by. He began rapidly remembering memories upon memories upon memories of thousands upon thousands of adventures. Of searching and looking and researching and fighting. As the fragmented shards of memories staggered him, racked his body and convulsed his mind, he let out an almighty, piercing scream which shook the very walls around them.

'I'm so sorry, my friend,' the king breathed. 'One last memory wipe,' he said, turning to Zear, who raised the memory elixir up to The Librarian's quivering lips. 'Do it. Before the memories break his mind.'

'Are you sure we can afford to administer it to him another time?' Zear asked over the moans and screams, his own typically steady hand giving off the smallest of quivers.

'No. But we have no choice,' replied the king, taking the elixir from Zear and placing it himself to the lips of The Librarian. 'If there's any chance for us to win, for Daffodil to succeed—we have to. Or Skutlish's plans will come to fruition. One last attempt. One last wipe… For the return of the Conductor.'

And he poured.

Chapter 45

Memory

A day will come when all the puzzle pieces will fall together and the knowledge of this land amalgamates. Realise then that discretion is key. Otherwise, I am sure these books and notes will be meaningless.

Unnamed Black Notebook #3, remembrance eight

Haradan and Daffodil walked through an endless train carriage.

The train was the doorway to all places, Haradan had explained. Not many people realised, he had said, but the train was the key to understanding Aethril.

He spoke sporadically, yet Daffodil wasn't fully listening. She kept her hood up and walked at a distance.

Opening a door, he led her off the train and to a new location, somewhere north of The City. From there, they followed the south road down towards the Northern Gate of The City.

Daffodil simply followed along.

Nearby were huts and encampments—the makings of a small village. *Was this Sherlotte's village? Had Riyul and Marwa made it?*

Daffodil recognised that Haradan couldn't be trusted. However, the last thing she could do was put her parents in danger by not leaving with him, by not pretending to be fooled by his claims.

How had Haradan even found her?

She thought back to what she had read and heard about tracing. But that still didn't explain how he found her; he never had any of her possessions. And then it hit her. The flask she drank from before they had discovered Riyul for the first time. He had always had a trace on her.

She had made a simple decision, based on a singular realisation: if this man had the ability to track her down like this, to come into her hospital back in her world, a world with clocks on walls, whilst her parents were probably in the very same building, then he would clearly stop at nothing to keep her from revealing to the world the existence of Aethril. She couldn't fight back just yet. Wisest to play along.

She also realised she felt something new. After everything she had been through, she felt a new emotion.

Fear.

She realised, looking at this man marching on, that he was without a doubt what she should be thoroughly scared of. Not Zear. Not Notra. But Haradan.

Sure, she had been worried, unsure, even heartbroken before her escape, but now it was pure, unadulterated fear. Haradan was clearly capable of anything. It was all starting to make sense. Even that cane of his—she hadn't paid it the slightest bit of attention before, but who knew if it wasn't like the staves Zear and Notra were wielding.

But there were still so many questions. Why hadn't Haradan found her sooner? Had it been an act when he had been sucked out of the doorway? Or was that an unexpected hiccup by someone else?

Daffodil breathed in deeply.

She couldn't fathom why he had said so many of the things he had said, shown her the things he had shown her, taught her the things he had taught her, but the best she could do was to work out his plan without him catching on.

She thought back to her parents. Daffodil had to trust them. They'd gotten this far. She oh so hoped they could find a door again. And if she could just find her way back to her friends, she'd work out how to contact them discreetly.

Then came her, and her memories. That was indeed a worry. Yet she felt something else—small, hidden, barely there. Along with the fear and worry, she felt a tiny spark of confidence: a certainty in her own thoughts and memories she had not felt in—well, she couldn't say how long.

A veil had been lifted. A block. Her memories sat better than they had ever before, and whether the train really could affect one's memories, or whether this was another one of Haradan's tricks that the people of the train actually bought into and let themselves believe, Daffodil felt more sure than ever that her mind was in the right place. She felt sure in herself. Her memories were her own.

In some ways, she was glad she was back.

The plan to escape had worked, just as The Librarian had predicted. But they hadn't anticipated Marwa and Riyul having to split ways.

Daffodil looked sidelong at the village they were passing. *Would Riyul and Marwa have reached Sherlotte by now?*

The Librarian had wanted to ensure escape for everyone in Aethril, and now that Daffodil could confirm it was possible, she would show everyone how to get out.

As they walked, she furtively brushed the barely perceptible bulge in her jacket's outer pocket. The Librarian's notebook. His secret book that he'd entrusted with her to take out. With it came an empty vial of duplication balm. She still didn't know what was written in the notebook, but she hoped that duplicating it in the hospital while Haradan's back was turned, and leaving the replica for her parents, had been the right thing to do. She felt like somehow this all—the book, Haradan's betrayal, and everything else—connected. Now she'd need to work out how under Haradan's watchful eye.

Haradan had fooled her many times. Why he had played this the way he had, she could not work out. However, at least for now, she finally had an advantage–she was aware of his lies, and would make sure to keep that knowledge hidden for as long as she could

Despite her fear, Daffodil knew what to do. This was about more than her now. This was for everyone in this land. Riyul. Safa. Marwa. Seul. And all the others.

Daffodil closed her eyes and saw the darkness of the world around her, laced with a fluorescent green grid, shimmering in the darkness. She could hear the light thrumming of the world at work beneath her feet and around her.

She was going to follow along with Haradan for now. Let him think he was in control while she figured everything out. It all seemed to be connected. Riyul. The markings. Marwa and the icing. And time. The train and time and every loose end… If her hunches were correct, she may have even figured out who the conductor was. And if so, she could help him return, and thereby help all in these lands.

It was all starting to make sense—like a puzzle half completed. And once the pieces fell into place, with the help of her friends and family, she would do what she had come back to do.

Daffodil was back to free Aethril.

END OF BOOK 1

Epilogue

Hoffman jerked awake.

Chuka-chuka-chuka-chuka-chuka.

He looked straight ahead at the ceiling above him. Wood. Carvings. Swirls and indentations and marks the likes of which he'd never seen before. Years with the police had made him quick under pressure, and so he took in this information in a few blinks of his eyes.

A shuffle nearby.

He turned—body aching. He was in a bed. A barely passable bed, with... a red patchwork blanket covering him. He squinted. This blanket looked familiar.

Nearby, random crates were littered around the box-shaped carriage (how was he in a carriage, and why did it look so old?). There was wood everywhere, from the panelling to the floor to the ceiling, but ... *nothing looked like this nowadays.*

And on the other side of the carriage were three others. *Impossible. Was that...?*

Three more beds. Three more people waking up. Clarice, Zakariyya, and a third man whom he did not recognise.

Blinking, he tried to remember the last thing he recalled.

The boy at the exhibition… The train station… James…

Hoffman was thinking back to James at Moor Street, connected with the shadows, when he realised where the shuffle had come from.

His eyes grew wide.

A shadowy figure emerged seemingly from nowhere.

The man looked completely different with his hair combed, wearing a flowing leather jacket and wielding a polished cane and winning smile.

This was not the homeless man Hoffman remembered, yet for some reason … He was sure … *Those grey eyes* … They twinkled in the exact same way.

'James?' Hoffman said.

'Please…' the man replied, extending a hand out for Hoffman, 'Call me Haradan.'

PREPARE FOR THE FINAL
INSTALMENT OF THE DUOLOGY

THE ETERNITY TRAIN
BOOK 2